BOOK 2

THE
HIDDEN
WORLD
CHRONICLES

Live Your Adventure!

BOOK 2

THE HIDDEN WORLD CHRONICLES

THE SECRETS OF THE SWORD

RICHARD NANCE & RHONDA ROTH

Tate Publishing & Enterprises

Published by Tate Publishing & Enterprises, LLC
127 E. Trade Center Terrace | Mustang, Oklahoma 73064 USA
1.888.361.9473 | www.tatepublishing.com

Tate Publishing is committed to excellence in the publishing industry. The company reflects the philosophy established by the founders, based on Psalm 68:11,
"The Lord gave the word and great was the company of those who published it."

Published in the United States of America

ISBN: 978-1-61566-833-5
1. Fiction / Christian / Fantasy
2. Fiction / Action & Adventure
10.01.05

DEDICATION

This book is dedicated to all those who were nice enough to take time out of their day to read a copy of our first novel. It was with great pleasure that Rhonda and I heard the great comments of all of our family and friends. It might be noted that we did not receive even one bad comment from all of those critics. Not even from the ones we didn't know that were told, "You've got to read this!" by those same friends and family. With great reviews coming from all ages of men and women, we were encouraged to write *The Secrets of the Sword.* Each one who read the first book demanded to be able to read this one. Here it is. We want to thank all of you and let you know that this book is for you. Enjoy the next adventure.

PROLOGUE

BY GAVIN GRAHAM

My involvement with the stranger known as Charles Jennings began on a North Carolina beach in 1964. At that time I was only eleven years old. I wasn't like other kids because I had an incurable disease. The finest doctors had given me only a few weeks to live. This all changed when a stranger came out of the ocean and walked up to where I was lying in the sand, having fallen out of my wheelchair. He took my hand. At that moment, some strange warmth went through my body and I found myself healed. The pain that I had suffered with for so many years was suddenly gone. I knew this was a miracle, but the stranger said something very strange. He told me that miracles were only wonderful things that can't be seen, and that we would meet again. At the time, I had no idea what he meant. I would understand later. Thirty years later.

It wasn't until 1994 that this same man came up to me with a journal. He said he wanted me to transcribe his journal and make it ready for publication. He would let me know when. The journal that he left

7

in my possession chronicled the journey of him and four others. They were Sarah Parker, William Patterson, Cindy Shephard, and Peter Black. This journey told how these chosen few were to enter into the mysterious and wonderful place that was the Hidden World. This was a world hidden since mankind inhabited the earth.

After reading the journal, I traveled to Seattle, Washington, where I completed the transcription of that journal. It took the first two of those fourteen years since then to write and edit the manuscript while I patiently waited for our next encounter. At Christmas time each year I have received a strange Christmas card with a royal crest on the front. On the inside was a message: "Patience is a virtue that all men should strive for." The card was always in my mailbox with no return address or postage marks. Each card was identical to the first and found me at the many addresses I had during my wait. That touch on the beach not only healed me but changed me in some miraculous way. Since that day I haven't aged physically and no longer get sick and it has left me with an awareness of future events when they pertain to me. This is very much like Charles in his early years as he too had this same awareness. My intelligence quota is now much higher than it should be.

Due to the sensitive nature of the manuscript, I placed the original and my copy into a safe deposit box where I knew it would not be seen and kept safe. I placed the key to that safe deposit box on a chain around my neck and waited. I knew I had not been forgotten, and due to that inner awareness, I knew that my wait would soon be over. Someone was coming.

It was January 2008 that the wait came to an end. That was when I met the most incredible person I have ever known. I met Liz. She was beautiful. She introduced herself as the daughter of Charles and Sarah Jennings. I knew that Sarah was pregnant at the end of the journal and that would have made Liz forty-three years old. She looked nineteen. This is where I became involved with the "Hidden World." I was now a part of the story I had been writing about, and it seemed that I would soon have another story to put to paper. It is important that I take you back to that eventful day when I met Liz.

MEETING ELIZABETH JENNINGS

It was a sunny but cold morning. I was having a cup of hot chocolate at one of the local ski resorts. I tended to keep a close eye on the mountains around Rainier since I read the first journal. It was because of that journal that I chose this area. I knew that an entrance to the Hidden World was near here. Though I looked long and hard for many years, I had not been able to find even a clue as to its location.

I was sitting outside the lodge when a beautiful redhead suddenly sat down in the chair across the table. Her shinning red hair was in contrast with her white ski suit which made her even more striking. The air of her presence gave her a special glow. She dropped a large folder down on the table.

"Hello, Gavin. I've been looking forward to meeting you. I've heard a great deal about you. Mom and Dad said to say hello." She smiled a disarming smile, and her eyes sparkled. I felt she was enjoying my discomfort at her sudden appearance. She was waiting for a response, and I had no idea who she was.

9

"And just who are your mother and father?"

"Charles and Sarah Jennings," she responded, without batting an eye. She stretched her hand across the table to me. "I'm sorry. I should introduce myself. My name is Liz. I was named after my grandmother Elizabeth. You may have heard of her. Drake and Elizabeth were the parents of my dad." She leaned across the table and reached over and pulled the chain and key out of my shirt. "He says that it is now time. He also said you'd know what that meant." She shoved the large folder over to me and continued. "You have more work to do."

It was then that I noticed an amber pendent dangling from her neck. Embedded in the amber was a scorpion. I recognized the necklace from a description found in Charles's journal. It was the necklace worn by Sarah Jennings. It was given to her when she became an adult. I could only assume that this was the same. I could tell by the construction that it was a one-of-a-kind pendent. I felt that there was a story behind all this, and I couldn't determine if it was sitting before me or lying on the table in front of me.

"I've read and written a great deal about your father and mother. Are they all right?" I was looking for more information. I wanted to believe her. This would mean my long wait was over. She was indeed beautiful and had a smile that would warm the heart of anyone. Could I dare to believe that she was who she said she was?

"I don't blame you, Gavin." She said, as if she had read my mind. "Mom and Dad are great. I was only a babe unborn when you met my father the first time. I was in school in Avalon when you met him the second time. Mom and Dad are both fine and are now back home." She turned her head sideways and looked at me with those bright green eyes. "You've waited a long time to hear from us again." She thought for a moment and continued. "I've been sent by my father because he has many more responsibilities than you can imagine, but he really wanted to be here to see you. You still have a manuscript to publish. Everyone, including Dad, thinks that we can't wait any longer. Events have unfolded pretty fast. We've done a great deal of work making UFOs more believable. It's now time to let people know from where they come from and what we're all about."

She stopped talking suddenly and stood up. I felt it too. Something dangerous was coming. Liz looked up into the sky to the west. "We're going to have company. Better get ready, but stay out of the way. This shouldn't be happening. I haven't been compromised, and no one should know about you. They have been sent for both of us."

A cold chill went up my spine. The other guest on the patio suddenly heard it too. It was a chopper coming low from the west. I could see even at this distance that it was black and didn't have any markings. Liz stood watching with her hands on her hips. "There will be six of them. They are a paramilitary group. All of them are ex-marines and have been hired to take us both out." She looked over at me. "That's military slang meaning—"

"I know what that means," I interrupted. The hair on the back of my neck was standing out. This was not good. I knew that the military was in good terms with the hidden world from Charles's Journal. Not many people outside of the President even knew about the hidden world. If these mercenaries weren't hired by the government or anyone on the outer rim, who was left? They were only carrying out an assignment. They truly believed they were doing a patriotic duty for some reason. I could tell by Liz's face that she was wondering the same thing, or was it my awareness of her feelings?

She walked around the table and stood beside me as she surveyed the chopper. "They will disembark below and come up over the wall. They have automatic weapons and don't care about collateral damage as long as they get us. When the shooting starts, get under a table and stay there. Things may get a little hairy."

She was right. The chopper stopped short of the lodge and disgorged six military-looking personnel. They wore dark green masks over the lower portion of their faces. The twenty or so people on the patio had turned to see what was happening. We had no time to warn them of the danger. The six from the chopper came over the wall of the patio and scanned the area. They immediately saw Liz standing in the open, well away from the other people who were now becoming concerned. The leader let loose a spray of automatic fire at Liz. She wasn't there. The bullets bounced off the rock on the opposite lodge wall and out over the mountain causing no more damage. Liz was now halfway to the group of men. They had scattered out, and Liz, seeing the opportunity, stepped between the men. Three were now on her left and three on her right. They dared not fire for fear of hitting their comrades. Bad mistake. The leader on the left and his two companions pulled knives from the scabbards strapped to their legs and started for Liz. I had read in Charles' journal about how adept the hidden world was at martial arts but I had never expected to see it in person. Her moves were fast and graceful. The attackers were rough and awkward. The result was three two-hundred-pound men lying at her feet. As they attacked, Liz moved as if by magic and gave each a slight blow just behind their ear and they crumbled at her feet not moving. I couldn't tell if they were unconscious or dead. The other three started for Liz as soon as they saw the first group attack. They arrived just in time to join their comrades at her feet. She stepped on top of the pile of men and looked them over carefully. She stood there with her hands on her hips like she had just finished her afternoon tea. She wasn't even out of breath. The patio erupted in applause.

Liz smiled at the group on the patio and stepped down off the pile of men and came over to the table. She leaned over and whispered, "They'll soon figure out that this wasn't just a scene from a movie. We need to get out of here." I got up from behind the table where I was hiding, and we left. Liz grabbed the large folder and we walked casually to Liz's car. Her red Ferrari was parked in front of the lodge in a loading zone. She stuffed the folder behind the front seat. There was a frown on Liz's face as though she was deep in thought. She didn't speak, which was just as well, because she was taking the curves much faster than I felt comfortable with. This was the first time I had ever ridden in a Ferrari. I hoped it wouldn't be my last. Any other time I would have really enjoyed driving down the mountain in this classic automobile but my fear of what happened at the lodge had been replaced with the speed we were now going. I had to hand it to her, she really knew how to handle an automobile, which eased my fear somewhat. I could now appreciate what I was experiencing. The car and the woman were both classics.

She reached into her jacket and pulled out a cell phone. *I can't believe she is going to talk on a cell phone while taking these curves at this speed.* She pressed a preset button on her phone and spoke. "We've got problems. We had a reception committee. No, we got away without anyone getting killed, but six of them will have a mountain of a headache when they wake up. No, I think we need to get the local authorities to pick them up. This is the same terrorist group that the CIA has wanted to break up for a long time. They have no idea who they work for, so they won't be any help to us. They just work for anyone who has the money." She looked over at me. "No. He's Okay. Yes, I know. We have a leak. Gavin's not safe now. Yes, I agree. We have to go to plan B." She listened for a while and said, "Okay; that sounds like a good plan. And Peter, thanks. We'll be there as soon as we can." She closed the phone and put it back in her jacket. We continued on down the mountain, and I was thankful that we hadn't met any oncoming traffic.

As soon as we got back on a major highway, we headed in the direction of Seattle. "Which bank do you have your manuscript in?"

I told her, and we headed downtown. She slid to a stop outside the bank. "Get your copy of the manuscript. Leave Dad's journal; we don't want both copies with us at the same time. We might have to use the original as a backup. Right now we have to leave town."

I got out of the car on shaky legs and went into the bank. It took several minutes to retrieve my manuscript. The people in the bank didn't seem to understand my urgency. I came out and found that Liz had disappeared. I stood there, wondering what to do next, when Liz finally came around the corner of the block and again slid to a stop. "Get in. We have to go to Las Vegas. We have a plane waiting."

13

As soon as the door closed, we were on our way. We hit the interstate and headed south. Liz finally sighed in relief and looked over at me. "Sorry for all this. I had hoped that our meeting would have been a bit more uneventful. I talked to Peter Black. He used to head up the Black Opps at the Pentagon. You should know all about him. He said that it's much too dangerous for you to personally get the manuscript published. We'll find someone else to do all the legwork for you." She smiled. "So much for you being a famous author. Right now we have to get you to a safe place. You have to work on Dad's new journal. It takes up where the first one left off. Dad had me keep a diary as well. You might find it interesting if you ever get around to reading it. He thought it would be good for people to know what was happening with me in the inner world and how I got back to the outside and what I've been up to." She continued to drive on in silence. I knew she was still in thought. Something was bothering her.

I finally asked, "Why are we going to Las Vegas?"

"We have to go to Groom Lake. Most of the activities there have been moved, but Jarod and his group are still around. A great deal has happened since the first journal, and you'll be able to read about that later. Right now, we have to get you back to Mom and Dad's place. You'll be safe there, and it'll be a lot easier to do your work."

Was she for real? Did she actually mean that we would be heading into the Hidden World? I felt my heart speed up. I was being awkwardly invited to the original garden of Eden. I had never dreamed that I would go there myself. I noticed that my knees were shaking. I wondered if it was from the news of our destination, or was it Liz's driving?

"We'll have to travel the rift. You know, the channel between the Atlantic base and the inner world. We think that whoever is calling the shots will be watching the northern and southern gates. Using the gate here in Washington State would be out of the question. They will certainly be watching that one. We have a big leak. What's more, it looks like we have a traitor. What bothers me most is that the traitor knows who we are. He also knew where we would be. He or she has to be someone we trust. No one else could have gotten that information. I can only hope there is some other explanation."

It took us some time to travel across the state of Oregon. We talked for several hours. I found out that she had first gone to the inside as a young girl of four. She mentioned her training at the university of the inner world. From there she spent two years at Atlantic Base. This was an underwater base off the coast of North Carolina that was used for research and a stopping off point from and to the inner world. This was impressive, as I knew how intense the training was at both locations. She had come to the outer rim and became a student at the University of Southern California. I found this amusing. She could have taught any curriculum there. While there she joined their ski team. Her abilities would have put other skiers to shame but she knew better than to become too obvious. She was put into the university for a reason and now both that reason and her ski career were over. She would not be able to go back to her life on the outside and neither would I. She had joined the university's ski team. They didn't have much snow on the inside, and she enjoyed the sport. Her dad was concerned. Charles told her that she could never place any higher than second in competition. Otherwise, she would draw too much attention. She could have set world records in any of the events. She was now angry that the events on the mountain wouldn't allow her to return to the university, much less the ski team. She would not be able to go back again until the source of the leak had been found and eliminated one way or the other. We stopped for gas and grabbed a bite to eat. I needed more to eat than Liz, as I had not been raised in the inner world.

I suddenly awoke and looked over at Liz. She was still at the wheel as she did not need sleep as I did. I had fallen asleep some time in the early part of the night and was surprised to find we had arrived in Las Vegas. There was a private plane waiting for us at the airport. Liz got the folder out from behind her seat, and I took my manuscript. We boarded the plane just as the engines were started up. It wasn't much later that we arrived at Groom Lake. Liz had been sitting with the pilot

15

during the flight. I wondered if she could fly. She came back to where I was sitting as soon as the plane stopped. She gave me an identification badge that had my picture on it. "Pin this on. You'll need it while you're here." It seemed that the pilot already had my ID when we boarded. I noticed that Liz had one too. How in the world did they get a picture of me, much less get it on an identification tag? I was finding out that things happened fast around Liz. Nothing about her was average. She surpassed average the moment I first saw her. She took my copy of Charles' journal and placed it in an aluminum case that she had brought from the front of the plane.

The pilot came back and opened the door and let down the steps. We quickly left the plane. We got on a waiting jeep and headed deep into the base. The marine driver had been waiting for us and evidently knew his way. Liz had the case tightly in her grasp. We drove straight into one of the hangers. We then went to the back where we came to a guarded door. We got out of the jeep, and the marine saluted and left. We turned to the next marine, who stood guard at the door. With a quick check of our badges, the marine there let us enter. We then went down a long passageway. From its direction and length I knew that we had to be going back into the mountain behind the base. Here we got on a blue electric cart. Liz ran her badge over a scanner on the dash. The cart started up, and Liz headed further back down the underground roadway. I was thankful that the cart didn't go as fast as her sports car. No words had been spoken since we first arrived and the silence was unnerving. We finally reached a bank of guarded elevators that I had read about in Charles's journal. The guard stepped aside as Liz placed her hand on a palm reader and the door to the elevator opened. The guard saluted and again took his place at the outside of the elevator. We entered the elevator, and Liz again placed her hand on a reader and entered several numbers on a keypad. The elevator started down.

It must have been several hundred feet down before we stopped. When the elevator opened, we entered a very large underground complex. It was obvious that all work at Groom Lake had not been moved.

There were several hundred people working down below the catwalk that we had stepped out on. We hurried down the ramp at the end of the catwalk where we came to an office that had another guard standing at attention beside the door. It seemed that there were an awful lot of guards here. This fact seemed to bother Liz for some reason. She showed the guard something that she had taken from her jacket, and he knocked on the door. "Come in" was the immediate response. We heard a metallic click, and the door slid open. We walked in.

A white-haired elderly gentleman looked up from his desk, and a broad smile came on his face. "Liz! What in the world brings you here? I haven't seen you in ages." He had gotten up from his desk and trotted over and gave Liz a big fatherly hug.

Liz backed up and returned the gentleman's smile. "It's great to see you again, Jarod. I'm sorry we had to come unannounced, but it couldn't be helped. Jarod, I'd like for you to meet Mr. Gavin Graham."

Jarod looked over at me in surprise. "So this is the carrier of the truth that I heard about back at the university. It really is a pleasure to meet you, Gavin." It seemed that I had picked up a title that I knew nothing about. I would have to ask Liz just what "the carrier of truth" meant. Jarod came over and shook my hand. *This couldn't be Jarod of Charles's journal. He couldn't be over fifty years old.* He smiled. "Don't look too surprised, Gavin. Much has happened since the time of your journal. Thanks to Charles and Sarah, I finally got a chance to go to that mysterious world that you have read about. Due to that trip, my useful years have been greatly extended. I am now ninety-six."

"I can't believe it. You don't look a day over sixty, and I'm not just saying that to be nice."

He smiled. "Something must have happened for you to bring Gavin here," he addressed Sarah. "He was not supposed to get involved." His frown was obvious. He knew something was wrong.

"Yes, Gavin and I were attacked in Washington State. They knew who we were and where we were to be found. They intended to eliminate us for good. They should not have known about either one of us.

I have to get Gavin to a safe place and come up with a new plan." Liz walked back and forth, evidently thinking about something.

Jarod interrupted, "He'll have to be taken inside. That is the only safe place. If they know who he is, they also know what he carries."

Liz looked up. "Yes I know. That second journal is very important. We have to get it ready for publication before this summer is over. Peter has found someone to take care of the first one. I'll be leaving it with you to get it to Washington. She handed Jarod the case containing both the manuscript and Charles's second journal.

Jarod took out my manuscript. "We need to make several copies. If the first one fails to make it, we'll have a backup. We can't send it over the usual internet channels. There are too many variables that can't be covered."

He wrote something on a piece of paper and pushed a button on his desk. A young woman came in about thirty seconds later, and Jarod handed her the manuscript and the note. Shooting a startled look at Jarod, she nodded before turning and leaving.

"I wrote that she was not to let either the original or the copies that she was to make out of her sight. She was to guard both with her life." Jarod closed the case gently. "We can't risk making a copy of this one. Gavin will have to carry it with him. Charles will need to make the decisions from here on out."

Liz looked over at Jarod. "We need to borrow the craft in the upper hanger. We have to travel to Atlantic Base."

"We've kept the craft ready. It's yours. It doesn't have the latest updates, but it should get you to the base." Jarod picked up the phone. He spoke quietly in the receiver and hung up. "You can leave as soon as it gets dark. What will you do for the rest of the day?"

"We need to get cleaned up and changed. Gavin will need some time to rest before we start. He may not get another chance for several hours. I'll take him up to the cafeteria and get him something to eat." She looked over at me and smiled. "He might be interested in what new developments are in the works." She knew I was curious. "Area 51 has made some great strides in the past fifty years. It may be a little too soon to make the latest finds public. I suggest you don't put anything you may see here today in your journal. We hope there will be plenty of time for that later."

That was good advice. What I saw after my rest period and before we left would have stunned even the most adventurous minds. We exchanged our lab coats for special uniforms. We were allowed into some special changing rooms beside Jarod's office. These were the suits that I had read so much about. It was only because of Charles's journal that I knew how to zip it up. It was a light blue color and fit me to a tee. Now I wondered just how they knew my size.

When I came back to Jarod's office, Liz had already changed. She was wearing a golden suit with a gold braid down the sleeve. Her suit fit even better than mine. She caught me staring and smiled. *I keep forgetting that these people can read minds.* I would have to be more careful.

Too soon, night had fallen, and we made our way to the upper hanger where I saw my first UFO. She was sleek and very shiny. The ramp was down. Jarod filled us in on the plan for getting us back to the Hidden World. This was the craft that we were to take to Atlantic Base. There we would change crafts, and a local pilot would return this one back to Groom Lake. We were to take a royal craft of Shambala to the inner world.

We entered the craft. I sat in a seat beside Liz. The restraint system gently encircled my waist. I heard the drives warming up. Liz brought up the ramp and closed the door. I knew what to expect, but the loss of gravity still caught me off guard, and I lost my breath. The feeling of falling was unnerving. The craft slowly rose, and the display of the outside came on. The three-dimensional projection was really impressive. It was true that the front of the craft seemed to disappear. The lights in the hanger went off, and the hanger doors opened to the night sky. We zoomed out at an unheard of speed. The result, though I could feel no acceleration, was still breathtaking. We climbed at the same rate until we leveled off miles above the highest clouds. We had to have been nearly in space before we headed east. The craft must have been going at least eight times the speed of sound, and we reached the Atlantic coast in just ten minutes.

After a few miles over the sea, we started down at the same speed. We stopped suddenly just over the surface of the ocean at the same time as I saw my life pass before my eyes. Liz flew just like she drove. We hovered over the calm ocean for a moment or two and then went below the waves where Liz turned on the craft's lights. I saw the bottom coming up just at the last moment. A shaft opened just under the craft, and we slowly settled down the shaft, and the door closed over our heads. We heard the air rushing into the chamber as the water was forced out. When the chamber was dry, the door to the airlock opened and we floated into a large hanger where I saw several workers in blue uniforms of a much darker shade than the one I was wearing running to place a cradle under the craft. The lights of the hanger swung over us as we settled down into the cradle. Liz sent down the ramp and pulled her case out from under the seat. We left the craft, and as soon as the workers saw who had arrived, a crowd of admirers surrounded us. Liz greeted them all with that bright smile. She seemed to know all of them by name.

The commander came up from behind the group, and Liz went over and shook his hand and talked quietly for a while. The commander looked over at me once or twice as they spoke. *It really makes me uncomfortable when I know someone is talking about me.*

The two stopped talking and came over to where I was standing. "Gavin, this is Jeffery. I don't know if Dad mentioned him in the journal. He is the commander here now. He will get the royal craft ready for us to leave."

It only took thirty minutes for the craft to be moved to the hanger. She was beautiful. She had better lines than the one we had arrived in, and her skin was a shimmering gold. There was a crest on the side. I supposed it to be the royal crest of Shambala. I soon learned that this was the one and only Zaron. This was Charles and Sarah's personal craft. The royal pilot had brought it here as soon as the interior heard of our little skirmish in Washington.

When we boarded, I heard Liz say, "It's good to be back aboard again, Zaron. Are you ready for a quick trip home?"

I really got a shock when Zaron sent me a thought. The first time I had ever received a direct thought from anyone. *Greetings, Gavin. My master wishes you well and welcomes you to his home.* I didn't know what to say.

"Thank you, Zaron. It's a pleasure to be on board." Liz sent me a smile over her shoulder and also sent me a thought of her own. *Well done, Gavin. Welcome to our world.*

I tried something new: I sent back a thought. *Thank you.*

"You're welcome," Liz responded as she lifted the craft off the floor and started for the airlock. I didn't feel weightless like in the other craft and remembered that Zaron had an auxiliary gravity drive that emulated normal gravity.

We went through the reverse of coming in, except that this time we didn't break through to the surface. We went a fantastic speed underwater in a southerly direction. It wasn't long before we started down, and I knew we were entering the rift. Even though Zaron had her lights on, the walls of the rift were too far away to be seen. This channel through the earth was truly large.

It wasn't long before the four-hundred-mile trip ended and we broke the surface into the sunlit world of the interior. We rose above the inner sea so I could get a good look at the mountains rising in the distance. They were majestic. They seemed to reach to the sky, which was a deeper blue than the sky on the outside.

We soon reached the base of that mountain, and I could see the tropical vegetation and giant waterfalls that disappeared into a swirling mist. The trees ran from the foot of the mountains to the white beaches of the seashore. Beautiful cities dotted the countryside. Roads didn't mar the breathtaking countryside. The need for them vanished long ago. The streets carried the local traffic, and the skies carried travelers from city to city or from one continent to another. There were no guarded gates or closed off compounds. All was open to anyone who wanted to visit. I found that there were no official papers or passports to hinder travel. This was a world truly at peace with itself.

"This is the land of Avalon. I wanted you to see it before we headed to Shambala." She turned the craft toward the sea and headed southwest. I didn't know the direction at the time, as there was no way to determine direction except for a compass.

Soon the towering mountains of Shambala came into view. We had traveled over six thousand miles in a matter of only a few minutes. We slowed so I could see the seashore and the villages nestled close to the mountains. The houses here were of a different architecture. The beauty of this place was exactly as Charles had described. The red tiles of the roofs glistened in the overhead sun. The white stucco terraces were lined with flowers and complimented the high turrets reminding me of ancient Turkey. There were ornate archways leading to streets lined with very tall trees that blended into the flowers along each side of the cobblestone streets. Each building seemed to compliment the surroundings. The higher ones seemed to move straight up the mountain. The lower buildings ranged out to farmlands that seemed to have numerous crops. Even at this height I could see the animals roaming the meadows. Everything below me was truly a work of art. Liz took me over the capital city as we headed south toward Charles and Sarah's castle. The capital's central castle was very ornate. Gold shone everywhere, and gems gleamed from the terraces. The flowered tiles of the streets glistened in the noonday sun. The gold on the spires and gates contained intricate carvings of flowers and mythical creatures that I could make out even at this distance.

I saw why Charles fell in love with this land. It would be a shame to see it change. It took centuries of hard work and dedication for this world to come to this level. Peace and tranquility oozed from the sight below me.

Too soon we were landing on the courtyard of Liz's home. Standing

22

below us were several people and a very large tiger. Soaring above us was a group of extremely large dragons. Liz was excited.

I had not realized that it had been a long time since she had been home. She ran down the ramp and into the arms of a woman who looked like her sister. That couldn't be Sarah. She couldn't have been over thirty, but the man standing beside her I recognized at first sight. Charles Jennings had not changed in forty-four years. He was busy kissing his daughter and giving her a heartfelt hug as he looked over her shoulder and saw me coming down the ramp.

He broke free and came over and took my hand. "It has been a long time since we last met, Gavin." He spread his arms. "Welcome to our world."

"You should have written more about it, Dr. Jennings. Your journal doesn't do it justice." I was busy looking up at the castle when suddenly I felt a wet lick on my face. I turned to see a huge tiger staring into my eyes. I froze.

"That's a good sign. Raja likes you. You have to be the first outsider that he has ever approached." Charles laughed as Liz also came running over and grabbed the big cat around the neck, almost knocking the big beast to the ground. The cat only roared with glee at seeing the girl. They had to be very close.

It was clear that Liz was happy to be home, but in a more serious voice she said, "Dad, we have to talk. I had to bring Gavin here."

"I know, Daughter; your experience worries me as well. We do have to talk. Right now let's get Gavin settled. I think we have time for him to see a little of the country before we put him to work."

"Oh, that reminds me. Your second journal is still on Zaron." She started toward the craft. She called back over her shoulder to me. "I'll leave the journal for you in the presidential suite." Liz had already picked where I'd stay. I learned that the suite was named in the honor of the late President Kennedy who had sent Charles and Sarah back home. Visiting kings usually stayed there. I thought to myself, *I guess the kings and presidents will have to stay in the guest room while I'm here. They must think I'm pretty important.*

Liz came from the craft, and the gleeful crowd started back toward the castle. That was when I saw it. Standing in front of the castle in the middle of the courtyard was a very large gold statue. The man in the center bore a striking likeness to Charles and on his right was the one and only Raja. On his left was another man dressed in golden armor and shield. That had to be Prince Verl. In Charles's hands were the Staff of Aaron and the Sword of Truth. Behind the three with his back to his friends had to be Eric, the trustworthy guide that went into battle with Charles. This was a depiction of the battle between the sons of light and sons of darkness. Below, written in English, were these words: *To Aaron and Sarah, son and daughter of light, with gratitude from the peoples of the world.* It had to be the best piece of sculpture the world had ever seen. I just stood and looked at it for several minutes before I realized that everyone else had stopped to look at me.

Charles came over and placed an arm around my shoulders. "You should have been here when they presented that to us. I had tears dripping off my chin. I have never been moved as much in my life. These people here are undoubtedly the greatest, most generous, and loving people the world has ever seen. You'll see why when you get to know them."

Charles looked me in the eye. "I got word from Peter. He was worried about your parents after what happened to you and Liz. He said for you not to worry about them. They were under the best protection the world has to offer. They won't even know they are being protected."

I felt guilty. I had not thought that Mom and Dad would be in danger. "Tell Peter that I really appreciate what he has done. I'll never forget it."

Charles smiled and nodded. "I'll let him know."

I felt someone take my hand and turned and looked down into those big blue eyes of Liz. "It's time we showed you your new home."

She led me through the great archway into the palace. At least it looked like a palace, because no home that I had ever seen looked like this. There was no door, which surprised me. At home a building like this would have a massive door with plenty of security alarms.

We traveled up a spiral staircase to the second floor as I admired the numerous paintings and sculptures that lined the walls. The paintings were huge and reflected light from somewhere surrounded each one with sunlight. The sculptures were recessed in nooks with the same affect.

I hurried to catch up with Liz. We entered a very spacious room and this one had a door. It wasn't just a room but a suite with marble floors and walls that seemed to have just been polished. There were comfortable looking chairs and sofas surrounding the room. Near the window, which had no glass, was a large wooden desk and chair with what looked like a computer on one corner. It even had a small communication device. I was told it was a telephone that I could use to contact anyone here in the inner world or anyone on the outer rim that I needed to talk to. I was told that I couldn't let it be known just where I was.

I walked over to the open window and felt a fresh breeze coming up the mountain from the sea. The view of the valley below was breathtaking. The sea in the distance was glistening in the sun.

Liz showed me my sleeping quarters which contained a recliner instead of a bed. "You won't need much sleep after you're here for a while," she explained with a smile. "We want you to get some rest now after you get cleaned up."

She then took me to what would be considered a bathroom, except the bathtub was a large pool filled with a pleasant blue colored liquid. I knew from the journal that this was no normal water.

Liz smiled up at me and said, "When you're ready to come down, we will have something for you to eat. It will make you feel better." She turned and left, gently closing the door behind her.

I removed my clothes and soaked in the blue liquid for over what must have been an hour. I can't explain just how good that blue water made me feel. I wasn't tired anymore.

I looked over at the desk and there laid the second journal of Charles Jennings. I couldn't resist the impulse. I went over to the desk and opened the journal. I began to read.

THE SECOND JOURNAL OF CHARLES JENNINGS

USA, 1964

My wife, Sarah, has begged me to complete a second journal of our adventures. She still considers our stay here as an adventure after all this time. What has happened to us has been much more than an adventure. You'll see what I mean as you read further. The words may not do justice to the actual events.

I should start out where I left off with my first journal. I have put the first one in a safe place until I can place it into the hands of the one who will put my words into a more readable format. Later I will reveal how I got it into the hands of Gavin Graham. He was just a small boy. God himself told me that I would meet him and that I would soon meet the one who would carry the truth. At the time, I had thought that the carrier of truth was Gavin. I was wrong. It wasn't Gavin who would carry the truth. The "Truth" referred to wasn't even my journal. Even then I knew that I would again meet Gavin, but many years from this point

26

in my story. His future and mine seemed to be intermingled somehow. Time would reveal much.

Sarah and I were sent back to the outer world as envoys and watchers in 1964. We had developed a history on the outer rim already, which made us the perfect couple for our covert work there. We were to again place ourselves in the public eye. I was to return to my position as professor of history. With the help of some very influential people, both Sarah and I had gotten positions with the University of Southern California. We traveled straight to the west coast when we left the beach cottage in North Carolina. We had spent several days there enjoying the late summer while events were taking place to insure our positions. We also watched Gavin Graham as the young boy came every morning to the edge of the sea and stared out at the sunrise waiting for that stranger who had come from the sea. We could feel his excitement at his new freedom from pain and the yearning for a sight of the man who had given it to him. Both Sarah and I knew that God had picked him for a reason. It wasn't for us to know.

We now had to get back into the outer world society. Our past credentials as teachers and explorers were already known, and our new knowledge put us far ahead of any other scholars here on the outer rim.

Sarah's fame had already been established as a famous anthropologist. She would be teaching the science as well. She would not be taking the position until after the baby arrived. Oh, yes, I have not mentioned that Sarah was also expecting. The baby was due around February the fourteenth. Valentines Day. We both knew that it was to be a girl and both of us were excited about our daughter who would be coming soon. Sarah wanted to name her Elizabeth, after my mother. It was an honor and an inner world tradition. The other three that went to the inner world with us are all back on the outside. Peter Black is back at the Pentagon. Cindy Shephard and Billy Patterson were married on the inside. They both now reside in LA. Cindy is doing research at the Denney Research Center on the University Park Campus of the

University of Southern California. Billy is now out of the Marine Corps and working as technical consultant for a major computer manufacturer in the valley. He also teaches martial arts at night to aspiring young athletes. We try not to contact each other unless we come across something very important, because of the risk of compromise. It was helpful that Cindy would be working just across campus from myself should we have to get in touch. Peter was our main contact. He would keep us informed on events.

We were to lie low for some time. I don't know if it was to make sure we were safe or the planning of what was to come would take a great deal of time.

Here I have to mention that it has now been over four years since that day on the beach with the young Gavin. We soon moved to California to a very nice house near the campus. Not only had we both received government grants, but also a very large inheritance was at my disposal. It was really from the inner world. It was thought that a rich professor would be able to swing more influence than a struggling one. We would have to pull strings when plans were in place, and here, on the outside, money made it much easier.

I have to mention here that Liz was born right on Valentine's Day just as predicted. She is now three, soon to be four, and beginning to take over the household. Her nanny is named Jenny Harrison. She has taken it upon herself to be Liz's teacher and mentor. She comes from a very good family in Avalon, and a graduate of the World University. Peter pulled a few strings to give her a false background on the outside. After all, California is a far cry from Avalon. If you know anything about Avalon graduates, you'll know that this means that she is more knowledgeable than all the professors at USC combined. She thinks that Liz needs to start her training because she has been showing signs of advanced awareness and exceptional learning skills. She already reads at a high school level and keeps Jenny busy answering complex questions. We knew that we would have to train her outside of regular school. A savant would soon arouse too much notice and she is not really a savant, just slightly ahead of a normal child from the inner world. She already has a great deal of poise and grace which she shows off with here acrobatic skills. Right now her favorite activity is visiting the zoo. She thinks the animals need someone to come see them while they are in prison. I tried to explain that they were not in prison, but she was not to be deterred in her appraisal of their situation. It didn't help that she could communicate with them via thought. I had not reached that point of awareness until I was fully grown. I wondered if this was a portent of things to come. She would really love the animals running free in our home of Shambala. I missed our castle and the people there, but work had to be accomplished here on the outer rim. We had not yet told Liz that she was not of this world. Keeping that secret was not easy as she was developing the ability to see our thoughts. I wondered just how long the shields on our thoughts would keep our true home from her.

She shouldn't be ready for the university for several years. We would then have to send her to the inside for training. We had to enjoy our little girl while we could. We couldn't hide everything from her because she knew we were not from California and she asked us many times about our other home. We told her as much as we could and promised to take her there some day.

I had been in touch with Jarod at Area 51. He wanted to meet us both again for old time's sake, but I sent word that it would be too dangerous at that time. Jarod is the head scientist who is knowledge-able of the inner world and has helped us several times before. It was there that I flew my first inner-world craft. You know those crafts as UFOs. Jarod and his crew had just made their first one on my last visit to Groom Lake. It was pieced together from a crashed craft from the dark forces. They still had years of development before they reached the level of technology of the interior races. Their first craft was crude, but with some help from us it was operational. I think it may have been spotted on test flights over the desert. The government is still trying to cover up the sightings or making the people who see them look like crackpots. It seems that all of them think these crafts are aliens from outer space. Even the military aren't quite sure what they are. There are only a few people in the United States that know the real source. There are also thousands of us from the interior working on the outside trying to bring knowledge and science to the people here while trying to keep them from killing themselves in the mean time. A covert worker that was working for Jarod is also from the interior. His name is Brian. Jarod and his crew don't know his true origins. It is through him that I keep in touch with Jabril at the University of Avalon. Jabril is headmaster of the university and calls the shots for all those working on the outside. No one really knows just how old he is. It is said that he was head of the university when King Dresden attended the university. I know for a fact that King Dresden is over a thousand years old.

The longevity of the people of the inner worlds greatly exceeds those on the outside. I'll try to fit in things from my first journal as we go along so anyone who reads this can fully understand what we are all about and just why we have to be so careful.

It seems that our lives have been one adventure after another since that day when I saw my first unidentified flying object. I was flying a small plane when it appeared just off my wingtip.

Now I need to tell you about the event that I mentioned above. I was teaching class as usual. As much as I enjoyed ancient history, I now found it rather dull, even though many of the books used in the course were my own. I was getting deep into the Mayan culture when I felt it. Someone in the class was probing my mind. I let the probe move freely in areas that I would let him look so as not to give myself away. I could have blocked him immediately had I wanted. I wanted him to expose himself. I scanned the room. A student sitting at the back of the room was the person doing the probe. He was not of this world, but his ability was still crude. He definitely was not a graduate of the university as the others on the outside. He was looking for information on South American tunnels formed by a superior race. He was a worker for the dark forces, working here on the outside. I probed his mind as he thought he was probing mine. I found out a great deal more about him than he had learned from me. I caught his eye as he looked up from the notebook he was writing in. He stopped the probe and I could see he was very proud of himself for his ability to look into my mind. I could tell from his mind that he was sent to find information for his superiors. He was also the kind of character that I wouldn't want to meet in a dark alley. I now knew who he was and where he lived. I also knew from what complex he had been sent. He would have to be watched. I also needed to know why he was so interested in tunnels beneath the planes of Peru. I knew they had massive tunnel complexes in several places on the outer world, so why would they be interested in those particular ones? Jabril would know about these and what danger they posed. I needed to get in touch with Brian. It looked like the dark forces were again on the move. They were still very vengeful for the defeat of Belial and the dark forces on the inside. They had lost their leader and thousands of comrades. They also had lost their access to the interior world. They had now turned their attention on the outer races. They want this world and will put up every effort to gain control of it and that is just the reason why we are here. We are going to make sure that this never takes place.

Fortunately, this was my last class for the day. I was going to follow my new student when he left, but he left before the class was over. I would have to find some other way to see what he was up to.

I dismissed the class and left the building. My car was over in the faculty parking area, but I didn't see the fellow anywhere. I saw from his mind that he was Greg Jordan. He had a student ID that had to be faked, for he was never a student here. It bothered me that he was so close to Sarah, Cindy, and me. I hoped that it was just a coincidence. I sent out a scan of the area to see if I could sense him anywhere. Either he was long gone or was now very much improved at blocking my mental scan. I went on over to my Jag and threw my case over onto the passenger side and waved at the students who were admiring my car. At least these students thought I was just a dull professor with a real neat car. It helped to spread the illusion that I was wealthy.

My mind mulled over the possibilities of why that young man was in my class. Every scenario that I came up with wasn't good. I'd have to talk it over with Sarah as soon as I got home.

I drove the car up the circular drive to the front of the house. I left the car out in front, as I might need it later. I went inside through the front entrance and was nearly bowled over by Liz. She jumped in my arms and gave me a big kiss. "Are you coming to my birthday party tomorrow? Miss Jenny said that we were going to have a big cake and a clown."

I looked into her bright blue eyes and noticed that they were starting to turn green, just like her mother's. "I wouldn't miss it for the world. So my little girl is turning four. You're growing up much too fast."

"Miss Jenny said the same thing. She also said that you wouldn't get much older if you forgot that it was also Valentine's Day tomorrow. What did you get Mommy?" She leaned back and stared into my eyes. "You did forget, didn't you, Daddy?" She shook her head back and forth. "I'm afraid you won't get any cake tomorrow." She paused then continued with a very serious expression. "You may not even get any dinner." She wriggled out of my arms and jumped to the floor. "I won't tell Mom if you go back out and get her some flowers." She smiled. "You know how she likes flowers. She says they remind her of home." She turned her head sideways and looked at me with a frown. "Can I go to that home with you and Mom someday?"

"I promise you that one day we'll take you there and we'll have a nice long vacation." She beamed with glee. "Now, go get Miss Jenny and tell her that I have to go back out for a few minutes."

She smiled and ran back into the kitchen where Jenny was busy baking cupcakes for the party. I left the house and made a quick trip to the florist. I made sure all the roses were long stemmed and had no thorns. After all, none of the flowers back home had thorns.

I got back to the house just before Sarah arrived. She had been giving a talk at the university concerning the missing meanings of several Egyptian hieroglyphs. She also was contradicting several meanings previously taken as gospel from the academic world. She had made quite a name for herself since our return.

Sarah came in and sighed as she put her briefcase on the entrance table. When she saw the flowers on the table she went over and smelled the flowers and read the note. With a smile she came over and gave me a hug. "You remembered," she said with a smile and gave me a kiss. "I'll have to remember to give Liz an extra cupcake tomorrow." She turned and went back to the kitchen to see how the girls were getting along with their cupcakes.

I decided I would tell her about the stranger later, when she wasn't so wrapped up in happiness and family.

She poked her head around the door with a questioning look on her face. "What stranger?"

Giving up, I told her what had happened in the class. She thought for a moment and responded, "He couldn't have known you were from the inside. He would never have tried to scan your thoughts and give himself away. He was just trying to pick up information." She paced back and forth. She always did that when she was thinking hard.

Her reasoning made sense. I told her, "We need to let someone know about this." I watched for Sarah's reaction. She looked up and nodded.

"Do you think that it's important enough to contact Jabril?" She knew that it had some significance but didn't know how much.

"I don't think it's worth the risk. I think my best bet is to contact Brian at Groom Lake and let him take it from there. He has direct contact with Peter at the Pentagon and Jabril back home."

I stopped Sarah from pacing back and forth. It was hard to talk to her when she was going back and forth like that. "Stop worrying. I'm sure it's nothing to get upset about. After all, that's why we're here. We're supposed to watch and wait." I smiled at her, and she forced a smile back. She wasn't so sure that it was nothing to get upset about.

She felt the same feeling as I did. Our premonitions tended to come true. Our feelings about this stranger were ominous.

"I'll tell Brian what I was able to pick from his mind so he can get his undercover boys out of the coffee shop and doing what they do best. They'll be able to find out what he is all about. He'll let us know what he finds out, and we can go from there." My assurance didn't make her feel any better.

After Sarah put Liz to bed for the night, I used the secure line in my office to contact Brian. Sarah came down and listened in. "Brian, I hate to bother you so late, but I need for you to get in touch with Jabril. Yes, we're all fine. Tell him that he needs to find out as much as he can about a certain Greg Jordan at 455 Cedar Lake Drive, this city. He attempted to read my mind in class today. He is working for the dark forces. No, don't have him picked up. I don't want to tip off his superiors until we know more. No, the information he was trying to get from me was information about ancient tunnels under the planes in Peru. I knew about them but didn't disclose anything to our stranger. Yes, he didn't know I scanned his mind. Thank you. I'll tell Sarah. Yes, Liz is getting to be quite a handful. Yes, I'll tell her. She wanted to know if Uncle Brian would be coming to her party tomorrow. Okay, I'll tell her. Let me know what Jabril says. Yes, I'm sure our friend will be back. He didn't get what he came for. I'm sure he'll try again. Okay, goodbye." I hung the phone up.

"Brian thinks this is important. He's heard rumors of the dark forces trying to get to the inside. The interior still doesn't know why they want to go there. Brian thinks Jabril will want to follow up on this information. By the way, he said to tell you he sends his love and to give Liz a big kiss for him. He also said that he was taking a break from work tomorrow for a long weekend. It'll give him an excuse to come to Liz's party, and we can talk face-to-face about what Jabril thinks.

"I only have one class tomorrow, so I'll be home early. This is a class of seniors studying ancient Greece. We'll see if our stranger has multiple tastes." Sarah didn't smile. I knew how she felt. We spent the rest of the night preparing for the next day. Sarah had another seminar to give, and I graded papers and made an outline for tomorrow's class. I need to mention here that Sarah and I don't sleep like normal people. We only require a couple of hours of meditation once a week. We spend much of our out-of-class time reading technical journals. We do this mostly to assist Brian and Jarod at Groom Lake. We try to find technical information passed on to the outside from the dark forces. Brian has been very busy working with Grumman on the LM5. That is the lunar lander that will be used on the upcoming manned moon landing.

The next day everything went as usual. Five minutes into my class I noticed Jordan slip into the back of the class. He was still trying to search my mind for ancient underground tunnels. I'm not so sure that he even knew why the information was needed. I searched his mind for what he knew about the interior. He knew nothing. He had interior abilities even though they were crude. He had to have been taken outside when he was very young. He didn't know his mother or father. He was only a flunky of the dark forces. He thought they were aliens from outer space. I suddenly felt sorry for him. Again he left before the class was over.

I wondered just how many others were like Jordan were out there doing deeds for the dark forces. They have flying craft much like the interior, but are a smaller race. They have evolved gray, leathery skin and have unusually large eyes due to thousands of years of inhabiting the underground kingdom. They have no feelings of love, remorse, or empathy for the outer world. They thrive on fear, and through their feelings of superiority over the outer race of men they want to rule that world. Jarod thinks that they have been trying to breed a cross between themselves and the outer races so they can thrive on the outside. They fear water and have a great dislike for fire or sunlight. They have been instrumental in many disasters to the human race in the past and would have had even more had we not stopped them from the inside. The destruction of their leader and the many thousands in the underground cities on the inside world put a damper on their plans.

35

I killed the leader with one swift well-placed swing of the Sword of Truth. I had not realized it at the time, but that was the only weapon that could have even touched the evil master of the underworld. My grandfather, Apollo, once owned the sword. Despite his reputation as a Greek god, he was just a man who happened to have a very long life span. His son, Drake, was my father. The Dark Lord, Balail, killed him and my mother when I was just a small babe. It took nearly thirty years for me to avenge my parents' death. I may now be a hero in the inner world, but I am still just a man. Sarah and I were fortunate to be trained in the inner world with the help of some very talented masters at the University of Avalon. Jabril is the headmaster there, and it is he who I wanted to get the information about our little stranger to.

I left the campus right after class. I would have to miss a departmental meeting for later that afternoon. I would have to call and make some excuse. Right now, I needed to get home.

Sarah had beaten me home. She and Jenny were fixing up the dinning room with balloons and streamers and a "Happy Birthday" sign for Liz. Liz was outside playing with Jake, our German shepherd. The dog weighed more than Liz, but he wouldn't let any harm come to her. It was a warm day for this time of year, and the kids from the neighborhood would enjoy playing in Liz's playground. I had warned her not to show off on the unusual equipment she had there. Jenny had insisted that the special monkey bars and climbing wall were built to further Liz's training. Needless to say, that Liz was four foot of pure muscle with a smile that would melt a snowman.

I told Sarah and Jenny about the stranger. Jenny was afraid for Liz. She didn't like the idea of the dark forces being so close to her ward. Sarah and I didn't like it either. Sarah took my hand and looked up into my eyes. When she did that, she could have anything she wanted. "Why don't you go outside and keep Liz company while we get ready for the party. She wants to show you her new acrobatic routine. She's been practicing it all week." She let go of my hand and gave me a friendly push toward the patio door.

When Liz saw me coming out of the house, she ran and jumped into my arms. She, like her mother, had me wrapped around her little finger. They made my world, and I knew that I couldn't be any happier than I was at this moment. This was not the inner world, but this one was perfect enough for me.

"Daddy, you have to see my new routine. Jenny helped me with it." She jumped out of my arms and walked over to a small tape recorder. She turned it on, and Beethoven's Fifth Symphony came from the speaker on the side. She walked to a practice square on the lawn. She went through a series of tumbles and maneuvers that would have challenged an Olympic champion. Each movement was synchronized with the music coming from the speakers. It was quite a show. Her balance and coordination was far beyond her years. Today she was four. What would she be like when she was grown? It's a shame we couldn't share her artistry with the whole world. I was very proud of her, but I might have been just a little prejudiced.

After her final tumbling run I could only applaud. This was the only gratification she needed. She came running over and looked up into my eyes. "How did I do, Daddy?"

"I would have to give you a perfect ten. I have never seen such a great routine." I smiled down at her and saw the appreciation on her little face. I ruffled her shiny red hair and gave her a kiss on the forehead.

Jake came over and nuzzled my hand. He wanted a little attention too. "Have you been taking good care of my little girl, Jake?" I patted the dog on the head, and he gave me a reassuring bark. Liz bent over and hugged the big dog around the neck.

Jake reminded me of Raja, the white tiger from back home. I missed him. He too had been a friend to me especially when I needed him the most.

I watched Liz for more than an hour as she worked out on the bars. Her strength and balance still amazed me. She could traverse the top bar from one end to the other while walking ten feet above the ground. The length of the bar was over thirty feet, and it was only an inch wide.

At the end, she did a complete backward flip and landed square on the bar without a bobble. Her nerves were much steadier than mine. She did a flip off the top bar and landed the way she had seen the acrobats do on television. This was just for show. She turned around and looked over to me with a grin. She knew she was good, and she knew she was showing off. She also knew that it was all right for her to show off with me. I smiled back and gave her a thumbs-up.

I got a buzz from my pager. The window of the pager only said, "Priority One." It was a coded message from Peter Black at the Pentagon. It meant that he needed to see me as soon as possible. It must have been very important for him to risk communication. He was keeping a low profile after he returned from the inner world. Something must be going on. It looks like our days of watching and waiting were coming to an end. I needed to tell Sarah and get in touch with Jarod at Groom Lake. He could make arrangements for me to get to Washington with the proper credentials so as not to arouse too much attention.

Word had gotten around pretty quickly about our stranger. I couldn't believe that he could be responsible for this sudden urgent meeting.

I slipped back into the house and left Liz playing with Jake. She was deep in conversation with him. It's not unusual to see a child talking to her dog. People would be very surprised to learn that Jake was also answering back. Liz's abilities were growing by the day.

I found Sarah and Jenny in the kitchen. I told them about the message from Peter. Both looked uneasy. Sarah came over to me. "I don't like the sound of this. I've had a feeling ever since you saw the stranger that something ominous was in the works. I feel that it has to do with us directly somehow." She paused as she always did when she was thinking. "And I'm not so sure it had to do with that stranger in your class."

Sarah's premonitions were much more than just feelings. She had a foresight that was uncanny. It was far better than my own. But even I had a feeling that something was wrong. "I know. I have the same feeling. Maybe Peter can put some light on the situation."

My pager buzzed again. I took it out of my pocket, and both Sarah and I looked at it. It said "51–2." It was from Jarod at Area 51. The "2" meant that he needed to see both Sarah and I. Sarah frowned. "I don't like leaving Liz. I know Jenny can take good care of her, but I'm still afraid for her." I had learned that this premonition of Sarah's was something not to be taken lightly.

Jenny tried to assure Sarah. "It must be very important for you both to go to Groom Lake. This overrides your request to go to Washington. This must be more important as Jarod knows that you don't want to leave Liz. If danger comes around while you're gone, you can be sure that I will take good care of Liz. Please keep me informed. I can't hide anything from Liz like I used to be able to do. She can see right through me." I could tell that Jenny was worried as well. Her awareness was almost as good as Sarah's.

Liz came bounding into the room and stopped abruptly as she saw our faces. "What's wrong, Mom?" The question hung in the air as we considered how much to tell Liz.

Sarah came over and hugged Liz. "Dad and I have to go on a little business trip after your party. We have to leave you with Jenny while we're gone." Liz was silent. She looked first at me, then at Jenny.

Liz then turned back to Sarah. "Mom, you're worried about me. You think that something is going to happen soon. You don't have to worry so much. I will make sure that Jenny is all right. You go with Daddy. What you have to do is very important." She smiled over at Jenny and me. What did she know that we didn't?

Jenny looked over at me and said, "I've told you she is brighter than she should be at this age. She is one of the sages, born to see into the future. I feel sorry for anyone who tries to harm her or one of us. Her powers are formidable for one so young." She turned to Sarah. "Your mission here is more important than Liz or me. We need to see how the future plays out. We've learned that the future is only in God's hands. We have learned that we must live for the future, not try to change it. If worse comes to worst, we still have the resources of the inner world at our fingertips. We'll be all right while you're gone."

Her words were meant to reassure us, but her mind was busy trying to come up with some way to keep Liz safe. She could not hide her worry from us. Sarah frowned over at me and sent me a private thought. *I don't know what I would do if something happened to Liz. I have a feeling that she will be safe though.*

Liz was watching us closely. I could see her mind racing. She knew something. She was also blocking it from the three of us. What was she planning?

I knew she was right about Liz being all right, but I could not see any solution to the problem that I too sensed in Sarah's and my future. I also knew for the same reason that Liz would be all right despite the danger we sensed. *Every one of us will be in danger, but I feel that for some reason it is meant to be.* My thought was true, and Sarah sensed the truth of it. Liz had also picked up the thought, and she was nodding in the affirmative in my direction. My daughter truly was a mystery. None other could have seen my thought to Sarah.

This surprised Sarah as well. "Just what other surprises are you keeping from us, young lady?"

Liz didn't answer the question but just smiled in the knowing way that we had been accustomed to seeing from her. I knew that Sarah was probing her mind, and, from her expression, she was getting nowhere. She did get an assurance from her that everything was according to some mysterious plan.

The doorbell suddenly interrupted all this.

Liz jumped for the door. "The clown is here!" She opened the door, and there stood our rented clown. He came in and looked over the entranceway. He was rethinking the amount of tip he would get for this little gig. He was harmless, but just a little bit greedy. Brian was right behind.

While the clown was surveying his new client's home, Brian took me to the side. "Peter sends word for you to go directly to Groom Lake. You will be updated there."

Liz finally took her eyes off the clown and noticed Brian. "Uncle Brian, you did come to my party. We are going to have a great time."

There had been several times over the past few years that Brian and I had to make some decisions on the processing of information or what the general outside world needed as far as technology was concerned. Mostly it was to keep me updated on the spread of the underground world of the dark forces and what they were up to.

Brian picked up his favorite niece and gave her a big hug and kiss. "I wouldn't miss it for the world, Princess." Brian had always called her this. He found it amusing that she really was a true princess.

Our attention turned to the clown who was still wondering about his bonus for this little party. He really was a greedy person. I just hoped he was a better clown for Liz's sake.

We took him to the backyard by the pool where he again re-evaluated his tip. He started setting up his balloons and tricks while more visitors started arriving from the neighborhood. Some of these where just friends of Liz's, and their parents and the others who had children Liz's age were just curious about the Jennings family. Some of the men who came along were there just to try to get me to invest in one of their "sure thing" schemes. We smiled and greeted the parents as the kids started playing in the grass with Jake. You couldn't tell that Liz was any different from the other kids. She really enjoyed playing with them.

We were enjoying drinks by the pool. Some of our guests expected alcoholic drinks, but we assured them that it wouldn't be good at a party for the children. We didn't relate to them that we didn't indulge in the practice of drinking either.

The clown was now busy making a doggy out of balloons. Liz found this fascinating. She watched intently as the clown passed out his crude creations. He didn't see Liz busy behind his back making her own creation. When he turned around, a perfect monkey made from balloons was sitting on the table with his tail slowly going around. His ears were overlarge, and she had stretched the balloon of his head so he had the semblance of a nose and eyes. Soon the tail stopped wagging as the bal-

41

loon finally unwrapped itself, and the air was released, and the monkey shot into the air and made a loud pop as it came apart. The parts drifted back down to the grass. Some of the parts fell into the open mouth of the clown. He was too astounded to speak. The children laughed and said they wanted to see the flying monkey again. The clown just stared down at Liz with his mouth still open. "How did you do that?"

She just smiled up at him and said, "You just showed me how."

I sent over a warning to Liz. She just looked back over at me and smiled.

Brian and Sarah were only amused. I could see that Brian was trying to figure out our little girl. I hope he has better luck than we have.

The party went on without any further complications. I assured those wanting me to invest in their schemes that I would think it over very carefully. The others we thanked for making Liz's party such a success. I don't think that their visit had satisfied their curiosity about the Jennings family.

We sighed with relief as the last of the guests left. The children were very pleased with the presents they had received at the party. By some mysterious way, each child had gotten something they had always wanted. We discovered that this was Liz's doings. The parents were told not to bring presents, which didn't hurt their feelings at all. All left happy, except those that saw their moneymaking schemes going down the drain.

Liz was happy. She had found another fascinating thing to do with balloons. She and Jake went on upstairs to the playroom. She was explaining what balloons were to him as she ran up the steps. That had to be a new concept for Jake. I wish we were as unconcerned as she was about what was going on. We would know more when we reached Groom Lake.

Brian said that he had to get back. There were some jobs that he had to do before we got to Groom Lake. Jabril had given him certain tasks that he didn't want to discus in an area that might not be secure from prying ears. He had gotten very cautious over the past few years. He told us to give Liz a big kiss for him and left. We would see him again very soon.

OUR VISIT TO AREA 51

It took us some time to make arrangements and to get an early morn-ing flight to Las Vegas. From there, we would be going to Groom Lake once more. Sarah had been there many times before, and we had changed into our naval uniforms. We were both commanders in the United States Navy, complete with service records and credentials containing crypto clearance. We didn't realize that this very item that we had used previously as a cover for our work would be the key to the predicaments which were to come. Even the best cover for our covert movements would have flaws.

We landed in Las Vegas and found our plane ready for takeoff to Area 51. It was sitting in the area outside the private hanger that we had come to recognize. The pilot, who we also recognized from our previous visits to Groom Lake, greeted us. He saluted us as we came aboard. He didn't speak a word but settled into the cockpit and, after a short time, had clearance to taxi for takeoff. The takeoff was almost immediate as this flight had priority. The flight to Groom Lake was short, and after we landed, we taxied to a waiting jeep. The air force airman that was driving jumped out of the jeep and saluted. "I am to take you to your

43

quarters," he said with self-importance. He had to be new on the job. We got into the back and darted into the complex of buildings as we headed for the hanger that led back into the mountain.

We were dropped off at the elevators and picked up by the marine guard who took us down the elevator to the large passageway that led back into the mountain. After placing his palm on the reader outside one of the elevators, the door opened and he motioned for us to enter. He saluted and turned and left. We already knew which floor our quarters were on. Our little guide and housemaids met us on our floor to show us to our rooms. We followed without any words being spoken.

When we entered our separate rooms we both found that the red light on our phones was blinking, which indicated a message was waiting. It was Jarod's voice on the phone and he was overly excited as he told us to come to level eighteen without further delay.

I left the room to find Sarah leaving her room at the same time, and that worried look was on her face again. She needed to stop doing that. She'd have frown lines before she was three hundred.

We went to the elevators, and Sarah put her palm on the reader. The door stayed closed. "It probably needs both our palms. Things have gotten more sophisticated since we were here last." I placed my palm to the reader, and the door opened. We punched number eighteen, and we dropped like a lead balloon. The thought made me think of Liz.

Jarod met us as the door opened. He grabbed Sarah and gave her a big hug and vigorously shook my hand. "Well, if it isn't my two most favorite people in the world. Glad you could come." His cherry greeting hid his true concern. "Come on. We have to talk, but not here. Too many ears have sprouted around here since you were here last. We no longer have a say so as to who is to work here. The selections, we are told, are handled by those that are more capable of making those kinds of decisions."

We could tell that this insult was eating at him. "Jocko is here. He came in from Washington just before you." He started to say more, but

44

after a quick look around, he thought better of it and just motioned for us to follow.

We soon reached his office, and after the palm reader allowed the door to open, we entered and received much the same greeting from Jocko as we did from Jarod. What would bring the head scientist at CIA headquarters out of Langley? He looked concerned as well and maybe a little frightened. "It's really good to see you both. I just wish it could have been under better circumstances." We waited for him to explain. "Some very unpleasant things have been taking place where we are concerned. It seems that we are all being replaced. There was a big speech about it being for the good of our country. There is a new face emerging from the military contingent at the capital that is taking control of all covert activities. He is Major General Theodore Wesley Vanderhoff, known by his subordinates simply as TW and his enemies as Teddy Bear. Grizzly would fit him better. Thank God that he thinks he is dealing with extraterrestrial aliens from outer space."

Jocko was interrupted by a knock at the door. "Our other visitor has arrived." He opened the door and in came none other than Peter Black himself.

A big smile came over his face as he spotted Sarah and me. "I was beginning to wonder if I'd ever get a chance to see my two best friends in the world again." He came over and gave Sarah and me fatherly hugs. "I sure am glad that we could get together again. There are two others coming down the elevator that will be glad to see you, and they should be just outside."

On cue, the knock at the door announced more visitors. Peter opened the door and in came Billy and Cindy. Billy let out a hoop when he saw us and came over and grabbed me with a big hug that lifted me completely off the floor. "Boy, are you two a sight for sore eyes." With that, he grabbed Sarah with a gentler hug as Cindy took her turn hugging Peter, Sarah, and me. Billy was busy shaking hands with Jocko and Jarod and introducing Cindy and himself. I now realized that this was the first time they had met.

45

Billy stepped back and looked at us. "That's the first time I've seen you two in naval uniforms since that last night on the submarine before we entered the inner world." He smiled. "Who are you trying to fool? You two are just not the military types. You make a much better mom and dad."

Cindy came over and put her arm around Billy. "We may be a mom and dad too before long." She smiled up at Billy's stunned expression. "No, I'm not expecting. But I can sense a little one in our future."

Billy knew that Cindy's awareness had grown since they had arrived in this world and the look in her eyes told him that she was right. Peter was the first to break up the reunion. "I guess I'm responsible for getting you all together. It seems that the seven of us in this room are the total number of people who know the truth about the inner world. The president knows of its existence but little more. For the future of all mankind on the outside, he has been sworn to secrecy. He will keep that vow."

Peter walked back and forth in front of the door before he continued. "Jocko has told you about Teddy Bear Vanderhoff. I filled in Cindy and Billy before we came down. Had a little trouble getting them through security."

Peter paused again as he tried to think about where to start. "Vanderhoff is a real sore spot in the Pentagon. He is from a rich oil family in Texas who bought his appointment to West Point. He was about expelled four times for cheating, but all charges were dropped for some reason. He has been buying his way ever since. He has big contacts in Congress. He wangled his way into the Black Opps after losing his command of the Special Forces. He was a real headache there, and it took some doing to get him booted out. It had to come in the form of a promotion that he didn't deserve. He now has the ear and eyes of the CIA and FBI as well as counter intelligence." You could tell that Peter had no love for Vanderhoff.

Peter looked over at Sarah and me. "I'm sorry to say that one of his spies told of a couple of naval officers with special privileges had come to Area 51 and had actually assisted in the design of some sophisticated equipment that was used on alien spacecraft. It'll only be a matter of days before he will be able to track you two down. He already knows about your visit to the White House. He has your pictures from surveillance cameras. It is from these that he also knows of the involvement of Billy and Cindy. Lord knows how he got them. The president can't intervene without tipping his hand. Other conspiracies would be nothing compared to your secret visit there, not to mention the Dalai Lama's."

Peter took a deep breath. He looked over at Jocko and Jarod. They had been listening in disbelief. Both had their mouths open. "You two are next. I think Vanderhoff wants you both to permanently disappear. Much the same way people who knew too much back in the fifties did."

Now Jocko and Jarod were becoming nervous.

"You will indeed have to disappear. With the help of someone you will soon meet, I have been in contact with Jabril on Avalon. You will take the craft in the upper hanger along with an inner world spy we have here at the base and relocate to the inner world. Jabril will contact us with details later." Peter paused again to let Jarod and Jocko take in their situation. The prospect of going to the inner world suddenly hit them as they looked at each other in disbelief. They hugged each other and slapped each other on the back.

Peter smiled at their elation and continued. "You will soon know what it's like to live in a perfect world. Your lives will never be the same. You may be required to return once we get this mess straightened out. I also know for a fact that you will not want to."

Peter's other comment finally hit Jarod. "Spy? What spy?"

"You remember Brian, who is now helping with the lunar lander for the moon mission?"

Jarod nodded slightly and cocked his head to one side. "I knew that character was someone special. He's the spy from the inner world, isn't he?"

47

"Yes. He has already been contacted, and I'm sorry to say that the next time the craft that you built tries to take off, the gravity drive that you reconstructed from that crashed craft will blow up. This is from strict orders of Jabril's. It shouldn't cause any major injuries, as the craft won't get that high. He has had his hands full eliminating any technology that could fall into the wrong hands. If all goes according to Jabril's plan, the intact craft will be in Avalon and Teddy Vanderhoff will be left holding absolutely nothing. We can't let a man like him get what he thinks is alien technology. It would take centuries for him to create another drive. The outer rim's technology is far too primitive. Charles, Sarah, Billy, Cindy, and I have other matters to take care of. Jabril is now working out the details. Our dear friend Vanderhoff also thinks the space race is a waste of military money, and we found that he intends to do as much as he can to divert money spent on the space program to his causes." Peter took another deep breath. "It seems that the dark forces have the same idea, except they intend direct action. Jabril needs for us to make sure that this doesn't happen."

Peter had that worried look that we had seen when we first entered the inner world. "Jabril has promised to keep us informed on any new developments." Here he smiled. The new Peter emerged as he said, "Jabril said that he would give us a call. I asked him how, and he replied 'Why, by the phone closest to you at the time, of course. He thought that it would be obvious. I'm sure he can do it."

I am also sure he could do it. Nothing would surprise me about my old friend and headmaster at the University of Avalon. He was much more than we could realize.

As if by cue, the red phone on Jarod's desk rang. The red light on the top was flashing. Jarod looked shocked. It was a direct line to the president. He went over and picked up the receiver and said, "Jarod here." He listened, and a strange expression came on his face. He looked over at me and said, "It's for you. He said it's urgent!"

I went over and took the phone from Jarod and was surprised to hear Jabril on the other end. "Hello, Charles. I hope you're doing well.

It seems that events have escalated since my last communication. I really would like you and your whole team to come back home for a meeting. I can't rely on current communications, and this is the only secure line in your area. I have already contacted Jenny, and she and Liz are being made welcome in your castle as we speak." He paused again, and I gave a quick look at Sarah. She suspected something was up.

Jabril continued. "I want you to take the craft there to Atlantic Base tonight. It might be a tight fit for all of you. Brian will be coming along. He will arrive there shortly. Brian, Jocko, and Jarod will fly directly to Avalon. You and your four companions will pick up Zaron and go to Mount Rainier for a special meeting. You will know more when you get there. After your meeting, you will come directly here."

It would be good to see Zaron again. The golden craft from the royal house of Shambala was not only the smartest craft of the inner world but also the fastest and most powerful. Sarah and I had considered that machine a close friend, if you can accept that concept.

Jabril closed up by saying, "Remember your training, and be careful. May God protect you until we meet again." The phone went dead. Jabril had finished.

Everyone had stopped, and all were staring at me. I suddenly realized that only Sarah had any idea to whom I was speaking and that I had not spoken a single word since I took the receiver from Jarod. I suddenly noticed that it was still in my hand and gently hung up the phone.

"That was Jabril, back at the university. He wants all of us to go immediately to Atlantic Base. He must have already contacted Brian because he said he would be here soon. Jarod and Jocko are to go from there directly to Avalon with Brian." I looked over at Sarah. "We five are to take Zaron and go directly to the western entrance on Mount Rainier for a mysterious meeting of some sort. We are to be updated when we get there. We should learn more at Atlantic Base as to the time for the meeting."

I saw that Sarah was thinking about Liz. I smiled at her as if she had

49

not seen my thoughts. "It seems that Liz and Jenny are safe at home." I was amused at the question in Sarah's eyes. "When I say home, I mean Shambala. They are at the castle now. It seems that Jabril got them to safety for some reason. This whole thing is getting very complicated."

Jarod had to have one of his cups of coffee. He was pacing back and forth, and Jocko was at his side. They were very excited and were chatting back and forth so fast that I don't think either one of them knew what the other was saying.

Billy and Cindy were excited too. They had longed to go back to Avalon. They now considered that as their home. Peter was just as anxious to see the inner world again, but his serious nature gave his face that worried look. He was thinking forward to our mysterious meeting at our base at the western entrance.

To update you as to the entrances that I speak of, you would have to revert to the original writings about the garden of Eden. The garden was placed at the east of Eden and not in it. God placed Cherubims at the eastern gate after Adam and Eve were cast out. With flaming swords, they guarded this eastern entrance. This garden utopia, which contained the tree of life, had eternal spring and all that man could want. It might also be good to mention here that there was no night. We were to find out that this garden was never destroyed, and we also found out why man could not discover its location. This garden was an entire world complete with continents and oceans with five entrances. One, which was the eastern entrance, was within the temple of Shambala near Lhasa, Tibet. The western entrance, of which we were just speaking about going to soon, is located within Mount Rainier. The next two are at the north and south polar regions. These are huge. The access is over three hundred miles from rim to rim. The fifth, that Jocko and Jarod are soon to travel through, lies beneath the sea in what has now become known as the Bermuda Triangle. A large rift below the surface goes through the crusts of both worlds in a place where the molten material of the earth has frozen all the way through. This allows the inner sea to join the outer ocean through this rift. It is through this rift that the inner world travels to access Atlantic Base and the outer rim. A much better explanation exists in my first journal. Atlantic Base is located north of the rift just a few miles off the North Carolina coast.

There was just enough time for all that had happened to start sinking in when a knock at the door announced Brian. When Jarod opened the door, Brian stuck his head inside and said only three words: "*Time to go!*"

BACK TO ATLANTIC BASE

This time it was Jarod and Jocko's time to follow as Brian led the way to the elevators. The other five of us tried to keep up. The tables and labs were empty. I had not realized it had gotten so late. There was no one there to see us enter the elevator to the upper hanger. Brian had bypassed the views of the surveillance cameras so our movements would never be seen.

This time the hanger was empty, and it was totally dark, except for a dim blue light emanating from the interior of the now critical UFO. The hanger doors were already open to the night sky. The outside lights were off, indicating the base had made ready for a covert night flight. They would assume it was time for the Black Bird to take off on some mission over Russia. It has been flying out of this base since '65.

Brian had indeed been very busy. It must have taken some doing to make all these preparations without alarming the rest of the base as to what we were up to. My admiration for the man went up another notch.

We followed Brian to the craft and went up the ramp. The craft had already warmed up, and the gravity drive was ready to engage. Brian slipped into the pilot's seat and brought up the ramp and closed the door. We all had flown before and was not surprised when the gravity drive came on, causing that falling sensation that sudden weightlessness brings. Brian easily brought the craft out of the hanger, and we shot at tremendous velocity to the upper reaches of the atmosphere. Jocko and Jarod were impressed with the way Brian was handling the craft. He spoke not a word as we huddled together and viewed the earth below us. The moon shining on the clouds gave an unreal peaceful feeling. The three-dimensional view projected before us gave that familiar feeling that we would all fall out at any moment.

Brian was wasting no time as we sped east toward the North Carolina coast. It was close to midnight, east coast time, when we started down rapidly toward the ocean that had suddenly appeared beneath us. Brian stopped the craft just above the waves. A late winter storm had given the surface white caps, and the wind was strong. We felt nothing. The craft felt no wind at all. It was not the weather that had stopped Brian but the cautious habit of making sure the air, surface, and below the surface was devoid of any human activity. After he had satisfied himself that our arrival had not been observed, he dove beneath the surface. Jocko and Jarod caught their breath. The three-dimensional view of going under water made them suddenly hold their breath as the sea came up over the craft. We traveled another ten miles east underwater before Brain again started straight down. The outside lights of the craft came on, and we saw the bottom coming at us really fast. This brought another gasp from our two novices. The craft stopped, and the huge doors of one of the complex's airlocks opened, allowing us to slowly drop down. We paused as the doors closed and air replaced the seawater in the large chamber. When a green light indicated all was safe, the main doors to the complex opened allowing Brian to gently move the craft over to a waiting cradle and gently settled down.

Brian shut down the craft and opened the door and let down the ramp. The view screen faded, and we could not see the bustle of activity our arrival had caused.

Jarod and Jocko stood looking around at this underground city. This room alone was the size of a good-sized football stadium. They suddenly became agitated when they saw several, what appeared to be, guards rush forward with strange-looking weapons pointed right at them.

We all froze, not daring to send out any thoughts or make any sudden moves. Security had become tighter since my last visit. It was probably because of the war with the dark forces.

A smile suddenly spread across the face of the guard nearest me. He turned and yelled as loud as he could across the room, "It's Aaron!"

The weapons disappeared, and all the work stopped in the hanger as people came running from all directions.

Jarod walked over to me and whispered, "They seem to know you."

After graduating from the university, selected students are required to work here at Atlantic Base for a minimum of two years. About every person in this room had been with me at what had become known as the final battle. They were either flying from this base or fought with the students from the university. They were my brothers, my sisters, and my friends. Of course they knew me.

We shook hands for what seemed an eternity as we introduced the two friends we had brought along. Sarah and I were surprised to see so many familiar faces from the university, and Cindy, Billy, and Peter were also catching up on what news they could from the inside as they recognized some of their old friends also. I guess we five were as close to celebrities as the inner world had. The admiration and respect we felt from the crowd around us made us feel very humble.

I had lost sight of Brian but finally saw him over the heads of the crowd talking to Jeffery. Jeff had been the commander of a flight out into the solar system that Sarah and I had been lucky enough to catch a ride on. We had actually walked on Europa, one of the moons of Jupiter. Jeff had a great big smile on his face as he and Brian gave each other a great big hug in greeting. They were about the same age, and they most likely spent their internship here at the base together; both now doing what they thought needed to be done. Jeff and Brian were both a cut

54

above even the superior intelligence of the inner world. It's not such a surprise that they were friends.

Suddenly a girl came running into the complex and jumped into Brian's arms. They hugged and kissed and both were crying. With a quick probe, I saw that it was Brian's wife. She had heard that he had arrived. They had not seen each other for over two years.

The sacrifices that these people make for the betterment of man are awesome. It's too bad that the human race doesn't know and can't appreciate what they are doing for them.

This brings us back to the reason we're here. We too have a task. We just don't know what it is yet.

Sarah slipped over and gently took my hand. "It's really good to see all of them again. I've really missed them over the past few years. I had almost forgotten just how great the people of our world are. I hope our task will allow us to spend some time with all of our people back on Shambala. I would like to also go to Agartha and visit Mom and Dad."

I gave Sarah a hug and kissed her on the forehead. I knew how she felt. After all, she was the true princess of Agartha and heir to the throne. Her father and mother, though king and queen of Agartha, were still just mother and father to Sarah. That would make me a prince of Agartha, a position that held some prestige in her homeland. I was also the former prince of Shambala, as my father and mother were once king and queen of that land. My true name is Aaron, Son of Drake and Elizabeth. Even though they were no longer reigning at the time they were killed by Balail, my family is still held in high esteem in the lands of Shambala.

We suddenly realized that all had become very quiet. A passageway had opened in the middle of the increasing number of people in the hanger. A craft was making its way from one of the elevators. I recognized the golden craft right away. It was Zaron. Whispers were going around the room. "Aaron is to fly Zaron once again."

I had not realized just how much of a status symbol that Zaron had

55

become since our battle in the interior. Zaron was flown by Sarah in the battle and blasted a very large number of the dark force's battle craft. Zaron was specially refitted with armor and screens as well as weapons at the top of the line of the inner world's technology. Her super speed is unmatched by any craft here, and I had personally seen one reach near light speed. I still don't know Zaron's top speed. There is one other thing that is super about Zaron. She received her artificial intelligence from Jabril himself. She was more alive than most humans I had ever met and much more intelligent. Sarah and I both loved the craft and indeed felt she was a close friend.

The cradle halted several steps away from us. Sarah and I went over to the craft and admired her sleek lines and shinny gold exterior. The crest of Shambala emblazoned on her side. *Greetings, Masters. It is good to have you back.* I smiled and patted the craft as one would pat a faithful friend.

It's good to be flying with you again, Zaron. Sarah and I have missed you. The ramp came down, and the door to the craft opened.

I will be ready when you are, Master, and I have very much missed you also. Zaron's engines seemed to purr as she got her systems warmed up.

Could a machine really miss her human companions? I told you her artificial intelligence was super. Maybe it is more than that. Only Jabril knows. This technology alone could fill several journals, so I'll move on.

Following orders, Brian said his goodbyes to the crowd and started to do the same with his wife. She then informed him that he was to take his period of rest and relaxation back home with her. These orders were from King Dresden. He hugged his wife, with an even bigger smile on his face, he and his wife, along with a very happy Jarod and Jocko, entered the craft. It rose and moved to the waiting air lock. Soon they were gone.

I just wished I could be there to see Jocko and Jarod's faces when they saw the inner kingdoms and the beauty of the interior world. They were in for a real treat. Their lives, like our own, would be changed forever.

We were to wait until we received word that our meeting was ready to take place before we could leave, so we joined Jeff and several of our friends from the university in the recreation room where we could just sit and talk.

Much had happened since we went to the outside. The forces of Shambala now controlled all security. They insisted that it was their duty to maintain the peace that their prince had made possible. They would not fail him.

This caused a lump in my throat. The people of my kingdom were valiant peoples with many backgrounds. It is the kingdom that holds the eastern gate. That gate opens to the corridors that lead to the land of Tibet. It is from here that messages are sent to the Dalai Lama when urgent issues arise. His temple guards the other end of the corridor and the golden gate at that end. A son or daughter of light can only open the golden doors of this gate. Not even His Holiness, the Dalai Lama, can do this. When he needs to contact the inner world, he holds a ritual where the temple of Shambala is drawn with colored sand. This is a very sacred time. If you are a student of history or eastern customs, you are already aware of this. This creation of the mandela usually takes five days by a team of lamas. On the evening of the fifth day, the doors to Shambala open. The Dalai Lama is greeted and, on occasion, enters Shambala itself.

My last visit to Avalon was on one of these occasions. He had assisted us on more than one occasion and was an emissary to the inner world.

I had paused as I thought of my homeland. Sarah's punch in the ribs brought me back to the table. I vaguely remember hearing Jeff asking about our daughter.

I smiled and responded. "She's doing great. She just turned four. She is just like her mother and won't listen to a thing I say." This got me another punch in the ribs. I started to mention something about Sarah just now proving my point and suddenly thought better of it as I rubbed my ribs. I continued on a safer note, "She's back in Shambala now. We hope to join her soon."

I was curious as to what new developments were going on at Atlantic Base. It was here that the new technologies of the inner world were developed and put to practical use. "What new work are you into now that we might be interested in?" I saw a smile come on Jeff's face. I knew that he relished anything new as far as inner technology was concerned.

He reverted to the old language as he described his latest project. Most of what he went over is not translatable to English, and I don't think the outer world is ready or could even understand the project that Jeff went over with us. It was fascinating, and we could have talked for many hours on the consequences of the project. A pat on the back from an old friend interrupted our interesting lecture. It was Dorin, commander of the base.

"Good to see you again, old friend. Sorry I couldn't meet you sooner, but you know how Jabril is when he's on a roll. Can't get away from him. He's been on the communicator for more than an hour outside time." He shook our hands, and I introduced him to Peter, Billy, and Cindy.

"It's good to see the 'mighty five' together again. I hope you don't mind the tag. The university gossip group gave you five that label very soon after the final battle. The title is now imbedded into inner world history. All of you heroes are still whispered about in awe at the university. I just hope all the rumors don't interfere with your mission when you return."

I saw Billy nudge Cindy. I picked up his thoughts, quite by accident, to Cindy. *See I told you I was something special.* I saw Cindy's smirk but didn't pick her return answer to Billy. It must have be a good retort, as Billy's ego seemed somewhat deflated.

My attention returned to Dorin. "Did Jabril mention anything about our mysterious meeting at the western gate?"

Dorin halfway smiled as he replied, "Yes. He knew you five would be anxious about a strange meeting, but he said you'd understand once you got there. We couldn't speak about the nature of the meeting, and you'll also understand why when you get there. He did say for you not to worry. It's more in the order of a protocol than of dire necessity."

Well, that really cleared up things. The meeting was now even more mysterious than before. I noticed that Sarah and the other three outsiders, as we liked to call ourselves, were thinking the same thing.

Dorin appreciated our curiosity but got up and shook our hands. "I really would like to stay and visit, but the base really keeps me busy. We'll let you know when it's ready for you to leave. In the meantime, please let Jeff show our newer guests around." He nodded toward Peter, Billy, and Cindy. I saw Peter and Billy especially perk up. This was right down their line, so to speak. Cindy was curious as well, but more from a feminine point.

Sarah squeezed my hand and sent me a thought. *I wish they could travel to the outer solar system as we did. Wouldn't that be exciting for them?*

I smiled back at Sarah. *I don't think we'll have that much time. I feel our departure will be very soon.*

Sarah suddenly smiled. *Can you feel it?* She seemed excited. *They will return here very soon for an extended stay. They will never forget it.*

Yes, I felt it too and so must have Dorin as he looked over to Sarah and sent her the thought. *Yes, I guarantee it.* He had picked up on Sarah's private thought to me, and it left Sarah stunned.

She spoke aloud to me as we watched Dorin go out of the room. "He's more than he seems. He may be more than he should be." She paused as she thought that over. "I'm glad he's on our side."

"Me too," was my assessment. I thought back to the time when I had first met Dorin. Even then I knew there was something special about that man.

Dorin's visit seemed to break up the conversation at the table as Peter, Billy, and Cindy were excited by the news that they would get a tour of the facility. Jeff was eager to show off the complex. The term *base* was really misleading as this complex was the size of a large city. There were over a hundred levels, and the hanger we arrived in was one of the smaller ones. We toured most of it when Dorin showed Sarah and me around on our first visit. There were over fifty thousand workers, students, technicians, scientist, pilots, mechanics, and other trades people here. Most were semi-permanent and lived here with their families. None considered this their permanent home, and they took their periods of rest and relaxation back in the inner world. We would call this vacation. Each of these periods usually lasted for six of our months or more. The people of my kingdom liked to take this period during harvest and festival time when they could help with the gathering of the fruits, vegetables, and grains before the celebration of the harvest festival. This was looked forward to with great anticipation, and the celebration lasted for weeks. If you had ever lived there, you wouldn't want to miss it either.

As Jeff got up from the table, he motioned across the room to a technician that was having one of the fruit drinks favored by the people of my kingdom. Jeff leaned over to me and whispered, "I wanted to show you our latest project, but there is someone here that is tied up on the project that would never forgive me if he didn't get to show it to you himself. Bargon is a student from Shambala and would be glad to escort you two to the projects facility."

Bargon came rushing over and spoke to Jeff for a moment. He was excited to get to show the prince of his kingdom and the princess of Avalon to the facility.

Bargon came over and bowed and started talking and didn't stop until we reached the facility. By that time, we knew about his whole family and what he was working on at the base and where he was expected to go when he left. He said there would be a surprise for me when we got home. He wouldn't speak of it any more, and he hid any thought of it very well.

The project's center was on one of the lower levels. We entered a rather large room that was arranged in much the same way as the labs were arranged at Area 51, but on a much larger scale. We approached a man deeply engrossed in his work. He suddenly sensed our presence and stood up and rapidly turned around.

There was only one person in the inner world that had a smile that big. Eric, my true friend and guide from the university, was staring at us in disbelief. He was by my side during the final battle and protected my back during my fight with the dark lord. I thought about him often, as he never left my side during most of my stay in the inner world.

"My lord, I did not know you were here. Why didn't someone tell me? I should have been there to greet you." He looked excited to see us, but the thought he had let us down by not being there when we arrived was also in his mind.

"I'm sorry, Eric, but we came in unannounced. We will be heading back home shortly after a short mission here on the outer rim first."

He came forward nervously to shake our hand. He held us in awe, much the same way he had in the inner world. Sarah sensed his feelings and gave him a big hug. A blush spread across his cheeks, and a sheepish smile followed it. He felt the same affection for us but thought it out of place to show it. He was truly honored by our greeting.

Sarah spoke for us as she said, "Eric, everyone should have such friends as you. We hold the honor of your friendship dear and would not trade it for the world."

Eric's smile grew, and I could see his old ego building. He truly felt it a great honor to be called a friend by the two of us.

I put my arm around Sarah and said, "I don't know if anyone has told you, but we now have a little girl. She will be waiting for us back at the castle."

This news excited Eric even more. "Wow, I hope that I will get to see her before she gets all grown up. I bet she sure is beautiful." Another blush crossed his cheeks as he looked at Sarah and realized the implication that she should look like her.

I felt the same way, but I couldn't keep letting Eric put his foot in his mouth. "Jeff sent us down and said that someone would show us this new project he was telling us about."

Eric's old self-confidence came back as he started showing us what he had been working on.

We were walked through the phases as he reverted to the old language. I can't go into details about the project, as it is not ready for disclosure to the outer world and, from what we were seeing, the outer rim would not be ready for it or understand it for centuries. Sarah and I both found it fascinating. We spent several more hours with Eric going over details of the project until a worker came with a message from Dorin. We were to follow him back to the hanger.

A younger student came running to catch up with us. "Dorin sent these down. He said you might want to change before you go home." He had the now-familiar golden uniforms we had worn before while on the inside. This time the golden jumpsuits contained golden braid, which indicated royalty. Our escort showed us to one of the quarters for the personnel at the base. We changed, and when we left, we gave the naval uniforms we had worn to the young worker who hurried back off.

When we reached the hanger, we found that our three companions had also changed from their civilian attire. Peter wore a gold suit much like ours. Cindy and Billy had the sky blue suits. All seemed ready to leave.

MEETING AT THE
WESTERN GATE

When we arrived at the hanger, our three companions were waiting. We could see the excitement in their eyes from their tour of the facility.

Billy seemed to be the most impressed. "Do you know that they have an elevator here that is a mile across? Imagine . . . an elevator that could carry half of New York City up and down like a bunch of freight."

The size of the larger craft here evidently hadn't been shown to Billy. The crew alone totaled five thousand and could go for years in the outer reaches of space. Even I didn't know how far they had been or had planned to go, but from some of the technology here they could go very far in a very short period of time."

Billy, Cindy, and Peter were able to go aboard one of the larger triangular-shaped research vessels. They thought these were large. Peter kept going on about their ability to monitor any communication and see the smallest details more than ten miles underground. "Not only can they see what's going on underground but can hear, smell, and feel what

63

they are monitoring and can replay it as if it was real time in a simulator that will seem to actually take you there."

I was very aware of that technology, as I had used it to tour the dark corridors and chambers of the dark lord before the final battle. When I went forth with Eric, Prince Verl, and the royal tiger, Raja, I knew just where to find him within the mountain. It was also this knowledge that allowed my escorts to rapidly destroy the ambush that the dark lord had set for us.

But I am getting away from what is taking place in the hanger. We had reached Zaron, and a courier was there waiting with a message from Jabril. "You are to arrive at the western gate Dome of Greeting at two in the morning Pacific time." We all looked at each other. None of us knew the time or carried a watch. The courier saw the questions on our faces and in our minds. "That's exactly one hour from now."

We had plenty of time. We only had to fly across the United States in one hour. To put it into context, that would be considered the very slow lane.

We shook hands with everyone, and Sarah gave Eric a big hug before we went up the ramp. He had followed us up to say goodbye. His work could wait. This was much more important, especially for him.

We settled into our seats and were greeted by Zaron. *Greetings again, Masters. Jabril has preselected our route. We will arrive exactly on time.* I felt the warmth of Zaron's greeting from the controls as I once again became part of the craft. I could feel her power and her need to once again fly with the masters from Shambala.

We eased into the small airlock and waited impatiently until the water again had flooded the chamber. The door above opened, and we streaked to just below the surface. When Zaron was sure that the area was clear, I gave her complete control of the craft. It was a little more complicated than an autopilot. We shot to the upper atmosphere and proceeded west for our still mysterious meeting at the western gate.

A United States geological survey team discovered the western gate in the early forties. They thought it to be built by an ancient civilization that no one had heard of. That much was correct.

Later, a secret military base was built there with underground tunnels leading to the large chamber, which was the true entrance to the inner world. This entrance or gate was, and still is, the Dome of Greeting. Access to the dome from the underground chamber has been one of the nation's better-kept secrets. Only a few have ever known about its location or its existence and still fewer would ever know what it truly was. Even these would never be able to go beyond the solid onyx statue of Apollo, which stands in the middle of the room. They would not know the significance of the golden tipped spear with a scorpion on its blade, which was held in his hand. They would not know why he was carved out of pure onyx. They would never know that he was my grandfather. They would not know that the dome would open to the sky to allow crafts flown only by the sons of light to land directly inside. Would those who waited there understand any of this?

We talked over what had happened to us up to this point, wondering what events were to unfold. We were used to surprises, as our first visit to the inner world had contained nothing but surprises from the time we arrived to the day we left. When dealing with the inner world, one can never be bored.

All too soon, as we were enjoying the flight, Zaron started down into the darkness. With the outside night view on, we saw the mountain coming up fast. We hovered over the west face, and Zaron communicated with the mountain, and the dome entrance slowly opened. The blue light from the interior gave an ominous glow to the surroundings. We slowly moved down through the opening and hovered just short of the surface as we surveyed what lay before us. Two men sat at a round table near the center of the room. Two marine guards with weapons stood on each side of the corridor leading into the room. I got an unexpected greeting from one of the guards. *Greetings, Aaron, son of Drake. Welcome to the Dome of Greetings.* It was a thought that only someone from the inner world could have sent. Zaron too, sensed no danger and

65

extended her tri-landing gear and gently settled to the floor. The door was opened, and the golden ramp was let down. *All appears safe, Masters* was the only cautious response of Zaron.

I got up and took a deep breath. "Well, let's not hold up the meeting." I led the little group out of the craft and headed toward the table as the two that had been sitting there slowly stood up.

It was not until we got closer that I recognized the two men. I had not tried to scan their thoughts, as I was busy looking for any hidden dangers. There before us stood two presidents: Lyndon B. Johnson and Richard M. Nixon. Both seemed to be much more anxious than we were.

Side by side we slowly approached the men. Johnson at once recognized Peter Black and surmised the identities of us other four. He was the first to speak. "I suppose that we have been honored to be meeting the famous five that I have heard so much about." His deep southern drawl seemed to be more at ease. Nixon, on the other hand, was still confused as to just who we were. He was still stunned at seeing a UFO. A gold one with a royal crest on the side must have been just a little over the top for him. Only one other president had ever seen one. Jimmy Carter admitted to the encounter but didn't know what he had seen. This was before he was the president of the United States.

Johnson came over and shook Peter's hand, and Peter in turn introduced us, starting with me. He used our outside names with no interior titles. He used Sarah's maiden name and did not infer in any way that Sarah and I were married. There must still be things that should be kept even from the president of the United States.

We followed Johnson and Nixon back over to the table where five other chairs had been placed. Someone knew who would be coming. A quick glance over to the entrance at the marine guard confirmed my suspicion. I got a quick smile in response. He was a plant and a personal guard to the president.

Johnson started the meeting. "As you know, there is a time when the outgoing and incoming presidents have to meet. This is where critical secrets of the presidency are passed on. Dick was sworn in last month, and much information has changed hands. Some of the information we get at this time is very sobering and tends to age each president far more than normal. The stresses on each of us are far more than the average citizen can comprehend."

Here he paused and looked over at Nixon. "One secret that is passed on is never written down. That secret is of your world. We must meet face-to-face for this to be passed on. Unfortunately, the Dalai Lama and Peter Black passed on this secret to me. Dick now has the reigns of leadership, and I don't covet his obligations, especially with the war now being waged in Vietnam. If politicians knew what they were getting into, they would never run for president."

He looked over at Nixon. "Mr. President." This was the first time he had addressed him by his title. "I hate to inform you that as president of the United States you now have to take orders from someone not of this country. Should you get any request from the inner world, they are to take top priority. It is for the sake of all mankind. You will not receive any orders unless they are of the highest importance. Thus it has been since our first president. George Washington also worked with this world and kept the secret. He did not know the capabilities of this world at that time, as the outer world was nowhere near able to understand what lay beneath their feet."

Even for a politician, Johnson was stretching this out for the benefit of the incoming president. Nixon remained in stunned silence. "These five people here, a few years ago, saved the entire population of our word from complete destruction. They each deserve Congressional Medals of Honor, but they can't be recognized for their valor. They did this with the unselfish goal to only help mankind with no thanks in return. They continue this work, and you, as our new president, are to give them every bit of assistance possible."

Nixon responded for the first time. "I am convinced that what you say is true, and they can expect my complete cooperation. It is also reassuring that someone with their level of technology is also working for

67

the protection of mankind." Here he looked at me. "That also brings us to the next reason for this meeting. I understand that two scientists who worked with you have now disappeared. It coincided with the replacement of Peter here at the Pentagon. His location could also not be found. I'm glad that Peter is okay, but I'm afraid something foul has occurred to the other two due to the reputation of the person responsible for having them ousted from the positions."

I answered the president, "We knew of their danger, and they are now safe in our inner world where they will remain until it is safe for them to return to continue their work." I could not at this time tell him more.

"Thank you," was the president's response. "I would have hated that an unsavory group of our military would have been responsible for something else."

"You refer to General Vanderhoff," I stated as a matter of fact.

Nixon looked stunned. "Yes."

"We can not interfere with normal operations of your government as the exterior has to learn to deal with situations like this on their own."

I looked straight into his eyes as I continued. "The inner world has struggled many thousands of years to achieve what they have. They will watch over the development of your world in much the same way a parent does a child."

I paused, trying to find the exact words. "You should be aware that a child who is protected from all harm and is given everything they desire will grow to never know the value of anything or even respect the hand of the giver. Their love will be only of themselves, and they will believe the world owes them. They will never know happiness or love. They will never add to the knowledge of the world but become a burden on society. We don't want that to happen to the child, which we watch. You will have to struggle and solve your domestic and foreign squabbles before you can grow and become a unified people once more. Each president takes on this responsibility, and it is not for us to interfere with his choices—good or bad. It is only when, for some reason, the fate of mankind is in the balance that we will not only interfere, but issue commands that will be followed. We all hope that such times will never come."

I paused once more. "It is from the child who has learned to give, especially of himself, that a future great leader is born."

I got a thought from the back of the room. *Excellent!*

It was immediately followed by another, *Sorry, my lord. I could not help it.*

I saw my dear wife's half smile. She had heard the thought also.

I sent a thought back. *It's all right. Thank you for your support.*

Nixon seemed sobered by my words. I tried to bring him back to the topic of Vanderhoff. "What can you tell me of General Vanderhoff that we should know?"

Nixon looked through some papers on the table to refresh his mind. "We have been monitoring him for some time, and his ties are deep and his influence is great. We have to find a way of taking him down without bringing down half of the Congress, the military, and several large corporations. This could destroy the confidence of our citizens toward our country in general." Here he paused as a major worry surfaced. "Lynden here has informed me that General Vanderhoff wants the failure of the space program so funds can be diverted to his newly acquired projects at Area 51." A frown creased his forehead as he continued. "Knowing the reputation of this man, I suspect sabotage." He looked into my eyes. "Is there any way that your people could help us there?"

"His sabotage attempts are easy enough to stop. We will help you with intelligence information but nothing more. You must stop his efforts. You have resources at your disposal that can handle that. It's other forces that the interior world is concerned about. Be assured, we want your space program to be a success, and should you receive word of strange sightings around the space program, know that it is us doing just that." I knew the kind of person the general was, and I concluded, "As for General Vanderhoff, in the end his arrogance and conceit will keep him from seeing the instrument of his downfall. If it is handled right, no shadow will be cast on the government but only on the General himself."

Both presidents seemed hopeful that what I said was true.

Nixon smiled. "I will keep your secret." He didn't have a choice. He stood up and shook all of our hands.

Johnson too took his turn in saying goodbye. "This trip took much too long, as we had to take an unscheduled military helicopter from my ranch in Texas. Eyebrows will rise when we aren't there for breakfast later this morning."

I smiled. I looked at my companions and got a nod. I got a thumbs-up from the marine sentry as he saluted and took the other guard out the door.

Nixon looked concerned. "What's going on?"

"We're taking you home. We'll have you back on the ranch in fifteen minutes, and no one will even know you've been gone. You may have to travel a few hundred feet back to the main house. We don't want to disturb the secret service."

Both were very excited for presidents of the United States.

Needless to say, they were very impressed with their short flight in a UFO. They had hoped to be able to tell their grandchildren about it. Unfortunately, that would never happen.

BACK HOME IN SHAMBALA

We left two very disoriented presidents struggling back to their bedrooms in the main house, and silently lifted off for home. The secret service would wonder how two US presidents had gotten past their surveillance. They would not mention it this time for fear of reprisals from their superiors.

I smiled knowingly as we streaked out over their heads. Should they have seen us, they would have had more to keep from their superiors.

I gave Zaron orders to take us straight to the Atlantic rift and through to Shambala. She seemed excited to be going home. Can a machine also feel excitement?

Sarah and I had been through the rift several times, but this was our three companions' first time. They were amazed at the size of the corridor through the earth and were surprised at how fast Zaron had traveled from one world to another. Four hundred miles underwater was nothing for her.

Soon the darkness of the rift changed to the deep blue of the interior sea as we came through the surface and settled just a few feet above the surface. We had forgotten just how blue the sky was here. We rose majestically to a great height to where we could see the mountains of Avalon to our north and the sea to the east. We headed east toward Shambala. The sea below was a deep blue, and to the east it blended into the sky. I can't describe to someone who has not seen it how beautiful it is not to have a horizon as known on the outside. The different shades of blue in the distance were inspiring. Soon these gave way to a dark line of mountains. These mountains seemed to rise out of the sea as we approached. Soon the snow-capped peaks and ragged ranges could be seen. Zaron was taking her time. I'm not sure if it was for her pleasure or ours.

Below, the seashore passed beneath us as Zaron slowed. We were approaching the mainland.

Suddenly two scout ships with the Shambala crest came alongside. Zaron was very recognizable, thank goodness. I knew that Shambala had taken over security and was glad that we were not shot down. I soon discovered that this was not their intention. A royal craft of Avalon soon took the point just in front of us. It seemed that we were to have a royal escort home. This was soon made obvious by a craft-to-craft transmission through Zaron.

Welcome home, Cousin. This came in the form of a thought, and I recognized the familiar warmth of the prince of Avalon.

Good to be home. Thanks for the impressive greeting.

The greetings are yet to come, Cousin. A lot of people are glad to see you back. We got word from Atlantic Base some time ago of your coming. You have a reception committee.

As we neared the castle, we slowed and circled. This was to announce that we had arrived to the throng of people that had spread out below in the castle grounds. There must have been thousands.

As we slowly came down, I soon recognized King Dresden and his daughter and Verl's sister, Dreana. There, too, were King Vardan and Queen Zella of my homeland of Shambala. The heads of the other

72

lands joined the king and queen. Some of whom I had never met. We landed gently into a circle that the royal guard had cleared in the middle of the courtyard. Zaron gave the first greeting as she let down the golden ramp.

We filed down the ramp to a thunderous cheer from the assembled crowd. The front rank were all the dignitaries of the lands and in the back of these were the workers from the castle all with that familiar warm smile on each face.

King Vardan and Queen Zella came over and gave Sarah and me a royal hug. "Welcome home, my children. It's good to have you again back with us."

They then greeted Peter, Billy, and Cindy in like manner, which embarrassed Billy and Peter somewhat.

King Dresden and Princess Dreana came over and took their turn greeting us.

There seemed to be someone missing. This was obvious when the crowd suddenly separated to allow a large white tiger with a little girl on his back to come to where we were standing.

Raja let out a roar of greeting, which made the crowd step back another step. Normally they would have bumped into those behind, but they, too, had moved back.

Liz jumped from Raja's back in much the same way one would from a small pony. She came running to Sarah and me for a family group hug, and kisses all around. She soon noticed Billy and Cindy. "Uncle Billy, Aunt Cindy, I didn't know you were coming. Wait till you see Mom and Daddy's home. It's great. Wait till you see all the animals here. They are all free. There are no cages here at all. You've got to see my room. It's full of toys and books. I've never seen so many."

She was excited, and she looked over at Peter. "You're Daddy's good friend, aren't you?"

Peter simply answered, "Yes." He moved forward to shake the little lady's hand and was surprised when Liz jumped into his arms and gave him a big hug. That did it. Peter would now be her slave forever. It's uncanny how well she makes lifelong friends in only an instant.

Liz came running back to us and took our hands. "King Vardan has a surprise to show you. I would tell you what it is, but I promised that I would keep it a secret." She led us over to the royal couple, and King Vardan and Queen Zella were laughing at Liz's excitement.

"We do indeed have something to show you. It's a gift that was from all the peoples of this world. Many of them wanted to be here. Unfortunately, the mountain can only hold so many.

As he was talking, he was leading us to something large sitting in the middle of our courtyard. A large satin drape covered it from top to bottom. It was several feet high. The king stepped to the front of it.

The king spoke. "All the people of our world for centuries have lived in the shadow of fear of the dark forces of this world. The dark lord presented the only evil that we have known for many centuries. You, Sarah, and your three companions came back to this world, and together we have ridden our world of this evil threat. We, the people of this world, wanted to show our appreciation of this wondrous event. Something that would last forever and remind us of that moment."

Here he nodded to Liz, who was waiting patiently. She ran over to the satin drape and pulled. The drape came down around the base of an enormous statue.

It was a depiction of Verl, Eric, Raja, and me during the final battle. Raja was to my right, and Prince Verl was to my left, and Eric was protecting my back. I, in the middle, held the Sword of Truth high with my right hand and the Staff of Aaron in my left. The entire statue was of gold and the artwork was like none that I had ever seen. It had to have taken the greatest craftsmen of this world years to create. As my eyes drifted to the base, I read an engraved plate: *To Aaron and Sarah, Son and Daughter of Light, with Gratitude from the Peoples of the World.*

Sarah took my hand. As I looked down into her eyes she wiped tears from her cheeks. She was not the only one affected as tears of gratitude dripped off my chin.

We turned to the crowd and raised our hands in thanks and gratitude, as words could not express our feelings. The people of this world felt this. All of them could feel our thoughts; a cheer rang out, and the mountain seemed to echo the cheer. I don't know if it was from mutual gratitude or the noise but Raja joined in with a roar. I tend to think it was the former.

Liz was jumping up and down, clapping her hands. This was a real treat for her and a real blessing to Sarah and me. We marveled at the statue for some time, taking in every painstaking detail worked into every part of the image before us. It was as though somehow we were frozen at a moment in time and suddenly turned into solid gold. As Billy best put it, "It was awesome."

I felt a hand on my shoulder. I looked behind me and saw a wet-eyed Verl admiring the statue. "This is the first time I have seen this tribute, also. I have never been so honored to be a part of that great moment." A smile came to his face. "Our friend Eric has also not seen it. Once he has, we'll never be able to get his head inside a space suit again."

Knowing Eric as we did, we tended to agree, but Eric had shown much more maturity at Atlantic Base. Life tended to do that to people.

King Dresden and Princess Dreana joined Verl and told us that a banquet had been prepared in our honor, and it would be in bad taste not to attend. I think that he was looking forward to the banquet too as he led the way into the castle. A cheer came from the group outside. They too would party for many hours, outside time. Singing and dancing would announce the first of a new festival that would be reenacted many times from this moment on. It would be a celebration of good over evil and set an example for those who were yet to come and remind those that remembered of just what could have been had it not been for those who fought to put down evil for all time.

Our battle on the outside had only begun.

GETTING READY FOR OUR MISSION

The following three months were filled with many activities as we reacquainted ourselves with our surroundings once more. We caught up with what had been going on during our absence. We renewed old acquaintances and made new ones. We were mostly busy with the general running of the castle. Sarah and I hoped that we would be able to stay here for an extended period this time.

Liz, on the other hand, was having a blast. She played with the kids of the other workers, but she was happier with the animals that surrounded our lands. A group of them seemed to follow her wherever she roamed. We didn't discourage her, as this was increasing her awareness as her body and mind grew. Raja was never far way. He kept his distances most of the time out of respect for the smaller animals surrounding her. He still took her for rides through the country where the people had become accustomed to the sight and didn't run for cover. She always smiled and waved to them. She was making friends by the hundreds.

The reason I bring up Liz's activities is because of an event that made my heart race. You can only experience this if your own child has ever been in dire danger.

I was walking in the castle garden, thinking over many things that I needed to sort out, when I topped the hill and saw a tremendous dragon with Liz hanging out of his mouth. With my heart in my throat, I raced to the bottom of the hill just in time to see the dragon gently place Liz on his back. She settled there and leaned back to enjoy the cool of the sea breeze. I screeched to a halt as the dragon saw my arrival. He was suddenly agitated. He reached over and picked Liz off his back and gently placed her back on the ground.

Liz looked very confused until she saw me. "Daddy." She came running over and jumped into my astonished arms. My heart was again approaching normal rate. "Have you met Drake, my friend? He is very smart for a dragon. He has told me many stories. He is even older than you are."

Here she smiled, and I frowned. "What's going on here?"

Drake was confused. He first looked at Liz and then at me. I got a very nervous thought from him. *Your Majesty, I did not know that the little princess was your fledgling. It is with great humility that I offer this apology to the great dragon king. I should have known that the little one who offered such friendship could be none other.*

Drake spread his wings and bowed his head low. It was a great sight, and I knew that it was an ancient show of great respect. The respect was not for just me, but for Liz also. *Be it known that I will watch over her henceforth, as me and my kind have watched over your dwelling during your absence.* Drake straightened and looked deep into my eyes. Could this majestic creature also see into my mind?

I answered with a thought of my own. *There is no apology needed. One should not ever have to apologize for friendship. It is I who am grateful to you and your kind. Your friendship with Liz is not only allowed but also welcomed.*

Thank you, Your Majesty, was his immediate response.

Liz looked confused. "Why did he call you Your Majesty?"

"Drake and I have met before. I recognize him now. We fought together in a battle a few years ago. It was then that he called me the dragon king." I heard a friendly low growl from Drake as he, too, remembered that moment. I didn't need to send him thoughts as he could understand our language. I smiled at the big creature and said, "You truly are very intelligent." The creature bowed low once more in acknowledgment.

I looked down at Liz and saw the sparkle in her eyes. "Your choice of friends is well founded, Princess."

"I know," was her simple response, "and you're the famous dragon king."

I nodded with a smile. Her intelligence was only exceeded by her self-confidence. I didn't know if it was her ego or her education which she needed to work on. I thought that a little of both wouldn't hurt. Time would fix that.

Drake was anxious to leave to relate what had happened here. I saw his thoughts and gave him leave to go. The great beast spread his enormous wings and once again bowed, and with a gust from those same wings, he gracefully took to the air and was soon out of sight over the kingdom. I would learn more about Drake and his kin later.

Liz and I both walked together in the garden and eventually made it back to the castle where a very anxious mother waited. She had sensed sudden danger, and her child was nowhere in sight. She was angry with both Liz and me for hiding our thoughts. She had been worried sick.

Liz tried to explain what had happened as she and Sarah strolled on back through the castle. I'm not sure a mother would really understand. She knew not to be too protective of her daughter, but instinct sometimes took over her reasoning.

It was a week later that Jabril sent for me. He told me to bring

Sarah and Liz along. This seemed important. Jabril only wanted meetings when things were about to happen. Big things. Needless to say I was anxious, and Sarah and Liz picked up on my worried look. It was a silent bunch that traveled in Zaron to the kingdom of Avalon and the World University.

We landed in the garden below King Dresden's castle and walked down the walkway to the main tower of the university. Many students broke into agitated chatter as they recognized us and waved as we passed. Word soon spread as students started pouring out of the main library. We walked proudly through the crowd to the tower where we took an elevator to the top where Jabril had his offices, labs, and workrooms. As I mentioned before, Jabril was not just the headmaster of the university. It was one of his other duties that had brought us here.

We went straight to Jabril's main office. The door opened just as we came up to it. Peter held the door and with his usual smile indicated for us to come in. King Dresden, Jocko, and Jarod were with Jabril behind the desk looking at something on a wide screen that was mounted into the desk itself. They looked up with a smile. Cindy and Billy were there and were excited to see us. We all exchanged hugs.

King Dresden came around and shook my hand. "It's good to have you home, Nephew. Why have you taken so long to come to visit?" He didn't wait for an answer, as he knew we had been rather busy for the past few months. He gestured toward Jocko and Jarod. "I suppose you already know Dr. Grossman and Dr. Jessup. They have been having a great time visiting with our scientists here."

Both Sarah and I suddenly realized that we had never known their real names. "I don't suppose that Jarod and Jocko are their first names." It was more of a statement than a question. Jocko and Jarod smiled. Jarod was the first to come around the desk and shake our hands. "The first name is Henry. Named after my father's friend in the auto industry. Of course, he hadn't made any cars at the time I was born."

Jocko moved Jarod aside so he could likewise reintroduce himself. "Name's William, but I have always been called Billy."

So Jocko was Dr. Billy Jessup and Jarod was Dr. Henry Grossman. These new names would take some getting used to.

Sarah and I then noticed Liz. She hadn't paid much attention to our introductions. She had locked gazes with Jabril and had not spoken a word.

We could not have known at the time what was transpiring, but we found out much later. I will relate that strange meeting of the two now to make future events clearer.

Liz had already met many people of this world, and Jabril was something entirely new. She probed his mind and reached beyond that eternal block that we all had come across when we were with Jabril. Jabril suddenly realized that a powerful probe had penetrated his real personality. This intrusion should not have been possible. He stared at Liz, and she did not divert her gaze into his eyes. Only two others had been able to see this deep into Jabril's mind, and they were long gone from this world.

Liz sent him a private thought. *You are not of this world. Why are you here?*

He sent a thought back. *I have been given an important job to do. You already know from whom. It is also important that who I am remains a secret between you and me. You also see why. Will you help me by going along with events yet to come? Your training has to begin now, and you also know why. These things that you have seen in the future have to be between just you and me. We cannot interfere with those events. The purpose is not always for us to see.*

Yes, sir. Why do I have these abilities? I know I am too young to understand. Jabril sensed the fear in her thought.

I'm sorry, child. I don't know why you have the abilities you do, and I am very, very old as you already know. Jabril smiled at her as the others were busy greeting each other.

Liz smiled back. Yes; he was very, very old.

This all took place behind our backs, so to speak. When I saw Liz staring at Jabril, I picked her up and introduced her to everybody. I was proud of my little girl.

Jabril started off the meeting by saying, "You may wonder why I've asked you three over. There are several reasons, among which Liz is the first." Here he paused and pressed a button on the desk. The door opened, and Jenny came in. We were surprised to see her.

Jabril continued, "Jenny has become worried about not being able to give Liz the training she deserves and has asked me to give her some advice."

Here, he looked down at Liz. "Young lady, are you ready to attend school?"

Liz clapped her hands and giggled in her childish way. "Yes, I would really like to go to school."

Jabril probed her thoughts, thinking that this was an act. No, Liz was really excited. He also saw that she would never attempt to put on an act. Her thoughts and actions were pure and innocent. Her intelligence would have been insulted should anyone have thought otherwise. Jabril felt a little ashamed of his suspicion. The bright eyes and smile from Liz told him she understood and it was all right.

I looked over at Jabril and expressed Sarah's thoughts as well as my own. "Isn't she a little young for the university?"

Jabril gave us a reassuring smile and replied simply, "You should know now that we don't measure time here the way it is done on the outside. Wisdom comes in many different ways. When we find those with special abilities, we need to nurture those abilities. You two are a great example. You gathered more in one year here than most of the students of this world attain in a lifetime. This is very rare. You have to take my word for it that Liz is ready for her time."

Liz smiled. I could feel that Jabril was keeping something from us, and I knew that Liz was.

I tried to look into her mind and hit a wall of solid granite. Sarah had done the same and got the same result. We did get a feeling back

81

that everything was all right. How could they block us and still let us see that feeling?

Jabril brought us over behind his desk and showed us what they had been looking at before we arrived. "It seems that General Vanderhoff had been busy since you arrived here."

The screen showed the general and several crewmen in one of the hangers at Area 51. Vanderhoff and a pilot were entering the craft that Jarod and his crew had reconstructed. The hanger doors opened, and the small craft lifted off the floor and immediately crashed back down. The door flew open and out came a ball of thick smoke along with Vanderhoff. He was slinging his arms and stamping about. It was just as well that we weren't playing the sound back as well. I could just imagine what he was saying.

Jabril gave us a play by play. "We hadn't anticipated that Vanderhoff would want to fly in the craft himself but should have known that from his arrogance. He wanted the craft repaired at once. You should have seen him when they told him that it had taken them twenty years for them to make a perfectly good gravity drive work. It would take another hundred years for them to determine how it worked. It would take even longer to duplicate it. Vanderhoff was livid."

Jabril switched views. I noticed that Liz had squeezed between Jarod and Jabril to watch the screen and was holding Jabril's hand. Sarah noticed it too. We looked at each other in bewilderment.

The new view on the screen showed several people at a conference table pouring over papers and reports. "This is a special committee from the attorney general's office building up evidence against one General Vanderhoff. It seems that your little speech in the Dome of Greeting made an impression on President Nixon."

"You saw that meeting?" I asked.

"We don't miss much. Especially where you are concerned. Nice speech by the way. It's a shame that we couldn't tell them any more or give them any more assistance."

He looked at Liz and then again at us. "Will it be all right if Jenny takes the princess with her to Jenny's quarters? We have set up rooms there and brought all her things from home. She can visit Shambala during her regular breaks." He saw Sarah's worried expression. "She will have great fun, and this really is necessary in more ways than you can imagine."

We had to leave Liz with Jenny many times, but only for a period of just a few days. This was different. It would be months before her first break. Though that was a short time here, it was an eternity for a mother.

Sarah didn't answer but only nodded as her eyes became very moist. She bent down and gave Liz a big hug and kiss. I followed. We would miss the little rascal. She really was our little sunshine. The day was always bright when she was around, and there was no such thing as being bored.

Liz saw how sad we were, and she tried to cheer us up. "I'll send you messages all the time to let you know what I'm doing."

She waved goodbye to Peter, Jarod, and Jocko and just smiled at Jabril and left with Jenny. The door sounded unusually loud as it closed behind them. Sarah squeezed my hand.

Peter had come forward and joined Jarod and Jocko, who were looking over some information dealing with the government.

Jabril motioned for Sarah and me to look at the screen once more. There before us was a three-dimensional view of a complex of buildings in a gray, desolate, barren place. The buildings were hidden beneath a very large cliff. I suddenly realized that it was the lip of a very large crater and the crater was on the moon. The view zoomed in, and we realized that it was occupied. Several small alien-looking craft were lined up near one of the buildings. A further zoom at the fingertips of Jabril took us directly into one of the buildings. There were the creatures of the dark forces moving crates and boxes in the airtight enclosure.

Jabril informed us, "The dark forces have been trying to build up this base for some time. They think that if they can obtain further technology from us, they would be able to take over the solar system. They

83

think they can steal this science. There is no way that this can happen, but they are now under the impression that these moon trips will expose their plans. They have tried to destroy several earlier missions but have lost those craft and crew. Dorin and his bunch have had their hands full trying to protect these flights. Unfortunately, they have not always gone undetected."

Jabril continued, "We have found out that they will attempt to destroy the crew and craft of the United States on their next moon mission as they move to the back side of the moon in preparation for separation and landing. They know that no communication can be sent to earth from that position. They think that their deed will never be detected."

Here he looked at me. "Dorin needs for you to take Zaron and escort the moon mission at a safe distance. Only Zaron can respond fast enough and with enough firepower to counter any attack. Meantime, Dorin and his fighters will be busy destroying the lunar base. This is the first direct attack on the dark forces since the final battle. We can't get all of them on the attack. Some will definitely be in transit to or from the base. Some may escape. Zaron will have to rid space of these. Only you can move as one with Zaron. The bond between the two of you is very strong."

"What if we are spotted by the crew on board the spacecraft?" My question was obvious.

Jabril just smiled. "Who would believe them?" Here he sighed. "If we are spotted, it can't be helped anyway. The moon landing must take place for man to realize that he no longer is confined to that little speck of dust in the universe that we call Earth. It is true that it is only a baby step, but it is the first baby step."

The others had finished with the reports and joined us at the desk.

Here he looked at Sarah. "I know that you don't want to be far from Liz. While Aaron is gone, you will stay here at the university. It is not for Liz's sake but for yours. It's way past time that you should continue your training. Aaron will join you when he returns. He has a lot of catching up to do. You think that your previous training was intensive. Well, as the outer rim says, you ain't seen nothing yet."

Jabril smiled at his attempt at humor. It was dry and seemed out of place with Jabril.

He must have caught my thoughts. He smiled a knowing smile in my direction and sent me a private thought. *You and your daughter have a lot in common, son of Drake.*

He turned back to Sarah. "King Dresden insists you take your rest periods at the castle. He thinks you'd be more at ease there. Your inner world status has changed since you first arrived, Princess. It wouldn't be appropriate for an heir to the throne of Avalon to stay in an apartment at the university. I'm sure you and Aaron will be more comfortable at the castle."

He looked at Peter. "Sorry, my good friend, but as you further your awareness at the university, you will be staying here. I need you close should immediate personal contact with your former government become necessary."

The word *former* gave Peter a warm feeling. He was indeed now home.

Jabril gave Peter a friendly pat on the back and said, "Your training will be on and off for the next several years."

Cindy and Billy were wondering about what was to become of them. They too knew that many years of training were needed for them but didn't expect to get the opportunity. They were mistaken.

Jabril, in his wisdom, spoke to them next.

"William, Cindy, you have been welcomed to this world. If you could make the decision now, we would like for you to make this your permanent home. You need not go back to the outside except for the intern work that might be required of you there. Your status has changed as well since you first came to this world. This has not gone unnoticed by our population. Your names and faces are known from one continent to the other. We know you have no residence here. There is a vacant residence very close to university that is available if you wish to stay there." Here he looked at King Dresden and got a nod. "It is a small castle that was once used by visiting royalty. It is completely staffed and very comfortable with a beautiful view of the capital city and the sea. It is also a short distance from the university. You have many years of learning ahead of each of you. The staff will be more than happy to look after your son."

Cindy and Billy looked at each other suddenly. "What?"

Jabril for once looked confused. "I thought you knew. We really do take too much for granted here. I didn't mean to be the first to break this great news. I sensed that you were expecting him already."

Cindy spoke up. "We did sense a baby in our future but didn't know that it was already on its way." Both were excited about the start of their new family.

Cindy nudged Billy with her arm and a private thought. *We can't accept something as grand as a castle to stay in. We don't deserve such extravagance.*

Billy agreed. "Your Majesty, Jabril, we very much want this to be our home, and we are honored that you would let us stay and attend the university, but we can't possibly accept something as extravagant as a castle. We can't even pay the servants. How could we ever earn the right to stay in such a place?"

It was King Dresden's turn to look confused. A thoughtful frown creased his forehead as he looked at Jabril.

Jabril only smiled and said, "It's their lack of training."

King Dresden nodded knowingly and looked at our two friends. "It's not just a gift. We couldn't find anyone else that could take it over since we built the new west wing on the castle three hundred years ago. All dignitaries now stay there. The castle is always vacant and wasted. As for the servants, there are none. There are no servants on this whole continent. The workers at the castle are volunteers, and the ones who reside there permanently do so because they wish to. It is the same in my castle. We are all the same. I only rule. We work, play, eat, drink, and live with each other as friends. I thought you had noticed that when you were here before."

Cindy looked ashamed. "We did notice that there was a great friendship between those who lived in the castle and those who worked there, but we thought it was only because of the type of people they were."

Jabril smiled. "It is because of the type of people they are."

Jocko and Jarod were taking all this in. They had seen a great deal of Avalon since they had arrived and marveled at the university and the capitol city. They were amazed at the people. They were learning that his world was indeed different. They wanted to see everything. The curiosity of a scientist is somewhat greater than others of the outer rim.

I had noticed their silence and could feel their concern. I looked at Jabril. "When are we getting Jocko and Jarod back to the outside?"

Jabril continued, "As you already know, when we receive someone new from the outer rim, we must first determine their nature and give them time to adjust to our world. This period of time is set by our laws and cannot be changed. It is equivalent of three months of outside time. That time period is up. At this time, we will again take them to the outer world to resume their lives only if they are sworn to secrecy about our world. Those that we find worthy are given the opportunity to stay with us and become a new member of the inner races."

Jabril noticed Jarod and Jocko looking at each other. "You have been watched during your required observation period and you both have been found worthy and we would consider it an honor for you to stay here with us and learn all that we can give you. After your training, you also will be a great asset to our world. You also may be asked to return to the outside should the need arise, but only on a temporary basis."

Jocko and Jarod were elated. They had never dreamed that something like this could happen to them. I envied them the joy of first seeing this world all over again. They will still be astounded many years from now. There is so much to see and learn. Their bodies will also

87

change, and their life expectancy will be more than quadrupled, even at their age. They will certainly need that extra time.

Jabril pressed a button on his desk. He addressed Cindy and Billy. "Grace will escort you to your new home and help you get settled. She is also one of the best cooks on the continent. You got some of her preparations when you were here in the castle last. Perhaps you remember."

We did indeed. Grace came in with the now expected friendly smile. No false smile in this world. Cindy and Billy hurriedly said their goodbyes and followed Grace to their new home.

Jabril looked over at Peter. "Peter, would you escort Dr. Grossman and Dr. Jessup to their quarters as I need to speak to Aaron and Sarah?"

Peter nodded, and all three shook our hands once more and said their goodbyes. Each was eager to see what was unfolding in their lives. It certainly was exciting for them, and their lives would never be the same again.

Jabril smiled and pointed down at the screen on his desk. A young man who looked familiar was busy at a typewriter. Papers were spread out around him. He was only in his teens.

Jabril explained. "Mr. Gavin Graham. He wants to be a journalist. He's editor of his school's newspaper. He is number one in his class and wants to go to the University of Ohio School of Journalism. He looks up everything he can find on angels. He has even written a book on them and hopes one day to get it published. His parents will soon get a letter telling them that Gavin has won a full scholarship. He still scans every face he meets for that face that he saw that one morning at the seashore."

Jabril paused and looked at me in a funny way. I could not tell what he was thinking. "Gavin still thinks you're an angel, sent from God." He was looking at my thoughts. "This is something you should be thinking about in your future. God sent you. You did his bidding. Through you, God healed his body. You may be as close to an angel as anyone from his world has ever come. This is not something to be taken lightly. You, like the angels, must carry on God's work.

"Years from now you are destined to meet again."

This was stated as fact. How could he know that we would definitely meet again years from now? I don't know if my further education would ever get me to the point where I could understand Jabril.

I would find out later just how right I was.

King Dresden placed a hand on my shoulder. He could see my quandary and was a little amused. He too was more than he appeared to be, even for a king. He smiled. "I have to get back to the castle. I want to see you, Aaron, before you go back to Atlantic Base. There are some things we need to discus, and I also have something for you to take back to Shambala with you." He shook hands with Jabril and hugged Sarah and patted me on the back once more and left.

Jabril watch him go. "Good man." He was deep in thought. "This kingdom was in shambles compared to what it is now that he took over. He is the hardest working king that this world has seen. It is not by accident that we have a near-perfect world here. It is the result of men like Dresden and hard work."

Jabril got back to the issue. "Jeff, at Atlantic Base, has had some communication with me. He wants to talk it over with you personally when you and Zaron get there." He paused here. "I think it has something to do with the dark forces. He didn't want to discus it over our regular communication channel. He suspects compromise of our network, even to Atlantic Base. I'm sure we still have secure communications, but Jeff wants to play it safe to make sure. He too is a good man. He and Dorin have made great strides at the base. You'll learn much more after your mission and training. After all, you should enjoy your internship there. I can see that your ability to put to practice what you have learned is far greater than you have previously imagined. Don't confuse arrogance with self-confidence. Though both are considered the same by most, they are definitely not."

Jabril looked deep into my eyes. "It is of the utmost importance that you make confident decisions and eliminate any self-doubt. Your future and this world's future will depend on it."

Again, Jabril saw something in my future. I'm not sure just what it was, but I got a feeling of a great deal of confidence in me. I could see what he meant, but I felt the confidence was undeserved. Now I could see just how behind in my training I really was. Someday I would reach the sureness I felt from Jabril and King Dresden.

Jabril only gave me that knowing smile of his. It was the sign that I was thinking on the right track. I could not hide any thoughts from him. It was not until much later that I would know why.

He placed a hand on my shoulder and said, "I'm afraid it's time for you to go. Don't worry about your family. They could not be in better hands. Remember, no matter where you go, you also go with God."

I left the university deep in thought. There was much to consider and think about. It seemed that everything I learned brought about the fact of how little I knew. Ever since I had learned about this world I had been the center of some crazy adventures. I still don't understand just why my life has been changed so much from that simple professor. Now I'm involved with protecting a moon landing planned by the United States. Is this too going to be more than just a precaution against evil from the dark forces? Maybe this also will be the start of another unbelievable adventure.

I hoped Jeff would be able to fill me in when I reached Atlantic Base.

I suddenly stopped as I climbed back up the hill to the palace gardens. *We need to leave right away, Master.* It was Zaron. She had gotten a message from Atlantic Base and had already warmed up her drives. She was ready to fly. I smiled at the warm feeling I always got from her and climbed aboard.

"I have to see King Dresden before I leave. It won't take long."

I went into the castle and went straight to the king's private quarters. As I approached, a chime rang and the door opened. I went in and found the king sitting at one of his writing desks. He smiled as I approached and got up and shook my hand. Something wrapped in a soft satin fabric was lying on his desk. He noticed my curiosity. "Yes, that is for you. It is the sword of your grandfather that you carried into battle." He unwrapped the sword and removed the sword from its golden sheath. The blade caught the light as if it were on fire. We both admired the craftsmanship.

Dresden held the sword high and watched the light bounce off the walls around the room. "You may have heard that the blade is not of this world. The whole sword is not of this world. It is said that an angel of God brought it here. Of this I can't be sure. But I do know for a fact that no power on earth can stop its blow. No other blade could have fallen the dark lord. It was not by chance that you carried this sword. It was presented to Apollo as a symbol that God would forever be with the righteous. It is now yours. The sword is a part of its owner, and none other but the true owner of the sword could have used it as you did." Here he paused as I again admired the sword, this time with new eyes.

Dresden went on. "I'm not sure what battles you will be fighting in the future or what time you will need the Sword of Truth by your side, but from this moment on, it will be close at hand. A place has been crafted for it on board Zaron while you were at the university. Only you can remove it from its holder. Use it wisely. Only a pure heart can wield its power."

Dresden slipped the sword back into the scabbard and handed it to me. "I know you must go, but keep the source of the sword just between you and me. My father passed this secret to me. Your father would have done the same, but the honor was unfortunately but gratefully left to me.

"Go now and fulfill your mission, and may God guide your steps." The king shook my hand, and we said goodbye.

Outside, Zaron was sitting in the courtyard. I went up the ramp and found the special holder for the sword just beside the door. I placed the scabbard and the holder on it and heard a metallic click. It was locked in place. I tried to remove it, and it came away easily. It was keyed to my touch. It would take a nuclear blast to remove it otherwise.

I got seated in the pilot's seat. "Well, old friend, it looks like we have a new adventure in store for us."

ATLANTIC BASE OPERATIONS

Z aron glided smoothly over the inner sea as we headed south toward the rift that would take us to the outer rim. We still didn't use the polar gates as both the outer world militaries and the dark forces were watching them. Zaron could have avoided contact, but we didn't want to take the chance that the dark forces would recognize Zaron. She had gotten quite a reputation as Sarah flew her against them in the final battle. They would know that once again Zaron was in the skies. They feared her. Both the craft's and my reputation had been much exaggerated as the details of the final battle reached the dark forces on the inner world.

I was to find out later that Dorin and his crew had planted these stories. Jabril had surmised that fear of me would give me an advantage should I ever have to face them in combat. And now that moment could be sooner than I had expected.

When we reached the area of the rift, Zaron paused and scanned the area. *All is clear, Master.*

"Okay, let's not keep Jeff waiting." Zaron, without a moment's hesitation, plunged into the inner sea. Soon we were again streaking through the darkness of the rift. I could only imagine the extreme forces that were on the outer hull during the first one hundred miles. At one hundred seventy-five miles, the force was zero. At that point, there was as much mass ahead of us as behind us. That was the point of equilibrium. The gravity force field surrounding the craft kept us from feeling any pressure at any depth. It was not only used for propulsion but also acted as a barrier to all kinds of exterior forces. This field also interrupted normal electron reaction by our earlier craft. Electrical charges would be canceled causing strange things to happen in the everyday lives of the outer races as the craft flew over. Cars would stop. Lights would go out. Area blackouts would occur. Radio transmissions would completely stop. Compasses would spin due to the motor reaction to the field. Later, shielding helped to eliminate these reactions. The dark forces had no such shielding. I don't know if they didn't have the technology or just plain didn't care. I imagine that this has caused many plane crashes. I have to remind the reader that the dark forces have no empathy for the outer races. They could care less if lives were lost. They would not divert their flight just for the sake of human life. This is a group of beings that has never felt love, hope, or faith. They live in fear, oppression of each other, greed, and the only ambition they have is to rule the outer world. This is their other trait. That trait is the quest for power. I don't know how they survive when there is so much killing in their ranks as one or the other tries to gain more power.

It is good that they also fear water and fire. We wouldn't meet any of them going through the rift.

We soon emerged into the Atlantic Ocean. I had not realized we had left the rift, as it was still dark. It was night here. I had no idea of the time of day.

Zaron paused as she surveyed ahead. *Do you want to travel above the surface, Master?*

"Yes, I want the Atlantic Base to know we're coming."

Zaron must have had communication as she replied, *They know, Master.*

We stopped over the entrance of one of the smaller airlocks and then drove straight down to the bed of the ocean. Zaron paused as the door to the underground airlock slid back to reveal the hidden chamber below. We eased down to the bottom of the shaft, and the door overhead slid back over our head. The air rushing in replaced the water, and now we were hovering in the air waiting for the green light to indicate that all was clear. The opening of the airlock door followed the light. The open door revealed the small hanger that I recognized from my first visit.

We were expected, and a cradle was waiting for Zaron. All craft were landed on these cradles because it made it easier to move about within the facility without them having to take flight.

Before the ramp could be let down, a crowd had gathered. Zaron was back and so was Aaron. Word spread fast. I saw Jeff and Dorin at the front ranks of the workers. I left the craft with thanks to Zaron, who responded with, *It is always a pleasure, Master.*

I went over and shook hands with Jeff and Dorin. A crew went into Zaron. Jeff saw my concern and explained, "We want to equip her with our new sensors and another special device from Jabril. She will be able to detect danger from many miles away. This is something new from Jabril. He said that only Zaron is capable of using this device due to her advanced artificial intelligence." He looked over the crew going into Zaron. "We hope to adapt the device to our other craft in the near future."

He shook his head as he admired Zaron.

Dorin picked up the conversation, "I don't know if anyone has ever told you, but Zaron is unique. Most of her systems were designed especially for her and came directly from the labs of Jabril. It will be many years before our technicians will be able to duplicate what we've found within her systems. That is one of the reasons we requested her. The other is the fear the dark forces have of her." He placed his hand on

94

his hips as he eyed Zaron. "She also has more firepower than our best battle cruisers."

I could tell by both their expressions that they held this small craft in awe. That says something, especially when you realize the source. This was another mystery to ponder, and I'm sure that both Dorin and Jeff had pondered the same mystery.

Dorin's attention was suddenly directed to the rear of the craft as more technicians than were needed were excitedly entering the craft. A crowd had soon gathered and was going in and out of the craft. There were too many excited thoughts for Dorin to figure out what was going on.

He rushed to the back of the craft expecting something wrong, only to be taken by the arm and led inside. There a group had gathered around the Sword of Truth. None of them had ever expected to see the legendary sword, much less up close.

Dorin was just as impressed as the younger technicians.

Jeff, who had followed us into the craft, let out a gasp as he too recognized the sword. "It's amazing."

Dorin knew more of this sword than most. "People, you are looking at a sword that is older than mankind itself. Make sure you realize the significance of the object that you are looking at."

Suddenly there was complete silence in the craft as all took in the splendor of the sword.

Jeff broke the silence that had followed Dorin's statement. "I'm sorry Dorin, but we haven't much time, and we have gathered a few of our crew leaders together for a conference in the lower conference room. We need to bring Aaron up to date on what we've been doing and what is taking place now and especially our plans for the upcoming moon landing by the United States."

Dorin nodded and quietly left the craft. He was more astonished to see the sword in the craft than I could have imagined at the time.

I walked with Dorin and Jeff to the passenger elevators, and we took one down to the lower conference room. It was elegant and had a huge table in the center of the room with about fifty chairs surrounding it. All the chairs, but three, were occupied. Everyone in the room stood as we entered. I nodded to them as Dorin and Jeff took their chair and indicated the one at the head of the table for me.

As I took my seat at the table, the assembled men and ladies followed suit, each with their eyes focused on me. I got curiosity from most and excitement from others. This was the legendary Aaron. All wondered if all that they had heard about me was true. I tried not to probe their thoughts, but feelings around the room were too obvious.

As I looked around the room, I realized that I knew a good number of them. I especially noticed Brian. He nodded in my direction with his half smile.

Dorin noticed the silent greeting and frowned at Brian, who suddenly lowered his gaze.

Dorin explained the frown and Brian's sheepish grin that didn't escape Dorin's notice. "You may have noticed that we have several members who have been working on the outside present at our little meeting. You may recall that we have great concern about the Apollo missions. It should be appropriate to mention that a couple of our group have somewhat overstepped their authority." He looked across the table at a young man who also had his head down. "Greg here took it on himself to implant a notion that the entire program be called the Apollo Program to honor your grandfather. He didn't realize that this would further infuriate the dark forces, which it did."

Greg didn't look up, but a smile crossed his face. He wasn't ashamed of what he had done. This too didn't go unnoticed by Dorin, who frowned once more, and I realized that he too was suppressing a smile of his own.

"And your friend Brian over there took it on himself to not be outdone. He was working on the lunar lander at Grumman. The code name for the lunar lander will now be 'The Eagle' after the royal bird and symbol of Avalon." He scowled at the two. "They have to be reminded what our true purpose is."

Brian was not in the least bit sorry either. I saw the thoughts of Dorin, and he was actually proud of what they had done but couldn't show it. He was also surprised that I had seen this thought and a curious look came over his face.

He sent me a thought, *Only Jabril of all the inner world was able to see my inner thoughts as you just did. You are much more than just a prince of our world, Aaron. Let's keep the pride I have for our two scoundrels just between you and me.*

I nodded, and we both shared a knowing smile. There was respect both ways in those smiles, and we both felt it. Here was another good man who was more than the average. There was something in common about Dresden, Jabril, and Dorin. I felt it but could not quite put my finger on it. I felt a slight chill as I realized that I had felt the same thing in Liz.

My attention was brought back to the table and the business at hand.

Dorin looked over to Jeff. He stood. "As most of you already know, we have had trouble from the dark forces on previous Apollo missions. We have had to destroy three of the dark force's crafts before they could do any permanent damage. The Apollo 11 mission is another matter. From our reconnaissance ships, we have learned that they intend to attack the mission as it moves to the backside of the moon. They will launch a massive attack from their moon base to insure complete destruction of the spacecraft. We could not possibly keep up with such an attack and keep what we are doing secret. We have to attack the moon base and destroy both it and all of their craft before Apollo 11 reaches the backside. This has to be done after the mission is launched to limit the time the dark forces can send reinforcements to replace any of their lost craft. That's where Aaron and Zaron come in."

The assembly looked back over at me. Jeff continued, "We will launch the attack after Apollo 11 breaks earth's orbit and heads for the moon. We will wait until one hour before the mission reaches the moon. That will give us little time. Aaron will follow as close as possible from the liftoff to prevent harm to the craft from land bases or crafts already in space. We expect that there may be a few of these, and Zaron and Aaron are the only two fast enough and with enough fire power to take out these craft and still go unnoticed by the Apollo crew. We think if Zaron stays far enough away and follows at the same velocity, the crew should not spot them. Even if they did, they would think that Zaron was some kind of space debris or maybe even aliens. If they think it is aliens that are up there, they won't dare report it." Here Jeff allowed a smile to cross his face. "We've been mistaken for aliens for a long time. A little more won't hurt." He looked over at me. "It seems that we too tend to add to the alien conspiracy that the outside peoples have come to suspect."

Jeff looked over at Dorin. "It is now nearly dawn above Atlantic Base. My attack force will leave shortly and remain in deep space in preparation for the battle. We will come in from the outer reaches in deep space and will not be detected leaving earth. Today is the day that the moon launch is scheduled. Aaron will leave Atlantic Base as soon as the spacecraft goes behind the planet in preparation for firing their thrusters and breaking orbit. He will then escort our lunar mission all the way to the moon. He will monitor the landing and escort the crew back to the atmosphere. He is authorized a rescue should the crew run into trouble." Here he paused and shook his head. "And from what I've seen of the technology, that is a good possibility. We just hope it isn't needed."

"Now let's get going. As they say in the space program, God speed." The assembly left the room, leaving just Dorin, Jeff, and me. We had stood as the rest left the room. Jeff shook my hand. "I must change clothes and get on board my cruiser. I wouldn't want my crew to leave without me."

He smiled and left.

Dorin looked over at me. "That reminds me of another innovation that has been added to Zaron. She is capable of projecting a field twenty yards from her outer shell that can be and will contain an atmosphere capable of supporting life complete with normal earth pressure. Should you need this device for the rescue of the members of the mission, you must be aware that while it is deployed, Zaron is open to attack."

I was impressed. I knew that Zaron was capable of creating breathable air, as she did this all the time. She always carried a compressed supply of atmosphere for emergency use, but I did not realize that such a large contained area was possible even for Zaron.

Dorin smiled at my thoughts. "Another special innovation of Jabril's," was his quick response. No other explanations were necessary.

We made our way to the hanger where Zaron was waiting. There were others that had made a pilgrimage to see the ancient sword. We let them do as they wished as Dorin thought that the people here deserved to have the chance to see something that was beyond even the inner world's technology. The sight of the sword was actually a spiritual event for them that I had not come to understand. Only a few knew the myths about the sword's origins. Only Dorin and I knew that these were not mere myths but something beyond our mortal world.

It seemed that Zaron was also enjoying the attention. The crews here were just as impressed with her. I didn't know it at the time, but many concepts of Zaron were also not of this world. But that is another story and too complicated to get into at this time.

We strolled over to one of the large conference rooms on this level just off the main hanger. Here many of the people who had visited Zaron had gathered. Those that were off shift were watching a national broadcast of the preparations for the launch of Apollo 11 mission. The screen was very large and had better contrast and clarity than a normal television broadcast. Dorin explained, "We take the original signal and with computer enhancement achieve a much better view of what is happening. Our technicians watch all areas of the mission from mission control, sort them out, and project them to this room for us to watch. This should be very interesting."

We watched, and as this was the first time I had seen the Saturn booster that was to take the crew in space, I was impressed with the contained power sitting on that platform. I don't know if I would have had the nerve to climb on top of that amount of explosives and feel comfortable.

The countdown had reach T-15 and counting. The countdown continued, and a ball of fire and smoke announced the ignition of the main engines. *The Saturn* and crew slowly lifted off toward space with a cheer from mission control, as well as those watching on the outside at a safe distance. I was impressed with the power generated from the booster. It must have been rattling the teeth of the crewmembers. Soon they were experiencing G-forces that had to be uncomfortable. It wasn't long before the booster rocket was depleted and separated from the second stage. This stage fired, and the crew was on their way into orbit.

Dorin looked over at me. "That's your cue, my friend. The first critical phase of the mission is over. They have survived that, and it's up to you to make sure they survive the rest." He stood up as did I. "We have to get you on your way."

The room had suddenly become quiet as all in the room turned their attention to me. There was awe in the room as everyone there stood up and watched us depart. It was only then that I appreciated the true importance that these people placed on this event in human history. There were two worlds that were relying on me to make sure this happened. One of these worlds was to never know that I was even there. I carried these thoughts with me as I again approached Zaron.

As we walked toward the craft, I asked Dorin about something that had been bothering me. "How big is the base of the dark forces on the moon?"

"Very. I see what you're getting at. Yes, earlier missions have detected buildings on the lunar surface. They are suspected to be alien complexes. Consequently the photos taken of this area have been airbrushed to remove them from public view. This is not our idea but has been taken care of by the government independently of us. They don't want to alarm the general public about aliens. As of yet, aliens have not appeared to cause any harm. The less the public knows about them, the better. This alien conspiracy goes very deep in the government and is handled very delicately. If they knew the truth, it would really give them a start." Here Dorin smiled.

We had reached Zaron's side. Dorin shook my hand. "Apollo 11 will be leaving earth orbit in a little more than two hours. You need to be out there waiting at a safe distance when that happens. It's now 9:45 a.m. on the outside. You will have to leave with the reality that any nearby persons on the outside can see you. I recommend a rapid departure. If all goes according to plan, you and Zaron will be in space for nearly two hundred outside hours. May God be with you on your journey and bring you both back safely." Instead of shaking my hand, he gave me a fatherly hug.

I turned to enter Zaron as a group of very quiet technicians had made an honor guard and a path leading to the golden ramp. I passed through their ranks and started up the ramp. I turned and sent a thought to those below. *Thank you, my friends. I can never repay the tribute that you have shown to Zaron and me. It is my hope that I will see you all soon.*

As I turned back and entered the craft, a cheer rang up behind me. I settled into the pilot's seat and sighed as I anticipated the events that were to follow.

Shall we go now, Master?

"Yes, my friend. It looks like you and I are destined to go down in history once more. I just hope the story has a good ending." Zaron seemed amused, if that was possible.

Don't worry, Master, it will.

I think that Atlantic Base had given Zaron an ego-boost along with her other capabilities.

WE FOLLOW APOLLO 11

This trip to Atlantic Base had been very interesting, as had my previous visits. I hated to once again leave my friends, but it was now time to go.

We brought up the ramp and closed the door. Zaron brought on the view screen as we gently lifted off the cradle and headed to the waiting airlock. The crowd below had grown, and all were waving as we left the large hanger. A lump came to my throat. I would never get over the amount of love I felt for these people. What was really great was the fact that this love was not just one way. I hope that one day readers of this journal are able to meet some of these people so you can even come close to understanding what I'm talking about.

Zaron had taken us through the process of leaving the base without any help from me. We were now sitting just below the surface of the Atlantic Ocean off the North Carolina coast. I sighed with a renewed resolve and sent Zaron shooting straight up into space. We reached a hundred miles out in about the same amount of time it took to say it. It was still remarkable that I felt no acceleration at all, but I was again impressed with Zaron's capabilities and especially her speed.

Zaron reached out with her new sensors and found the spacecraft. It was now in a safe orbit. I could zoom in on the craft and see the crew even though they were hundreds of miles away. It was reassuring to know that I could cross that distance in only a matter of one or two seconds. I judged that about thirty miles' distance would be sufficient for an escort.

After about two hours, I saw the thrusters come on as the craft broke earth's orbit. It came back around the earth and headed straight for me. I would wait and scan the area and drop in behind it. I would be its shadow for the next four days before their attempt to land on the moon.

It was July the sixteenth, and Zaron and I were in for a very long, slow mission. Landing was not scheduled until the twentieth. We passed our time by monitoring all broadcasts from the craft and mission control. I kept a zoomed-in sensor activated at all times of the interior of the craft. This three-dimensional sensor was part of Zaron's new sensing system and allowed me to feel that I was actually in the craft with the crew. I saw everything that they saw and could hear everything that they said. It made me a little self-conscious being so intimate with the crew without them even knowing it. I felt that it was important to know if they had problems at the same time or before the crew knew it. Like Dorin, I didn't trust the technology of this craft.

I realized that Jeffery and his attack group didn't have Zaron's capabilities, so Zaron was relaying what I was seeing straight to his command battle cruiser. He sent back a message through Zaron that the transmissions were coming through clearly. The crew had adapted a screen to display exactly what we were seeing. Jeff was really impressed and said it helped to pass the time.

Jeff would not start his attack until the Apollo 11 spacecraft was twenty thousand miles from the moon. They had timed it so their attack would be accomplished and any stragglers would be removed before the spacecraft could reach the backside of the moon. Also, the moon base would not have enough time to send a distress call back to the planet.

They too did not have communications capable of reaching earth from the backside. It was my duty that none of their craft would reach line-of-sight to their bases back under the surface of the earth.

I had time to review scans of the base from previous inner world missions. These views were stored in Zaron's main computer. I use the term *computer* loosely, as it didn't really apply to that device, but the English language has no translation for what it actually is.

I had not realized just how extensive it was. They had a small city there. Most of their structures were above ground. That was for the ease of construction and not by preference. They did not expect humans to be able to see their structures for many years to come. Events had changed that, and the dark forces thought they had the solution. We too thought we held the solution for their base. Coming events would be very interesting, and things would be happening very fast. Jeff and his attack force would have to be through and space clear of all craft within one hour of the initial start of the attack. All this had to take place out of sight of the outer rim or the *Apollo* spacecraft crew.

The anticipation made me a little nervous. Zaron picked up on my feelings. As pilot, I was an integral part of the craft. Not only could I feel every part of the craft, the craft in turn could feel me as a part of her. This association can't be explained to one who has never experienced it. It truly has to be felt.

As one with the craft, Zaron sent me a thought. *Never fear, Master. We are in control. I won't let you down.*

Thank you, Zaron. I don't think that it would be possible for you to let me down. I just hope we don't let down our friends. I knew Zaron understood completely.

The rest of the day was uneventful except when I approached too close to the spacecraft. I was spotted.

I saw this on my sensors but knew if I backed off it would cause more questions. I watched as the crew tried to figure out just what I was. They were discussing just how they were to report this sighting to ground control. They knew that the world was listening. They decided to try to send a code that might give away their problem. They asked for the position of their booster. I watched as the command center members were scratching their heads. They made a quick check and sent back that the booster was six thousand miles down range. This confirmed to the crew that what they were watching was an alien spacecraft. Nobody else was up here. It wasn't getting any closer, but they tried to take pictures of me. The distance and the thick glass of the capsule prevented any clear detailed pictures, but they could tell that I was real and some type of solid structure.

I got a message from Jeff. "Slowly back off and move directly behind. I don't think that those three men want to tell their story to anyone. They don't want the world to think they have sent three lunatics into space."

We watched their reaction, and when none of the crewmembers were looking out the window, Zaron and I moved directly behind the craft. The next time they looked, we were gone and they now weren't sure that what they saw was actually real. This was good.

We continued on toward the moon as Zaron and I slowly backed off from the craft to a safer distance. Here I knew that we would appear as only a small speck in the night sky.

Nothing of any consequence happened for the next two days. We watched the night sky, and Zaron scanned space for the so-called alien craft. She saw only Jeff's force waiting in space. They were shielded from sight from the dark forces but not from Zaron. Her sensors were indeed powerful. I could see why Atlantic Base was so impressed with this technology.

It seemed like no time had passed when we got word from Jeff that the time had come.

BATTLE AT MOON BASE

J eff didn't waste any time. The whole taskforce came streaking in from space and came in on the base. I watched on the console as Jeff took out the main command center and moved on to the hanger facility. Those that followed were taking out grounded spacecraft and still others were blasting apart living quarters. Two other specially equipped craft came zooming in and opened up sonic weapons on the underground facilities. These weapons shook the thin shell of the moon and entombed thousands of the dark forces underground forever.

Two crafts had taken off from the surface in preparation of the attack on the *Apollo* spacecraft. These were ignored as each member of the task force had previously been given assignments with orders that their primary task was to take precedence over any other events. They knew that Zaron and I were watching.

I knew we had to act fast. Zaron picked up on this, and we were on the backside in almost an instant. The two crafts of the dark forces didn't know what hit them. There was only a fine mist where they once were. We surveyed the scene below. That same type of mist was slowly flowing back to the surface of the moon. The base was a shambles.

Zaron scanned below. No life of any kind could be found. Jeff and his crew were very efficient. Though thousands were killed, neither Jeff nor I could feel any remorse. This was not because we were so cold. It was because what we had eliminated was so evil.

Jeff pulled back his force and again headed for deep space to wait there. We didn't expect any more crafts, but Jeff wasn't taking any chances.

Zaron and I also pulled back and picked up the *Apollo* craft at a safer distance this time. They fired their retro rocket and assumed an elliptical orbit of the moon.

We all watched via Zaron's sensors as two of the crew transferred to the lunar lander and powered it up. Zaron monitored all the controls as the lander separated from the orbital craft. Slowly the lander moved away and started toward the surface.

Zaron picked it up first. They were not where their onboard computer said they were. This could result in disaster. We moved closer. We watched as the craft continued down. We could tell that there was more information being fed to the computer than the primitive device could handle. Fortunately, an error flag came on indicating this fact, but the crew was not briefed on this particular error. They communicated this fact to the ground. After a small period of time, they were told to ignore the error and proceed. I thought that this was not the best advice. They were still off course and heading for a landing that would be a great deal harder than they had expected.

I don't know if it was pure luck, chance, or intuition that they switched from computer control to manual. It was a decision that would save their lives. It was now that they realized that the computer had caused them to overshoot their original landing in the Sea of Tranquility. The lander was still heading down, and a steady hand was taking them over some very uninviting landscapes but was using up way too much fuel. There was only one-minute's worth of fuel left when a suitable site was seen and the craft eased toward the surface.

Mission control also saw that they had gone beyond the critical point

107

and were on the verge of calling an abort of the mission as the surface of the moon came closer. They were too close to turn back now. They settled the craft down in a cloud of moon dust and cut their engines with only a few seconds of fuel left.

A message was sent from the lander. "The Eagle has landed." I breathed a sigh of relief, as I am sure many on the ground had done. I also thought of Brian back at Atlantic Base. He would get a real kick out of his lander sitting on the moon and especially the phrase that was sure to go down in history. "The Eagle has landed" was a phrase that would soon be heard all over Avalon, and Brian would be credited with the title. The outside world would never know the true origin of the name of the little craft sitting on the moon. Brian wouldn't care. He and Greg would be congratulating each other about now. I smiled at the thought.

The crew had been scheduled to sleep. That had to have been scheduled by someone who had never just landed on the moon. Sleep was out of the question. The excitement of the moment was too strong. The two astronauts started making preparation for leaving the lander. They were going to walk on the moon.

We again watched with the world as the two left the craft and started on their list of tasks on the moon. Armstrong made a statement when he stepped on the moon, but even with our advanced equipment we couldn't quite make it all out. I'm sure he had prepared a memorable statement. We were much more concerned about their safety. All was clear. We were the only aliens in space. I smiled, as this was the first time I had ever referred to myself as an alien.

For all intentional purposes, we were very much alien to the outside world. We were just not the sorts of aliens that people had mistaken us for. We just didn't come from outer space. Or, on the other hand, maybe we had in a certain way. This was something to ponder, but later. We still had our jobs to do.

We continued to watch as the two finished their moonwalk and reentered their craft. We watched at a safe distance until they blasted off from the moon to rendezvous with the orbiting craft. There were no problems as they docked and made preparations for their return to earth.

It was just then that Zaron picked up six craft coming fast from the surface. The dark forces were not done yet. Zaron streaked toward them at incredible speed. They had made the mistake of lining up in formation. Due to the fantastic speed that Zaron was moving, there was no way that they had seen us coming. In less than half a second, all six craft were no more than a fine mist. We scanned again and did not find a repeat of this effort by the dark forces. They were wondering what had happened to their planned assassination attempt. It would be much later that they would learn that their moon base no longer existed. As for now, they would stay out of space. They couldn't understand why there was no communication from their moon base or the craft that they had sent out. None of them wanted to go look. They are very cowardly beings. No way were any of them going to venture into space for some time to come.

Jeff had picked up what had transpired and saw how quickly Zaron had dispatched the six craft of the dark forces. He was very impressed as he sent me a message. "We didn't need a task force to destroy the moon base. Zaron could have done it all on her own. I've never seen such power, speed, and firepower in a craft so small."

I sent back, "We know the extent of the facilities at the moon base, and only a force such as yours could have accomplished what you did in the time you did it. Zaron has hidden abilities even I am not aware of as yet, but we still need occasional help.

"I think the original risk to the mission is now and forever over. We only need to escort the crew back to earth to make sure of their safety. Zaron and I can handle that. You don't need to stay up here for four more days waiting for the dark forces. I'll join you back at Atlantic base when they splashdown and I know they are safe."

It was true. The next four days were very uneventful. Jeff and the attack force were back at Atlantic Base. They would be going over the attack for some time trying to determine just how sophisticated the base on the moon was from the scans obtained just before the attack. Their scans after the attack showed only desolation.

While Jeff and the others were going over their scans, Zaron and I got to know each other much better. I was able to get a better understanding of her new sensors and super drive that could take us to fantastic speeds. By the time of splashdown, I had just about gotten to the point of understanding the principal but not the application. I really had much to learn.

I had been in space for a long time. I had not eaten and only had energy drinks aboard. This was not uncommon. We can go for weeks without food because when we do eat, all the nutrition goes straight to our systems. This is also why there are very little waste products generated by our bodies. This is one of the reasons our life expectancy is so long, baring any unforeseen accidents or murderous attacks from forces on the outer rim. Such things just don't happen in our world. This will be hard for a reader such as you to comprehend. Just realize that it is possible. Maybe your world too will become like that.

Now back to what was happening.

I was only in the outer reaches of the atmosphere when the capsule splashed down and was safely back on earth. I turned Zaron east and headed back to Atlantic Base. It's useless to say that we were in the small hanger in no time and settling down onto a cradle.

We got a hero's welcome. Zaron's legend had grown since we had been gone. I'm sure her speed and power were greatly exaggerated in the retelling of our battle with the dark forces. Jeff would tend to play down his part. The group thought our fights were much more exciting. It was like one craft and one man against the entire forces of the dark. The sons of light again were triumphant.

After several meetings and several speeches to the workers here at the base, it was again time to leave. Though it was hard to say goodbye again to my friends here, I was anxious to get back to Sarah, Liz, and my home. I was hoping for a long period of rest. I should have known better. As Jabril had put it, my education was sorely lacking.

I went aboard Zaron again, and as the door closed to Atlantic Base, I received a message from my craft. *It will be good for you to be home again. I will look forward to seeing my other two masters.* She had referred to Sarah and to Liz. The little princess was now included as a master of this craft.

We soon headed through the rift as I sighed with relief and anticipation of seeing my world once more.

BACK TO THE
HIDDEN WORLD

The bright blue sky of my home world was welcome as we broke the surface of the inner world. The towering mountains of Avalon were to our north. I needed to see Jabril. I wanted to get an update on my family and what was in store for me in my immediate future.

We swung north and approached the castle of King Dresden at a much more moderate pace. I think we both were enjoying the deep blue sea and the glimmering seashore that was coming into view. We circled the city, slowly enjoying the beauty of the architecture below. We passed the huge waterfall that was cascading down the mountain to the stream that ran through the royal gardens and the center of the university. Students were roaming the gardens in the reading areas of the university library. It was a peaceful view below.

We landed just above the university on one of the patios of the royal garden. Again we seemed to draw a crowd. The royal craft of Shambala was very recognizable and all knew who it was that flew her. As I went down the ramp, several students came over to greet me. There were a thousand questions. Some of them I could answer, and many I could not. They wanted to know how long I'd be here and if I intended to come back to the university. The top of the list was, "Can we see the Sword of Truth?"

In any place on the outside rim, I would never have even considered such a request, but here was much different. "Yes, it is something that all of you should get a chance to see. Zaron will welcome you. Please take your time and make sure all who desires to can have time to see Apollo's sword."

The faces of the crowd brightened as the whole group headed for Zaron. Soon I was left alone, standing on the terrace overlooking the central tower of the university that housed Jabril and his staff. It seems that a sword had taken over center stage and left me in the wings. I smiled and walked down toward the university, enjoying the feel of the sea breeze and the smell of the flowers in the garden. If Jabril wasn't in, I would just sit right here under one of the large shade trees and wait for a couple of weeks if need be. Yes, it is that pleasant here. Learning here is not a struggle as in many outer universities, but pure pleasure.

Even when I reached the tower and entered, the pleasure did not end. Music flooded the hallways, and beautiful paintings and sculptures lined the walls. Even the ceilings were festooned with great scenes from the histories of this world. All of the art was far beyond the abilities of the outer world's greatest artist. I slowly went forward and took the spiral staircase to Jabril's labs and offices. I stopped in front of the door and sighed. I didn't have to knock. A student in a lab coat opened the door. "Welcome, my lord. Master Jabril is waiting for you."

I entered and looked around the large room. There were many students here working on different projects. Jabril was at his desk as usual. He looked up as I came in. He only smiled and motioned for me to come over. I approached the desk, and Jabril indicated a chair. "Sit down, my boy. We have much to discuss." *I am used to being call "my boy" here. Needless to say that I'm over forty and still considered a kid even with my inflated reputation here.* Jabril smiled at my thoughts.

"You'll get wiser with age, my boy." I think the "my boy" was one of Jabril's jokes this time. "Still, we have a great deal of material to go over before you can rejoin your family." He put away the scrolls and papers that had been on his desk. He sent a silent message to the staff in the room, and they filed out, leaving us alone.

It seemed that our discussion was to be private. He stood and started that familiar pacing behind his desk. He was deep in thought, and with Jabril, there was no way to determine what he was thinking about.

He stopped and looked at me. "Our old friend, the general, is boiling mad. He is pressing his old buddies in Congress to appoint a special committee to seek, obtain, and use alien technology from countries other than his own through any means possible." Jabril was shaking his head. "Some other countries have acquired some technologies over the past several years. None of them alone could make any headway in decoding the science they have uncovered. On the other hand, if talented scientists got their hands on all that is out there, trouble might be in sight." He started his pacing again. "The United States is the most obvious country to get this information, but only when they are ready. Under no circumstances should men like the general be in charge of such an endeavor. We have to move up our timetable for removing him. I have already had information leaked to the subcommittee investigating the general's activities. It seems now that he is suspected in the murder of two NASA scientists. One of these was working for the CIA, and one was working at Area 51. Of course, we are talking about Jarod and Jocko." He continued. "There is another case of a missing colonel in the United States Air Force that the general had fired, and then this colonel disappeared from sight." I knew he was talking about Peter. "We know that these men are very much alive, but due to the murders that the general has committed in his past, I think that, as far as the general is concerned, they should stay here and stay dead." There was now a scowl on Jabril's face. I had never seen him so upset. "That man and his goon squad, using the Vietnam war as a cover, killed the entire population of two whole villages. Men, women, and children died at his hand, and his superiors never knew of the incident. It would now be too hard to prove. I feel no guilt in letting the man answer for murders that he did not commit."

Jabril sighed as though he was trying to dismiss General Vanderhoff from his thoughts. He again sat as his desk and brought up his private screen. It was fed from the information-gathering complex of computers of the university. Again I must try to get you to understand that the term *computer* is used very loosely. These devices would make modern computers seem like children playing with blocks.

He was going over some very recent scans of the dark forces. "It seems that you have really put a scare in our old enemies. They are even afraid to come out of their underground tunnels, even at night. It will be some time before they get their bravery back. I don't think that we can expect any trouble from them in the near future. We do have to watch the outside. Their war should come to an end soon. There will be no real winners there. We think that the east and west have cooled down and the threat of a nuclear confrontation is, for now, not very likely."

Jabril smiled one of his knowing smiles. I knew something was up. "Now is a good time for you to go back to school. You know your education is very lacking. You have a great deal to learn and a short time to do it."

I smiled at Jabril's use of *a short time*. Time for him was nothing. This short time would last for twenty-five years.

Jabril continued with, "You really need some time with your family before you continue your training. Your young daughter has been introduced around the university and has made quite an impression with the staff. They have also been evaluating her. Their reports are impressive. I have just been going over them. I was not surprised at their appraisal. Liz is very exceptional. She needs training more than you do. Sarah is in about the same situation. You need physical, mental, and spiritual guidance for you to be able to face your future. Liz, on the other hand, will surpass her parents in only a few years. Her training will follow a different path. Only a few here at the university have the ability to pass on the knowledge that she needs. Her dexterity and mental skills are at a level that has not been seen in this world for many centuries. At four years old, she was able to penetrate my private thoughts. It is at this time that I saw not only her skill but also the wisdom that came with it. She immediately understood me and I understood her without words being spoken or thoughts passed between us. Jenny thinks she is a *sage*. This is a term we don't use lightly. Only the old ones had such skills. Her heart is true, and her thoughts and ambitions are pure. She holds you and Sarah in awe. You have raised her well thus far. It is up to you to hold her back on occasions, as we don't want to loose that spirit in studies. Her breaks with you and Sarah in Shambala will be more numerous than the average. She needs this time, and she should spend this time with the two people she loves most. Encourage her fondness for the animal kingdom. I see this as very important for growing her as a person and even maybe more."

He smiled at me and stood up again and gave me a fatherly hug. "Sarah and Liz are waiting in the student cafeteria. You will have to rescue Liz from all the stories the students are telling about you. You know how they are, and Sarah is much too nice a person to interrupt them." He walked me to the door. "Enjoy your rest period, and I want to see you when you get back. I'll let you know when. One other point . . . we had a message that an animal named Jake was picked up by an Atlantic Base scout at night from a kennel and taken to your home." He smiled and gave me a pat on the back as I went out the door.

My head was spinning with the implications of what Jabril had told me. I wondered what Sarah would say when I told her what Jabril had said. Things could get very interesting from here on out. I hardly noticed the staring students as I made my way down to the cafeteria. My thoughts were deep and confusing. I just wanted my little girl back. I would make sure that she would never change from the person I knew her to be. After all, that was the little girl that her mother and I loved. I knew that she was special, but I thought that it was just prejudice from a father's viewpoint. I could feel that there was much more in her future. I hoped that when she was a woman she would be just like her mother.

I sighed as I realized that time passed very rapidly here, hidden from the outer rim. It seemed only a few days ago that Sarah and I had come here. I'm sure that the change in Liz's life would be just as dramatic as the change in our lives. Liz is very young. She can take change as long as it isn't too intensive. She still needs play and friends. Not just her animal friends but human as well. Could she get that at school? I wonder if all fathers worry as much about their daughter as I did mine.

I shouldn't have worried about friends. As I entered the cafeteria, Liz and Sarah were surrounded by a large group of students sitting in chairs and on the floor. They were telling her stories about their world and the school and finally about her dad and mom. She was excitedly taking all this in. She seemed happier than I had ever seen her. I now realized that we had sheltered her from people more than we should have. Here she was free to talk and do all that she was capable of. Here she could talk about her animal friends to people who understood. Here she could do her gymnastics for an admiring crowd without reprisals from Dad. Here she could learn what real friendship means. She had already made conquests in this one room.

I smiled as I reached the table. Three students got up to offer me their chairs, but I just thanked them and sat on the floor with some of the other students.

Liz was very excited to see me. She ran over and hugged my neck so hard that I thought she would choke me. She was really strong for one so young. "Daddy, I have been having so much fun. This is really a great place, and they know so many great stories here. They told me that I was a real princess. I wondered why we lived in a Cinderella castle. They told me all the wonderful things you and Mom have done. All the people here are so nice. I don't want to ever leave."

I looked up at Sarah's smiling face. She was also glad to see me. She had been worried as usual about our mission. She would welcome me home later when we had less company.

The students were all smiles. They truly loved the little princess. She could not hide her feelings from them and all of them saw the pure heart and talent that was held in that little package. They knew that one day she was destined to be great. I thought that she already was.

I hated to interrupt the friendly group, but we had to get back to Shambala. "Well, princess, it seems that you will have to leave for a little while. Your mom and I have to go back to Shambala. We can't very well leave you behind. Raja and Drake would miss you. That reminds me. There is another friend there that will be excited to see you."

I smiled over at Sarah. I sent her a thought. *It seems that a scout ship out of Atlantic Base took it upon itself to rescue one German shepherd from a kennel one night and dropped him off at our castle.*

Once again Liz picked up on my private thought. Her eyes brightened and she was jumping up and down. "Jake is here?" She clapped her hands. "I can't wait to see him."

I stood, indicating the end of our little get together, and we said our goodbyes, and hand in hand we three walked back up through the garden to the waiting Zaron.

As we approached the craft, at least a hundred students cleared a path to the ramp. I saw Sarah's puzzled expression. Liz had already picked up on what it was. She ran ahead and up the ramp. Sarah soon joined her and watched as Liz was admiring the sword now hanging by the door. Liz was almost breathless. "The Sword of Truth is real. It isn't just a made up story, like in fairy tales." Sarah was just as amazed.

What happened next took me by surprise. I would have to explain why to Sarah later. Liz reached up and gently took the sword from its mount and held it out in front of her and admired the beauty of it. "This sword is very powerful. It is very, very old." She looked up at me. "Is it really yours, Daddy?"

"Yes. King Dresden passed it on to me before my mission. It once belonged to your great-grandfather, Apollo. You will learn much about him in your studies."

Liz gently, and with a sense of reverence, placed the sword back onto its holder. A faint metallic click showed that it was again locked in place. Liz should not have been able to remove that sword. Jabril himself designed that holder. A light came on in my head. Jabril designed that holder. It seemed that the Sword of Truth had more than one owner. This was something else to ponder. It seems like I'm always coming up with things that I don't understand.

Our friend Zaron interrupted my thoughts. *Greetings, Masters. It is good to again have you all on board.*

"Thank you, Zaron. Let's all go home." The ramp slid up, and the view screen came on. The door closed, and we watched the waving crowd as Zaron gracefully lifted up over the capital and headed east out over the inner sea toward Shambala.

R & R IN SHAMBALA

W e approached our castle from the south. Somehow Zaron knew that I would want to fly over the capital and the surrounding area. I was amazed at the number of people that had flooded the streets of the capital city. I found that the same was occurring near our home.

Sarah seemed surprised that I was surprised. "Don't you remember? It's harvest time. Everyone is taking their extended rest periods from their jobs, and students at the university are home on leave until harvest is over."

Yes, other things had taken over my mind, and I had not realized the inner time for harvest had come. This was a great event in our kingdom. Sarah was looking forward to it, as was I. This would be Liz's first harvest. It would last for over a month, outside time, and would finish up with festivals all over the land. Much to our enjoyment, Sarah and I were expected to participate fully. The whole land looked forward to this occasion, and their celebration at the end of harvest was extensive. There would be singing, dancing, eating, and drinking for hours on end. I need to add here that the drinking was not the kind referred to on the outside world. These people could not tolerate alcoholic beverages. Not on principal, but physically. Their drink was pure energy that gave a natural high. I think the high was more from the enjoyment than the drink. The best of the foods of the land were prepared, and these were enjoyed with relish. I can never put into words the taste of these dishes or how they fortified our bodies and I believe our souls as well.

We circled over the castle a couple of times and gently settled down in the courtyard to the place where Zaron always stood waiting for her masters. When she had let down the ramp, Liz was the first one down. Soaring down from the sky was Drake. He spread his great wings and landed with the grace of a feather floating down to earth. He truly was a graceful being. Liz ran over and rubbed his great nose. He seemed to enjoy this; after all, how do you pet a dragon? His scales were harder than any steel known to man. Liz didn't care. He was her friend. Speaking of friends, out of the castle came the German shepherd. He either sensed the presence of his little master or maybe just smelled her. He slid to a halt as he saw the great dragon standing in the courtyard. A low growl came from Jake. This brought an immediate rebuke from Liz. "You two have to become friends. Drake is my friend, and he will never harm any of us. He is here to help you guard the castle." Jake seemed to understand. Liz had understood too. She knew that Jake's nature was to guard the home of his master from any harm. His territorial nature didn't include a huge dragon. This would take some getting used to for him.

Sarah and I smiled at Liz's quandary and were impressed with the way she handled it.

Jake had once again started wagging his tail and gave Liz his usual welcome kiss, which amounted to a lot of slobber down one side of her face. We would have to teach him a more pleasant way of greeting. Liz didn't seem to mind at all as she gave the big dog a hug around the neck.

Jenny and the castle staff had come out to greet us. Jenny had taken it upon herself to make sure that Liz's rooms had everything she would need, including a bed for Jake. Her library was already filled with books from the university that she would need for her studies. The rest of the staff took turns hugging Sarah, me, and especially Liz. Liz was eating this up. She had never received as much attention as she had since coming to this world. I knew for a fact that she would never tire of it. Love can be felt and will last forever, and there was much love in our castle.

After we went inside, I went to my study to check on any messages that I might have received. I knew that there would be many. After all, my outside activities ran a close second to running the estate and the castle.

While I took care of answering the many messages, Liz and Sarah were preparing our welcome home dinner with the staff. We would dine well before we went below to the fields and vineyards to help with the harvest.

I heard a soft padding behind me. I had not sensed a large tiger creeping up on me. I turned around to find Raja, the royal white tiger, coming in to greet me. He had been hunting and had seen Zaron flying overhead and came straight back home. I gave the tiger a great hug around his enormous neck. He let out a grateful groan. "How have you been, my friend?" The animal sat on the floor and tried to lay his head in my lap. "Yes, I've missed you too. It is really good to be back home." The big animal understood. He sprawled at my feet and feigned sleep. He was not only my friend but my guardian. When he was around, I knew that wherever I went, Raja would be right by my side. I smiled and continued my work. When I had gotten caught up, I went downstairs to the banquet room and joined Sarah, Liz, and the staff just in time for our preharvest feast. Raja was right by my side. The people of my kingdom were now used to seeing us together. At first they had feared the great beast but now realized that not only was he my constant companion but my friend. After all, a five-hundred-pound tiger tends to go wherever he wants to.

We dined for more than three hours. It wasn't the amount of food we ate that caused so much time but the friendly conversations going around the table. We had to be updated on who had new babies and who had gotten married and who had just been appointed to classes at the university. Most of the people here attended the University of Shambala, which was run by my father and mother until their deaths. Only a selected few got appointments to the world university on Avalon. It is only there that the more gifted receive intense training. It is from the finest of these that assignments to Atlantic Base are given. From the elite of these go the ones that mingle with the population of the outer rim. So you can see that those working on the outside are quite capable of doing about anything asked of them. The outer world could never imagine what they owed to these people over the past several thousand years and especially in the past one hundred.

We know what man can become. Getting the outside man through his childhood is very difficult. He is so arrogant and knows so little. Sometimes it takes a great deal of effort not to just give up on him. This journal may help him understand just what he is capable of if he would only try much harder. For this reason, I will take you through our harvest time so you may get to know the people here and how we live and why we live that way.

In much of my journal I have only hit the high spots or points of interest and not gone into detail about life here. It would take much more than a book to explain it all. Maybe only a small portion of the life of a smaller portion of people of this world will give you some insight.

For this reason, I am going to take you with us to the harvest and festival in our little hamlet. Though this is only a small fraction of the people of this kingdom and an even smaller fraction of the people of this world, it may give you some idea as to why we love it so much here.

As for the rest of the five who first came here, we didn't get to see as much of them as we would have liked. Cindy, Billy, and now little Bill Jr. visited often. We watched Bill Jr. grow under the proud eyes of his parents. Peter stayed busy at the university, and we seldom got to see him. Jocko and Jarod seemed to be everywhere at the university. They seemed much younger now, and their minds were like sponges. The jolly two made friends easily and could be found telling stories to the students in the cafeteria for hours on end. They were having the time of their lives. They could not believe a world such as this existed.

THE HARVEST

As you have probably guessed, we needed to change clothes before we joined the other workers. Not only would our golden jumpsuits have been uncomfortable, they would also have been inappropriate. The suits are a requirement at the university for all personnel and are expected in court and state meetings. The other times, such as this, we dressed entirely differently. We had changed into our working clothes. There was nothing about them to signify that we were any different from all the other workers. When harvest time arrived, all were equal. Our dress was much the same as old European peasant clothing. They were airy, comfortable, and practical. All wore scarves around their necks to keep dust and chaff from going down their necks and caught the sweat that resulted from exertion. Yes, we do still sweat. We walked down from the castle to the foot of the mountain where all were gathering for their different tasks.

Jonas was handing out the tasks. Because of my size and muscular build, I was to go the wheat fields. I was to use the scythe and cradle to cut the wheat. You may have seen pictures of this instrument. It had a long curved blade at the end of a long handle. On the handle was a cradle that would catch the wheat as it was cut. When this cradle was full, the cut wheat was laid in a small pile that the ladies following the cutters gathered up and placed in tied-up stacks that would be picked up by the carts. The carts would take this grain to the thrashers, who would beat the straw against a large sheet spread over an even larger stone. This would separate the wheat from the straw. The straw was saved for the making of bricks and firing their kilns. It was also used to fire the kilns of the glass and pottery makers.

The separated wheat was then taken to the seashore where Sarah and others used huge wicker baskets and flipped the wheat into the air allowing the offshore breeze to take the chaff out over the ocean where a number of fish had gathered to feed on it. The rest would settle to the bottom and make the sea bottom fertile. This had been done this way for centuries.

You may be wondering at this point why a people so advanced were using such outdated methods to harvest grain. It is also a good place to explain why.

This world too went through its period of industrialization. Machines were designed to do everything. The quality of our products declined. The land was losing its richness, and the people were losing their touch with the land. The machines were polluting our air, and we were relying on them to do our work. The joy of the harvest had gone. We didn't need to harvest all of our fields in one day. We didn't need to plant thousands of acres to feed our world. We didn't waste half of what we ate and didn't eat five times what we needed. I wonder if that rings a bell. We soon realized that the old way was more efficient and much better for our souls. Now you will find no internal combustion engines anywhere. The grain is stored in much the same way it was done then, but now it is taken to the mills on the streams coming out of the mountains, and, using water, wheels it is ground. The wheat is ground into flour. The barley, oats, and corn are ground into feed for the livestock. They have enough surpluses to keep the millers busy until next harvest, and we have more than enough for all our needs.

We still use oxen and horses to move our harvest in carts or wagons. These gather the stacks of wheat, the grapes, and other vine-growing fruits from the vineyards, and apples, pears, plums, peaches, and other fruits from the various orchards. It has taken centuries to acquire the ability for all to become ready for harvest at the same time.

At the end of harvest, the trees recycle their leaves and bud for growing the next crop. We don't have a fall or winter here. The fields are turned under, and new crops are sown. When the next harvest time comes, all will once again be ready.

When the first rest period arrived, I realized just how badly I had neglected my body. I had been in the fields for fifteen hours. My arms felt like lead, and my back felt worse.

When Liz came in from the vineyards where she had been taught to gather the grapes and place them onto the whicker baskets, she was one big grape stain that had a smiling face. Jenny hurried to clean her up before we sat down for our first energy replacing snacks.

We would wait several hours, outside time, before we went back to our chores. By the end of what would be a week, my back and arms were feeling much better. Jabril was right. Not only was my mind sorely lacking, but also so was my body. The university would soon remedy that.

Liz soon joined Sarah and me at our table, and she was again our clean little girl. I hoped Jenny had brought several changes of clothes for her. She then gave us a play-by-play on how to harvest grapes. She talked constantly about what she had seen and what she had done. She said next week she would get to help stomp the grapes to extract their juices. For some strange reason, the children of the hamlet all looked forward to this. There were several stages in the harvest process and all was not done until the raw materials were processed in their various ways and stored properly. The rest of the season would be used in making the food products that we were so used to. The breads, jams, drinks, salads, and fruits that gave us so much energy and health would be ready for consumption. Is it any wonder what we eat here is so nutritious?

As one, we all rose from our tables and went back to work. Since

127

there is no sleep here, except for the smaller children, work would be carried on in this fashion for the next several cycles. Here I must explain that a cycle is about a day and a half outside time. I hate to keep giving times as outside times, but otherwise you wouldn't know how long I'm talking about. To make it a little more simple, harvest lasts for about a month and a half.

After the last cycle and the month and a half was over, it was time for festival. Liz found that she enjoyed the festival time more than she enjoyed stomping grapes, which was saying a lot.

It was time for all workers to gather in the town square. This is a really large area surrounded by shops and places to eat. The shops supplied us with many of the things we needed in everyday life. This is where it is made and picked up. You notice that I didn't say *buy*. Each of us here supplies the needs of others. Nothing is bought or sold. There is no money. This concept went out with the internal combustion machine. We also do not have street lamps. We don't have lamps of any kind. It is never dark here. We still use electrical power, which is generated by plants many miles from here. All power conduits have to be underground. Electricity is used for communication and cooking. No other use of it is needed.

The singing and dancing started almost immediately. Liz was busy learning new songs. By the end of festival, she knew them all. The singing raised our spirits, and the dancing loosened up our stiff muscles. The singing and dancing was only interrupted by the eating and drinking. It seems that everyone was taking turns as something was going on all the time. There was not a sad face in the whole gathering. The people here did not grieve for the loss of loved ones or let tragedy cloud their lives. They knew that what God had willed no man should question. Dwelling on the loss of a loved one not only was a waste of their lives but dishonored the one that was now gone. Their love was still there and felt. This could only bring a smile to the face of the ones who would normally be grieved. With the lifespan here, you can imagine that this was seldom.

The festival too soon came to an end. People started leaving for their homes or businesses. The students went back to the university. The people working on the outer rim, and especially at Atlantic Base, resumed their responsibilities. Many would be back next harvest. As they would say on the outer rim, vacation was over.

We stayed, as was custom until the last had left. Jenny gathered up her things and put them in a bundle, which she slung to her back. Liz and Sarah also gathered their packs and tossed mine to me. Sarah had been nice enough to pack it for me. Hand in hand, we all again climbed the mountain. We again enjoyed the scenery surrounding us. The view of the sea as we went further up seemed to stretch forever. Soon we were crossing the courtyard where Liz once again stopped to admire the statue of her dad and his friends and Raja. The golden statue glistened in the overhead sun, and I too admired the statue. It was the artistry and love that brought my admiration.

I hope you can now better understand the people that presented that statue to Sarah and me. You have to remember that harvest and festival is only carried out in Shambala. Other countries have their traditions, which are just as wonderful. We would have to go to each country and live with them for a time to really understand.

RETURNING TO
THE UNIVERSITY

We had changed back into our jumpsuits. Liz was excited as usual. Everything new to her was something marvelous. Zaron was waiting as usual. We got the usual from her, *Greetings, Masters.*

"Hello, old friend. It seems that we are destined to return once again to Avalon."

Jabril requests that you come straight to his office. She paused then continued. *All of you.*

Sarah looked across the seat at me. There was that look on her face again. Liz picked up on it too. When Jabril gets urgent, it means that something is up. It's not always good. I tried to change the mood. "Maybe he just wants to say hello." It didn't work.

At least the flight was pleasant. We landed as usual back in the courtyard garden just south of the university and overlooking the campus. We went down the path toward the tower. We didn't speak. Not even the little chatterbox holding my hand had anything to say. She too had thoughts of her own. We arrived at the master of the university's main office and were let in by another assistant. He stood to the side and allowed us to enter and left the room as he gently closed the door behind him. Jabril was now alone in the room.

He indicated for us to take some chairs on each side of his and behind his desk so we could see his now-famous screen. "You need to see this." It showed our friend the general sitting in front of a congressional investigation committee trying to answer questions concerning embezzlement, misappropriation of funds, extortion, and murder. He was sweating. We watched the whole session, which didn't go so good for the general. Liz had a frown on her face as she looked up at Jabril. Something passed between the two. Neither Sarah nor I could pick it up. The screen went blank.

I asked the obvious question. "When do you think he will be sentenced?"

That's when it got mysterious. Jabril's answer was one word: *never.*

He went on to clarify his statement. "Just after this viewing, our friend the general pulled a disappearing act. We had not expected this, and we were not able to find him right away. It took us two days to locate him. By that time, he was already in South America. He has some unsavory business associates there that will give him further aid in disappearing. Right now the United States government knows nothing of his whereabouts. All that we can do is keep monitoring his activities. Only when his activities concern this world directly can we interfere. Much to our dismay, this happens much too often on the outer rim. It seems inconceivable that their learning can cause so many people such distress." Again Jabril shook his head, and again some message passed between my little girl and the headmaster.

Jabril changed the subject. "It's high time you got back here. The masters are waiting for all three of you." He smiled a knowing smile. We said goodbye and started out the door. A look passed between Liz and Jabril. Both smiled at each other, and we left.

There was no pause between the time we left Jabril's office and when our training started. Each of us went out separate ways. We had no time off except for our rest periods, which the masters had scheduled so we three could take it at the same time. The only other breaks were during harvest and festival back on Shambala. We relished these periods and looked forward to them. Our training was furious, and the new areas I studied virtually made my head swim. There is no way I could possibly go into all the things we studied. I tried to keep up with where Sarah and Liz were in their studies but soon gave up. My load was heavy enough, and I was only starting. Liz was on an accelerated rate. Only her ability made her capable of such a load, but she loved every minute. As she learned, we watched her turn into a young woman. We never celebrate birthdays here and since a year passes so fast we never miss them. In outside time, it has been nine years since we had that last visit with Jabril. Sarah and I are not half the way through our training. Liz has already reached our level, and she is only thirteen by outside terms, but she is as tall as her mother and just as pretty. They now look like actual sisters.

I bring all this up at this point because we have gotten a message to come to Jabril's office once more. We haven't even seen him since that last meeting. Again all three of us were requested to come.

When we arrived, the door opened on its own. No student assistant was inside. Jabril sat behind his now familiar desk. Again he called us over. The screen popped up out of his desk. He moved some switches. "I need to show you something."

He brought up an area of the Brazilian jungle. He zoomed in to a jungle compound. He continued on down below the compound to a maze of tunnels and rooms. In one of these rooms were numerous members of the dark force and standing in the middle was a human. Jabril again zoomed in on his face. "Recognize him?"

It was our nosey friend from my class back on the outside. The one who thought he could read everybody's mind. "Yes, I do. Why do I get the feeling that he is again up to no good?"

"That's probably because that is just what he is up to. It seems that the dark forces are using our little general as an instrument. They are supplying him with advanced weapons and money. He in turn has taken over a very large drug operation with the intention of spreading out and taking over all of Brazil. With his new weaponry and his influx of murder-hungry recruits, it could really be possible. Let me show you what he has done so far."

The screen showed a small village that was near Vanderhoff's headquarters. They had rejected joining forces with him so the general personally led a squad of his goons to the village. The view showed Vanderhoff marching in, sweeping the area with automatic fire, killing everyone in sight. None of the villagers had any weapons of their own. When his goons got through, Vanderhoff walked through the village shooting in the head those who were only wounded. It was when he shot a small three-year-old girl in the head that we realized that it must be too terrible for someone like Liz. I knew it was too much for me. Sarah was crying, and Liz had fire in her eyes. I had never seen a look like that from her before. The gaze that passed between Liz and Jabril would have melted solid steel. I can only imagine what transpired between the two. I wouldn't know for sure until much later. Then it would be too late to stop what was to come.

All of a sudden Liz's face changed. The fire had been replaced with a questioning look as further thoughts were exchanged. Jabril turned to Sarah and me. "I'm afraid this is much too intense for our little princess. I think it would be best for her to return to the university and Jenny."

For some strange reason, she didn't seem to object. Without hesitation, she came over and gave both of us a hug and kiss and she told us that she loved us. There were tears in her eyes as without another word she turned and left.

When the door closed behind our daughter, a confused mom and dad looked for an explanation from Jabril. None was forthcoming. He had turned back to his screen and brought back another scene. "You may recognize this. It is the latest scan of the underground breeding facility in New Mexico. We had not realized to what extent they had carried these experiments. It seems that crossbreeds may now be traveling outside these facilities. They have not succeeded with very many, as their attempts are crude. The creatures that have survived seem to have taken on the same disposition as their makers. These cruel, unfeeling, and manlike creatures have made the mistake of continually breaking the local laws, mainly killing and taking what they want. Fortunately, most are now spending the rest of their existence in various prisons. It won't be long, with our help, that the others will be rounded up also."

Jabril looked at us. "This is where you two come in. I can't ask Aaron to go alone all the time. It's time that you, Sarah, go with him on his next mission. Jeff has worked out an attack plan on this base, but he needs three things to make it work. One is Zaron. Two is someone to cover the air to and from the base during the attack. Three is someone on the ground to infiltrate the facility and move to the fortified underground chambers and destroy them. We don't think that just an earthquake or our sonic bombs will affect these after what happened at the final battle. These chambers were built to withstand that. Only the abilities of Aaron can call up the power of the earth from within to seal these chambers for all time. Only from within can he detect the weak points of the chambers. This is the most dangerous part of the mission. Aaron is not indestructible. His own power could kill him." He was looking at Sarah as he said the last. I said nothing.

Jabril somehow knew that I would go regardless of the dangers. Sarah, on the other hand, was a mystery, even to Jabril.

Sarah saw the question in his eyes. "I'll go and do what I can to help. I'm just worried about Liz. She looked really shook up about what she saw earlier. What are you planning to do about him?"

Jabril seemed to be thinking over what he would say next. I could not see his thoughts, but he was holding something back. "We're working on the problem with the general. As for Liz, I can say without a doubt that she and Jenny will be kept very busy."

Sarah was not completely comfortable with the answer, and neither was I. We just didn't know at the time what keeping Liz and Jenny busy meant.

Jabril continued, "You have to go and prepare to leave. Jeff's mission is just about ready to leave. The attack is at night. It will be midnight in New Mexico when Jeff arrives there. You will have preceded him there. The mission has to be completed and you ejected from the complex before the final attack. The rest of the base is to be destroyed and all that are in it. This will hopefully be another blow to the dark forces. The whole mission has to be back at Atlantic Base before dawn. This doesn't give any of you much time. That is why Jeff has spent so much time on the details of the attack. He'll brief you on your part and time-table when you arrive at Atlantic Base."

Jabril stood up, indicating that the meeting was over. There was a worried look in his eyes. This didn't make me feel any better. We shook hands, and Sarah and I left for our quarters at the university. We needed to freshen up and take some food. This might require all the energy we had and then some.

We didn't talk much. Each of us had our own thoughts as we headed on back to our apartment at the university. It looked as though our training once again had been put on hold. I just hoped we had learned enough to get us through this next mission to the outside. I really didn't relish going into the underground of the dark forces. I could not see how this could be accomplished. Even if it could and even if I were undetected and not killed, how could I destroy the crossbreeding facilities of the dark forces and return to the surface? There were way too many "ifs." I really hoped that Jeffery and his crew had thought all this over very carefully.

Sarah was just as concerned. She knew that she and Zaron could handle her part. It was me that she was worried about.

It was only a short time later that, hand in hand, we headed up the path to the lower garden where Zaron waited. I could feel that there were many plans going on that we didn't know about. I also felt that most of them concerned us. These premonitions of mine seemed to be getting much stronger, and Sarah's awareness was just as strong. She gave my hand a knowing squeeze. It didn't take words to express our concerns and feelings for each other. We had gone way beyond that. Even with our increased knowledge and powers, we were still only husband and wife as well as mother and father. It seems that these concepts never change, as well as the feelings that go with them.

When we reached Zaron, her golden hull seemed to shine more than usual and her ramp was already down. The drives were already warmed up and ready to go. We got the familiar, *Greetings, Masters,* as we came aboard.

"Well, good friend, it seems that we are again on another adventure." It was a thought more than a greeting, and Zaron picked up on our doubts concerning the mission.

Her answer back was unexpected and gave us something to think about. *Never fear, Masters; the sons and daughters of light will always prevail.*

Both Sarah and I smiled at the optimism of our little craft. Could she have been listening to the fantastic tales at the university? "Thank you for the confidence, Zaron. It's time to again go to Atlantic Base. This time you won't have to have any more improvements."

None is needed, Masters. Our little craft also didn't have an oversupply of modesty. I think cocky would be more appropriate.

Our craft picked up on my thoughts. *Not really, Masters; modesty has nothing to do with the truth.*

I had not looked at it quite like that before. Sarah and I both laughed at our friend as we lifted off and headed again back out over the Crystal Sea. We could feel the pride which came from our little craft, as well as the pride in her masters, though we did not feel like her masters at all.

The rift was traveled without a word from any of us, and we were soon in the outer world. We came close to the surface and noticed that is was near midday. Being cautious on this trip, we traveled the rest of the way to Atlantic Base underwater.

When we finally reached the base, we were met with another underwater craft that preceded us into the channel of the airlock. We followed, and both crafts were soon settling down in the hanger.

BATTLE PLANS

Dorin and Jeff were both there to greet us as we came down Zaron's ramp. Jeff had just left the craft that had preceded us into the hanger. There were their usual smiles, but we both sensed something deeper in their thoughts as we shook hands. The usual curious crowd gathered. It was surprising as almost all of the crew here now we knew personally from the university. We spent over an hour shaking hands and renewing old friendships. It was a happy time that was over much too soon.

We sensed urgency from Dorin and Jeff. They were too polite to interrupt our greetings, but they were anxious to get on with why we were here. We reluctantly broke away from the crowd and followed Dorin and Jeff to the small conference room off this hanger. Here we met several people who had been waiting patiently for us to arrive. We apologized for keeping them waiting and seated ourselves at the table.

Peter Black was here. He smiled a greeting with a familiar wave of the hand. We wondered what would bring Peter here.

Dorin made his way to the head of the table, where he remained standing. "I don't have to introduce you to Aaron and Sarah. You all know them well by now. We have called this meeting to bring all the groups of this project together. It is a very complex mission that we have ahead of us. All of you need to know why you were performing the tasks that were assigned to you. We had to lay down the groundwork for this to be a success. All resources will have to be utilized during and after the operation. If all goes according to plan, none of us except Aaron will even be involved. If things go wrong, we will be Aaron's backups.

Dorin noticed the confusion from both Sarah and me. Surely he didn't expect me to take down the base all by myself. I knew that my self-confidence had improved, but not that much.

Dorin smiled as he saw our thoughts. "We have several factions in play. One is the dark forces and their breeding complex where half human beings are being grown from embryos obtained from captured pregnant humans. This isn't bad enough as they change these embryos' DNA structure so they are more like the dark forces than they are human. There have been hundreds of failures, and the creatures incubated there haven't lived very long. We don't think that they have made many successful beings, but we can't be sure at this time. Not only should all of these creatures be eliminated, but also the dark forces performing this evil against the human race. No sign of these labs can be left. All this has to be done by Aaron from deep within the base."

Dorin paused as he and the rest looked over at me. I suddenly realized that I had my mouth open in disbelief. I closed it and took a deep breath.

All centered back on Dorin as he continued. "That is the easy part." He caught my thought and smiled. "I'm sure Aaron is up to the challenge. It's the other factors that get tricky. We have human scientists working there who are under the impression they are working for the United States government. The upper levels of the base contain labs and quarters for the personnel. The second level is strictly storage. The ground level contains only hangers and garages for the private helicopters and trucks and elevator access for freight and people. This area, as well as the levels below to level five, is guarded by what appears to be United States Army personnel. The gate to the complex is likewise guarded. The sign says Government Biological Research Facility of New Mexico, and access is limited. Not only do the scientists think they are working for the government, but also the guards and workers there. They are retired or discharged army personnel that have been offered five times their normal salary to enlist for this duty. None ever go to level five.

The last group of beings is the most pitiful. These beings were once human. Their pasts, their presents, and their futures have been burned from their brains. They have no sense of identity or care. They are only biological robots that go between levels five and four to bring research, supplies, and messages to the dark forces working below. Unfortunately, we can't find a way to save these beings. Even if we did, there is nothing we could do for them."

There was a mumble around the room as the horror of what they had heard sunk in. These people have a very hard time realizing that such evil can even exist.

Dorin looked around the room. "We have to carry all this out without the destruction of the human personnel working there. We also have to do it without their knowing that we are even involved. To do this, we have to use a little of our pull from our friend Peter Black." All eyes turned to Peter. "With his help, in conjunction with the president of the United States, the army has organized a strike force to attack the complex. The cover story is that a terrorist group is manufacturing biological weapons that will be turned loose on the United States. We have gone through several ways of getting all of this accomplished. We need to extract the civilians before Aaron attacks the breeding complex. They have a nuclear reactor generating power for the base. We will use our technology to simulate a reactor leak. The radiation level will appear to be high enough for all personnel to be evacuated from the complex and taken to Area 51 to be decontaminated. At this point, Aaron will act. The complex from level five down must be destroyed completely. Aaron then has only fifteen minutes to get out of the complex before the air strike destroys the ground level of the complex with incendiary bombs and the underground areas with ground-penetrating explosives. The nuclear reactor is one mile from the main complex and should not be damaged. A special crew will arrive there from the nuclear regulatory commission to take the reactor down and disassemble it. Nothing will be left of the base."

Dorin took a deep breath. He looked over the group and continued. "As you may be aware, when allowing the outside agencies to carry on these tasks, human errors are sure to take place. This is where our special group comes in. We will have Jeff and one of our battle cruisers just out of the atmosphere above the base. The final attack will be at night. Should total destruction not be attained, Jeff will follow up. If the dark forces try to interfere from the outside, we have our greatest backup. Sarah and Zaron will be close by. Zaron will be shielded from any radar and will be on the watch for crafts of the dark forces. None of you need to be told just how capable these two are to the task. After the battle, if all goes according to plan, Aaron will be picked up by Sarah and returned to Atlantic Base. All human personnel will be decontaminated and returned back to society with instructions not to disclose what they were doing."

Dorin looked over at Peter. "Peter will fill you in on our timetable and just how we will get Aaron into the complex."

Peter stood. He looked over at me with concern on his face. "There are other issues that have to be solved on this mission. We have to determine just how far along the dark forces are on their program and just how big the complex is. We have several scans of the area, but the critical areas are shielded from our scans by a new technology of the dark forces. This has caused us great concern. Aaron will have to be in the complex for at least three days prior to the attack to determine what he has to deal with. To do this, he will be undercover as a guard on level four. He will at the last moments have to descend to level five and crush everything there without getting himself killed." Here Peter gave me a reassuring smile. "After that, he has to make it back out of the complex before the strike force destroys everything in sight. If he doesn't make it out with the human staff, Sarah and Zaron may have to intervene. This will be in full view of the strike force and the evacuating personnel and will be used only as a last resort. We have to assume that anything that can go wrong will. Jeff and his crew will follow up only when the area is clear of all humans, both military and civilian. It is one thing for these people to see a small UFO. It is another for them to see a giant battle cruiser coming from outer space. All this has to be accomplished on Aaron's third night at the complex and completed before sunrise." We could see the concern on Peter's face. He continued, "Timing is everything." As Peter sat back down, a new round of comments filtered around the room. They were concerned as much as I about the fact that too much of this mission was to be performed by the outer military forces. Their confidence in these was not very high. My confidence in them was also about as high.

Dorin again stood. He smiled and added, "You may be concerned about the safety of the innocent humans and of especially Aaron. We could not let this happen without a little help from us. Major Craig Austin is in charge of this military operation and is also one of us. It took a lot of undercover work for Peter to pull this off, but he insisted that he could not in good conscience go along with our plan without Craig pulling the military strings."

A collective sigh went around the room. A deeper appreciation of Peter went with it. I felt much better myself. This might just work after all.

Dorin concluded the meeting. "I have to say that I am proud of each of you in the jobs that you have done preparing for this. Those that are to be on the mission itself will report to Jeff for further briefing. Sarah will attend these meetings and be made aware of the exact battle plan of the US military. Aaron is to go to Washington to catch a cargo plane loaded with supplies and personnel heading for the base in New Mexico. Good luck to all of you. You all know how important this is to us as well as the human race."

All left the room except for Sarah, Peter, Dorin, and me. It seemed that I would be leaving soon, and this was my last chance to say goodbye.

Sarah was not really happy about saying goodbye. She could sense the danger that I would be going into. She knew, from what she had learned at the university, that the dark forces had formidable weapons. They had not been idle since the final battle. If I were detected, my life wouldn't be worth much. They had no compassion, and should they learn that Aaron was in their midst, there would be no escape. Jeff and his forces, nor Sarah and Zaron, could react fast enough beneath the surface of the earth. I knew that Sarah would react with total destruction should something happen to me, and she wouldn't care who saw her. Zaron alone had that much firepower. It was reassuring that she and Zaron would be close by at the final moment.

There were tears in her eyes as she kissed me goodbye. No words were spoken. Our feelings spoke much louder than any words. She left with Peter, knowing that Dorin wanted to speak to me alone.

Dorin was serious as he took both my shoulders and looked me in the eye. "Jabril insisted that only you could pull this off. I don't know why you keep being thrust into battles with the dark forces, but I feel there is a much deeper meaning that neither you nor I can understand at this time."

He slapped me on the back and sighed with resignation as he turned and led me back to the hanger.

We were soon approached by one of the new recruits from the university with some civilian clothes. I was to change into these immediately. It seemed that my time for departure was rapidly coming up.

I changed in Jeff's quarters and came back to the hanger with my guide. There was a small craft that had been brought up from below and sat on one of the cradles with her engines warmed up and ready for flight. It seemed that Jeff had requested to fly the craft and see me off. He seemed almost as worried as Sarah. He also had my final instructions. These were in the form of military orders to report, in uniform,

142

to Washington International where I was to board a military transport. My uniform and personal items were already waiting at the beach house on Emerald Isle. I had used this house before, as had many others. It seemed that this was an ideal way for our people to join the outer world. From there, they would take civilian positions throughout the world. Normally they would stay here for a few days and make themselves seen to give the impression that they were just normal people on a few days of vacation. I would be there only one day. The residents near there would see a soldier returning to duty after a very short leave.

Jeff and I left the base and traveled to the drop-off point where the craft stayed just beneath the surface about a mile south of the beach house. He scanned the beach for early risers, as it was a good hour before dawn. It was also now midsummer. Jeff put down a field that would allow me to move to the beach without so much as getting wet. This brought questions from one individual who had seen me on my first visit here.

I again thought of Gavin Graham as I once again walked out onto that deserted beach. I wondered what he was doing now. He had only been a boy of eleven that day so many years ago. It was not long before I was once again just below the beach house. From here I could see Gavin's grandparent's house. I could almost see once again that young boy running for the first time in many years toward the house to show his mom and dad that he was healed. He still thought that it was an angel that he had met that day on this beach.

I would see him again. This was one premonition that was very strong. We had something in common. The hand of God had touched us both. What other two people on this world could say the same?

It was with reluctance that I entered the beach house and made preparations to leave. I found all my papers and identification in order. It seemed that I was now one Barry Jennings. I smiled at the way our security had kept my last name. They knew that I would readily answer to my former name from the outside. A rental car was waiting in the driveway. It took me some time to pack as all my clothes were scattered about the house. It looked as if I had been there for several days. Someone had taken great care to make sure those who had to clean up the house after I left would think that a very messy individual had occupied it.

I smiled at the thought as I backed the BMW out of the driveway and started for Washington. It seemed that this sergeant was very extravagant. This would fit into the character of a discharged army sergeant that had just been offered to reenlist at ten times his former salary for a single six-month tour. How many others had fallen for this scheme from the dark forces? It didn't seem in character for them to pay so much money. I didn't realize just how right I was.

THE DESERT BASE

The trip up the coast was mostly uneventful. I eventually made my way to the airport with several hours to spare. I turned in my rental car and took the shuttle to the main terminal. I made my way to the private check-in at the far end of the terminal. Loading would be from the ground and not from the larger ramps for commercial jets. Since I was early, there was nobody at the desk leading out to the tarmac. I settled down with the Washington newspaper. It might be good to get the latest of what was going on in the world outside.

An item caught my attention. A group of eight young college grads had started up a software company. Brian had mentioned this to me back at Atlantic Base when I had asked him about the project he had started from Area 51. He was to start an international network of information-based computers. He said the seeds were planted and several of the people mentioned in this article would become extremely wealthy. It seemed that unrest was prevalent all over the world. The Soviet Union was having issues with its satellite states. The Middle East was still fighting each other as usual. *World unrest* seemed to be

145

the key words. Could this world ever be united as one? It would take a great deal of work.

I put down the newspaper and watched the people. It wasn't long before others arrived that were supposed to take the same flight. Almost all were army. The few others seemed to be workers at the base. A gentle scan of their thoughts confirmed my suspicions. All had been promised huge salaries. It was evident that greed had brought them all together.

Soon an army sergeant came to the desk at the head of the stairs leading down to the loading area.

I joined the line of military that were taking their orders to the sergeant. He took his time thumbing through each set of orders. As he finished, he motioned each down the stairs to board the waiting plane. I was next to last to board. The plane was packed, and I had to take a very uncomfortable rear-facing seat near the back of the plane. Cargo planes aren't known for their comfort. All the others resigned themselves to the fact and settled in for a very long flight.

The plane was a propjet, and her speed was not what I had become used to. The flight was boring, and nothing of importance happened during the flight. I spent the time looking over all the people onboard very carefully. None knew the true nature of the base. Many thought they were going to work in a government super secret complex. At least they were half right.

We landed on a small runway somewhere in the desert. I could not see any towns anywhere as we came in to land. We transferred to buses and started out over the desert in a convoy after the plane was completely unloaded. Trucks carried the supplies that had come with us, and buses carried the people. All were army green. As we didn't pass any populated area, our trip had gone unseen by everyone except a lone spaceship fifty miles above. I could tell Jeff was watching intently to the events below. I could not sense Sarah. She had to be still at Atlantic Base. She would only arrive just before the planned attack.

After more than an hour on the buses, the convoy arrived at the base and waved through the gates by the sentries on guard. Each carried submachine guns. I'm sure that no one that was not expected ever got through those gates.

Our buses drove right into the above ground hangers for the helicopters and trucks, and we left the buses under guard and were processed through a series of clerks who handed out instructions and destinations. Each of us wore a color-coded badge that designated our level. I was the only one issued a red one. I knew it was for level four.

We wasted no time at all topside as we were taken to elevators that were to take us to our proper levels of assignment. When the elevator finally came to level four, the only people on it were the armed guard and me.

Another guard who took me to indoctrination met me. Here I was given a big line of propaganda about how important secrecy was to the base and death was the sentence for those who did not carry out its policy.

I was glad that I only had to spend three days down here. It was not the most pleasant place I had ever been. My sleeping quarters were on level two. I shared it with ten other guards. I had to spend hours listening to how they were going to spend their money when they left. I also had to feign sleep as I lay listening to the snores of the other men who were off their watch.

My job was simple. I had to guard an elevator and let no one go on it without the proper pass and an environmental suit.

I learned that the suits were to cover up the identity of the individual and not for any environmental reasons. These individuals were the nonhumans that we had been briefed about back at Atlantic Base.

It was on the second day that I suddenly realized just who these zombies were. They were guards and other personnel that had finished their tour. Having their minds burned out paid them off. It seemed that these beings could not be kept alive for long, even with advanced technology. The dark forces had to replace most of the personnel at the base every six months. No one ever left. This fact gave me a greater resolve

147

to make sure I destroyed all of the dark forces. This travesty against the human beings of this world was more than I could take. There would be no remorse when I destroyed this complex and all that dwelt below level four. I spent the rest of my day scanning the crust of the earth surrounding the base. I knew every flaw and every way that could be found to crush this breeding facility beyond recognition. The earth was at my beck and call. I felt her respond to my thought. There would soon be an earthquake that would shake the area for miles around. I only hoped that the earth shield that I would be contained in would preserve my life. I would have to go down the elevator that I guarded when the time came. I would have very little time before the dark forces detected me. This would be very tricky.

The third day arrived. I was on the night crew. At least it was supposed to be night. One couldn't tell down here. Halfway through my shift, I was supposed to go down to level five. Jeff would be watching from above. I could already feel Sarah. She was stationed close by. I sent her a warm hello. I felt her concern ease a bit. The smile in her return thought brought me courage.

Very few ever came to this level for any reason. I had noticed that the stockroom on this level had plenty of environmental suits that were worn by the creatures below. I knew I had to wear one of these to be able to make my way to the breeding chamber. I could not tell from here what it would take to destroy the fortified chambers. Jeffery was right. I had to be there to determine how to take them out.

I left my post and donned the gear that was to be my cover. I came back to the elevator and entered. A scan of my hand was supposed to allow the elevator to descend to level five. I knew my hand would never pass this security scan. It didn't take me long, thanks to my training, to bypass the security and start down. The device was very primitive in our standards. The door opened, and I picked up the dank smell of the underworld. I made a straight beeline to the breeding chambers with a solid blank wall in my mind. There was no way the dark forces that swarmed this area would recognize an inner world presence. I was still amazed at how well organized this group was. Fortunately they did not pay any notice to my passage.

I reached the breeding chambers and realized that I had a huge problem. Even with several faults in the earth near here, there was no way I could destroy them at a distance. The fortifications of these tunnels were on the extreme. No normal earthquake could even touch them. Only from one vantage point near the facility could this whole area be crushed. Unfortunately, I would be in the middle of it. This was suicide. I could see no other way. The elevators would be over a half mile away, and, after the quake I was to bring, they would be out of commission anyway. This quake would have to be large. It would shake the desert for miles around. It would also seal me over a quarter of a mile below the surface with no way out. I think the bubble of protection that I would have around me would hold back the debris momentarily. I now wished I had Aaron's Staff to part the mountain of rubble that would be around me much like Moses used it to part the Red Sea. I kept my thoughts from Sarah. She had her job to do. Worrying about me would not help.

At the last moment before I reached deep inside the earth with my awareness, I would have to let down the shield to my mind. I had to be one with the earth, or this would never work. I would also be vulnerable to mind probes. At the last moment, all here would know who was in their midst. This was the only comfort in what lay before me. They would once more know that Aaron was to do battle.

It was time.

I let down my guard and reached deep within the earth with my awareness. I felt her in much the same way as one feels when greeting an old friend. She was ready. Sudden awareness also erupted into the underground. There was fear and hate mingled as they found Aaron in their midst. It was too late. The earth erupted with the force of a full-blown volcano. The underground chambers were crushed with the upheaval of a small mountain. Thousands of the dark forces were instantly destroyed before they were aware of what was taking place.

149

The bubble of protection around me somehow kept me safe, or was it the mountain itself? I would never be sure which. I could hear the sirens above me at a distance sounding the warning of a radiation leak. Jeff had done his job. The earthquake had shattered the nerves of all at the facility, and the threat of radiation didn't help. They all hit the stairs to the outside as the reactor and all electrical power was instantly shutdown. The generators topside gave enough light to the emergency lighting systems to get them all out.

It was then that I got Sarah's thoughts. She had been monitoring what was taking place. She also saw the circumstance that I was in. Needless to say, my wife was boiling mad. The thought was abundantly clear. *Are you completely crazy?* She didn't wait for the obvious answer. *You could have been killed. And how, pray tell, were you expecting to get out of there?* She again didn't wait for an answer. *Thank God that Zaron and I were here. Her force field was able to hold together an airshaft just over your head. You'll have to get into it in a hurry. The military are already moving the humans to Area 51, and their attack group will soon be plastering this area with incendiary bombs. The shaft goes up at a forty-degree angle to the surface. I just hope you can make it to the shaft. The surface penetrating bombs will follow, and I can't promise that we can hold the shaft open much longer. Zaron is already stretched pretty thin. By the way, she sends greetings.*

I didn't know if this was supposed to be funny or not, but it made me feel much better. *Tell her that the sons and daughters of light will prevail.*

I looked over my head and, sure enough, there was the opening to the airshaft. That was reassuring, but the steel bars that stretched across the entrance wasn't. I removed the environmental suit and reached into my jacket and removed the disrupter that I had smuggled with me when I came here. I used it on the bars. The bars vaporized, and I got a *Well done* from Sarah. The entrance was still over ten feet over my head. I looked over the debris at my feet. There was no way I could stack it up to reach the ceiling. All the blocks were over a ton. One block caught my attention; it was at an angle and positioned about six feet from below the entrance. I thought of Liz. I would have to use the block as a springboard and jump to the opening. I took five steps back and was stopped by the wall of debris. I would only get one chance. My training would again come into play. I mentally measured the distance and ran and sprang from the block. One-half turn in the air, and I had gone feet first into the opening. I grabbed for traction and turned and started for the surface much to the relief of Sarah. I got another thought. *Liz would be proud.*

It was none too soon as I heard the bombing start on the complex. The ground-penetrating bombs started just as I reached the surface, and I heard and felt the airshaft collapse behind me. A giant fan blocked the entrance, but due to the fact that all electrical connections were severed, it wasn't running. I stepped through the blades and came out into the filtered air-handling unit. A door led me out into the cool night air of the desert night. A mile away I could see the complex on fire as the attack group moved off.

I had not even heard Zaron quietly land behind me. I was too busy counting my blessings. One of which was my wife.

Thanks can come later. Now just get your tail in here. There was more relief in Sarah's thought than anger.

I gratefully turned to find a ramp coming down from out of the golden craft not six feet from me. I rapidly boarded the craft and got a *Greetings, Master* from Zaron. She didn't seem the least bit perplexed with the previous situations. Not so with Sarah. I couldn't tell if she was mad at me or scared. Maybe it was a little of both. Neither helped her disposition as we moved away at a safe distance and Jeffery and his crew moved in to remove any sign that a base had ever been here. The sonic probes devastated the remainder of the underground complex, and the disrupters shattered everything above ground including the airshafts that the military had overlooked. There was only a depression in the desert that indicated where the base had been. The reactor had been left. Destruction of it would have meant widespread contamination of the desert. The nuclear regulatory commission with the utmost discretion would handle it. The remaining structure would be destroyed in like manner. The desert would again reclaim what was originally there.

Sarah parked Zaron on watch not far from the base. We were to make sure that no other dark craft would come to the area. We would leave just in time to make it to Atlantic Base before sunrise. That would not be very long as the base was three hours ahead in outside time.

This gave time for Sarah to swarm me with kisses as tears streaked her face. "I thought I had lost you. I saw what you had to do. It was just by pure chance that Zaron picked up on the airshaft. I think that God was by both our sides back there."

We enjoyed these few minutes together before we had to again head back to the Atlantic coast. Zaron lost no time at all getting us back there. She had waited until the last possible moment before leaving. I think she realized that Sarah and I needed that time alone. We made it to Atlantic Base just as the light of a new dawn crept out over the Atlantic. It was good to be back among friends. Zaron moved to the waiting familiar cradle and gently landed in place. The golden ramp came down once more. We left as I gently touched the Sword of Truth at the door with a prayer of thanks to the creator for sparing our lives once again.

A cheer rang out from the crowd. News of our success had preceded us. Jeff's crew was probably responsible. I was later to find out that the staff here watched every detail of the mission. Jeff's sensing capabilities were much improved. The destruction of the base and the miraculous escape engineered by Zaron and Sarah would be talked about for years. They had all been able to see what existed below the surface and see just how far from human the dark forces were. It left a resolve to all here that the dark forces had to be stopped at all costs. The human race again would never know just how close they had come to being replaced by an evil counterpart. This half-human and half-dark force would be something no one would want to have in his or her neighborhood. We would make sure that from now on no such things as this would ever again reach the point of getting out of control. It must have taken many years for the dark forces to put together such a detailed and well-organized complex.

The next several days were passed recounting the events that took place out under the desert. The other time was spent meeting old friends and learning about their expanding families. Brian told us of his two children. One had already started in at the university, and the other was anxious to follow. Both were boys and from what I could tell, they too were as intelligent as their father but not near as proud.

These made us want to get back home to Liz. I'm sure she had gotten word that we were all right.

Much the same as before, we hated to leave our friends, but other friends and our responsibilities in the inner world were waiting.

We boarded Zaron, and the golden craft was again heading to Shambala. It would be good to again see those mountains rising from the sea to greet us on our return. This land was now a very big part of us. We could never call another place home again.

The dragons circled the craft as we landed at the castle. One great dragon had a human companion on his back. We knew it was our dear daughter. She wasn't and never would be again what you would call an average daughter. We had stopped being concerned about her dangerous pastimes because to her they were as normal as walking down through a garden of flowers. It still brought a gasp as she swooped down at fantastic speed to land gently beside Zaron. She jumped lightly down from the neck of the giant beast and came over to give us hugs and kisses like a normal daughter.

Even her pets were unusual. Drake spread his wings. *Welcome home, Your Majesty.*

"Thank you, Drake, and thank you for taking such good care of our daughter." I bowed slightly toward Drake. The gesture did not go unnoticed. The giant dragon spread his wings in a salute. I had impressed the dragon much more than I had intended because a bow from the dragon king was an honor not to be taken lightly.

Liz looked up at me and said, "Thank you, Daddy. Drake is honored beyond measure. I have never seen him so pleased."

Liz looked more at ease since her rest period here at home. For some reason, she had increased the intensity of her training, both mental and physical. It would have been much too much for an average student, but Liz was something special. Even she was reaching that saturation point during each session. Only her periods at home brought her back to normal. Neither Sarah nor I could tell what was driving her. She spent many hours one-on-one with Jabril on training that could not be found in any department at the university. There was no way to tell what kind of training this was for both Jabril, and Liz had a mental block that could not be penetrated. We had to rely on Jabril's decisions. He was the wisest person on both worlds. He would only do what he thought was best. Liz was not the only one who was under intense training. Sarah and I would soon resume our interrupted schooling.

Time would again seem to stand still as we immersed ourselves into our work. It was because of this that we didn't at first miss Liz. We had become accustomed to go for long periods and not see her, as her training was much different from our normal classes. We also hadn't missed Jenny. It was not until our next rest break that we noticed that Liz had not arrived home as usual and neither had Jenny.

When we started asking questions of other students returning to Shambala, we realized that no one had seen either of them for what had to be several months, outside time. Sarah was beside herself. We got on Zaron and headed back to the university. One person would know. Jabril.

He was expecting us. His face told all. He knew everything and had not included us. He had better have a very good reason, for Sarah was about as mad as I had ever seen her. You just don't mess with a mother's child.

THE MISSION OF ELIZABETH JENNINGS

J abril motioned for us both to sit. Sarah had a hard time calming down enough to sit. She finally submitted, and I joined her in the chairs in front of Jabril's desk. We both could tell that Jabril was keeping something from us. He was pacing back and forth behind his desk again as he looked for the right words. He suddenly made his decision and sat down at his desk.

He looked over the desk straight into Sarah's eyes and said, "Liz and Jenny are on a mission. Liz has been in training for it for some time now. She and Jenny are on the outside and have been for some time. They are alone and without support from the inside for fear of compromising their mission." Here he paused and watched for our reaction.

It was obvious. Both our mouths were open in disbelief.

"What sort of mission is my daughter on?" Sarah was on the point of losing control. That is saying a lot if you know my wife. She is about as self-assured as any person on the inner world. But this was her daughter we were talking about. That changed everything.

155

Jabril again stood up. "You already know your daughter is exceptional. You can never realize just how exceptional."

Here Sarah couldn't stand it any longer. "Where is she?"

Jabril didn't hesitate. "She has been kidnapped by General Vanderhoff." It was just a simple statement but might as well have been an atomic blast the way it hit us.

This brought both of us to our feet. We knew what kind of man this was. We were ready to start throwing things when Jabril unexpectedly smiled.

"Don't worry. Liz is in complete control. This whole thing was planned and carried out without a hitch. We needed to get someone into the general's camp, and who better than a spoiled rich kid of two American millionaires? She wormed her way into Colombia, South America, with Jenny where she let slip in several areas that she was the daughter of the rich and famous Charles and Sarah Jennings. We knew that sooner or later word would reach the general in Brazil. We knew with his greed he couldn't pass up the opportunity to kidnap the youngster for ransom. Which he did. Liz had played her part well, and both were taken to the general's base in Brazil."

Sarah was now standing and wasn't about to sit back down. "Vanderhoff is not the kind of man to turn Liz loose once he gets a ransom, no matter how much it is."

Jabril again smiled unexpectedly. "Of course he isn't. He plans to kill them both as soon as he gets the money. We knew this before we started. I don't think that it's Liz who is in the most danger."

This didn't make Sarah feel any better. Jabril continued his pacing as he spoke once more, "There are more factors in play here than you can realize at present. Liz has many tasks to perform while in the general's camp. These all have to be accomplished before we can bring her out." He looked over at Sarah as she slowly regained her chair. Her knees were now getting a bit weak. "This is where you two come in." He smiled his knowing smile. "You are a big part of this whole thing, and you have to be brought up to date on what has happened as our little girl crouches in a dark cell in the jungles of Brazil, playing her part, and enjoying every minute of it. She has overcome the urge to tear the general apart. This is to her benefit as well as the general's." Here Jabril allowed another smile. He was much more confident than we were.

Jabril came around the desk and took Sarah's hands. "Don't worry. Liz has become more to me than just a mere student. I would never let any harm come to her. I would call up every power in heaven and earth to keep that from happening."

We both saw the truth of it in his thoughts. We were allowed only that brief glance. Much more was there, but not for us to see. This made Sarah feel somewhat better. I was still a little hesitant with such trust in Jabril's ability. *I would feel much better if I were there myself.*

Jabril turned to me. "You will be."

I could hide nothing from this man. He looked over some papers on his desk and made another decision. "I need for you to come into the projections area where we will show you Liz's journey so far. She has been a very busy girl.

"Let me give you the background of our plan. Jenny and Liz were to go to Cartagena in Colombia where Jenny was supposed to visit a sister. The sister is one of us. Both, as you know, speak Spanish without any accent. They were accepted as locals. Liz played the part of a spoiled, little rich girl. She made known in the party centers of Cartagena of who she was and in particular who her parents were."

Here Sara stopped Jabril. "Why are you speaking in the past tense?"

Jabril looked surprised. "Because all of this has already happened. We didn't involve you because your part of the plan hadn't come up yet."

Sarah looked at me with that frown that told so much. She wasn't really pleased with what she was hearing.

Jabril continued as though he had not been interrupted. "We knew that Vanderhoff's crew liked to spend their ill-earned money in the bars and hot spots of Cartagena. We also knew that he had a large reward offered to anyone who could give him the whereabouts of Charles and Sarah Jennings. He still thinks that you two are in league with aliens. He wants the technology that you can supply him with, and with his greed, he saw the opportunity of killing two birds with one stone. He saw a way to get a large sum of money from you, and once you got there, he would get the rest that he wanted. Then he plans to kill all three of you as well as Jenny. Right now she is working as a slave in his kitchens. This played right into Jenny's hands. She has already picked up most of the information we needed about Vanderhoff's operation. There are some other parts of the mission that only Liz can accomplish. This is planned for later when you are supposed to arrive." He noticed the question in my mind. "You will arrive, but not the way Vanderhoff expects. But we are getting ahead of ourselves. I want you to watch your daughter at work before I explain your parts in the mission."

Jabril led the way to the projection area. He spoke over his shoulder as he went. "Liz isn't your little girl any longer. She would be fifteen in the outer world, and she has a mind of her own." He shook his head as in resignation. "That mind is the most astounding of any I have ever seen in this world. Great things are in store for her. This man, Vanderhoff, has affected her greatly. She has to face this man to be able to see the true evil there. This important lesson is a hurdle that she has to cross before she can fulfill her true potential. You, as parents, need to support her in this and turn loose the little girl and embrace the woman she has become."

These were powerful words from the headmaster. It gave both Sarah and me something to think about. We knew that Liz was special but assumed that it was just the pride of parents that was influencing our judgment. It seemed that she was more than we had suspected. Jabril had seen many great minds here at the university over the past several hundred years. This was no small observation he had just made.

We followed Jabril into the projections room. The room at first seemed to be just a dark hole in the wall, as there were no reflections at all. Jabril closed the door, and a bright city spread before us. The city

158

encircled a bay with a cruise ship sitting at anchor in the middle of it. "This is Cartagena. The cruise ship sitting in the bay is the one Jenny and Liz hopped aboard on its last port of call. It seemed that several of the more expensive suites were still available. They arrived in style according to Cartahena standards."

Jabril moved forward with a remote that he had removed from his lab coat. He liked to wear those coats because they could carry so many items that he was always looking for. We were used to his attire, and the lab coat seemed to suit him. As he stopped, it was evening and we moved closer to the ground near the rear of one of the local hotels. A shadow darted out of the darkness and again blended back into the shadows. We could feel the breeze off the ocean and the night sounds. We moved into the shadows, and there stood our daughter all dressed in black. She looked in our direction and smiled. Jabril chuckled. "She knew she was being monitored. This is only one aspect of her awareness that has manifested itself. Jeff was fifty miles into space when this was scanned. Yet she knew he had zoomed in on her face." We continued to watch.

I was curious. "What is she doing?"

"She is on a private mission of her own. While preparing for this mission, she monitored Vanderhoff and his drug trade with the Colombian drug lords. She has been making forays into their warehouses every night, planting incendiary bombs timed to go off in unison at the end of the mission. Not only will the cartels loose millions of dollars, but also these drugs will never hit the streets of the US or Russia. She hopes that it will cause an internal war between the Colombian factions and disrupt drug trade for years." Jabril paused. "It might just work."

We moved forward and watched as she expertly climbed the walls of the warehouses and entered into the upper windows. She planted the devices throughout the warehouse in predetermined areas. Some of these were right under the noses of the guards who were busy drinking and playing cards. She made no sound and left the same way she came. We again zoomed in on her face. She grinned up at us and gave

159

a thumbs-up sign. A signal she had learned from watching the space flights. Sarah and I grinned back at the projection. She was so real we could almost touch her. It was hard to believe that this had happened several days before.

Jabril moved forward again. This time it was an entirely different Liz before us. She was dressed in expensive-looking casual clothes and wearing way too much jewelry. She was in a local nightclub with a beer glass in her hand, and it was half empty. Sarah caught her breath. "She wouldn't."

"No." Jabril chuckled. "Half of it was expertly dumped onto a cactus plant. It is only for show."

Liz had picked up on the lingo of the southern California mall rats. She was laying it on pretty thick. We soon saw why.

Jabril zoomed in on a person sitting at a near table. "This is one of Vanderhoff's goons, and Liz knows it. It had taken her five nights before one of his goons arrived. Watch his reaction as Liz lets slip who she is."

We watched and listened as Liz starting bragging about her around-the-world trip with her mom and dad. She knew someone near was bound to ask who her mom and dad were. She then proudly pronounced the name of Charles and Sarah Jennings of California.

The reaction of the goon was almost instantaneous. He got up and headed for the phones. We followed. We listened in as the man finally got Vanderhoff on a radiophone at his camp in Brazil. The man was extremely happy. Vanderhoff had offered a half million-dollar reward for anyone who could give him the location of Charles Jennings. We monitored the phone line. Vanderhoff was about as excited as the man. He saw another opportunity here. He asked who was with the goon. The goon mentioned a Garcia and a Ramon. Vanderhoff told him to bring the girl to Brazil. Failure to do so would result in being shot on sight. This was pretty good incentive. The goon hung up the phone and stayed at the club and followed Liz's cab back to her hotel. He follower her in and was standing close when she asked for the key to the penthouse.

The rest was obvious as Jabril went forward to see the goon and his two pals enter the stairway to the penthouse. They broke down the door and found a startled Liz and a terrified nanny screaming. Waving a gun around, they finally got Jenny to shut up. We all smiled at that. Jenny could have torn all three apart without breaking a fingernail. Liz was still playing the spoiled brat part as she placed her hands on her hips and said, "Just what do you want in here? Take anything you want and get out. It's my bedtime."

The goon grabbed Liz and pulled her hands behind her back and tied them together. Liz stomped her foot. "Wait till my daddy hears about this. You'll be sorry."

This brought the gag. Jenny was thrust up as well, and they were taken down the stairs and out the back through the deserted kitchen. They were roughly shoved into the back of a military looking Land Rover. We watched as they left the city and headed for the mountains where they would pick up a helicopter bound for the camp in Brazil.

Both girls were careful. Both knew they could remove the bonds in only a matter of seconds if needed. Liz placed the idea in her captor's minds that if they were harmed, they might not live very long when Vanderhoff found out. After that, they were treated much more gently.

It seemed that nothing much else had happened until they got to the camp as Jabril skipped to that point. Vanderhoff was beaming as the girls were brought in. Their bonds and gags were removed as Vanderhoff walked triumphantly around them. "So Charles Jennings's brat has come for a stay, has she?"

Liz let out a retort, "Just you wait. My daddy will make you sorry that you were ever born."

Vanderhoff threw back his head and laughed. "Maybe he'll be the one who will be sorry."

Liz came back. "I don't care if he is all the way across the world in China. He'll find you."

She put her hand over her mouth as though she had let something important slip. This made Vanderhoff very happy. So Charles Jennings and his wife were in China. His spies would soon find them. All they had to do was search all travel records into the country for their names. He would know where they were in two days' time.

Liz watched Vanderhoff, and by her expression, we knew she was scanning his mind. A look of sudden understanding crossed her face. We were the only ones who saw it. Vanderhoff was studying Jenny and wondering what to do with her. Liz planted a suggestion that she could be used to cook and clean. This was planned many weeks before. The suggestion took hold, and Vanderhoff said to goon number one, "Take the wench to the kitchen, and put her to work. She can't escape through five hundred miles of jungle."

Liz breathed a sigh. Task number two accomplished.

He looked at Liz with disgust. "Take the brat to the cellar, and lock her up. She is not to have any food until she tells me where her father is."

Vanderhoff smiled. He didn't care if she talked or not. Torturing the brat would be payback for all the trouble he had gone through. Being the brat of Charles Jennings made it that much sweeter. He would take care of all three when he got what he wanted.

As Liz was taken to her cell and locked in, Jabril tried to bring us up to date.

"We chartered a yacht in your name in the Bahamas and hired a crew. We renamed her *The Alien*. They sailed her to Shanghai under your orders where they anchored her in the harbor. There they were to await your arrival in Shanghai. We left a trail a mile wide, and it still took Vanderhoff's spies more than four days to discover it. They were very proud when they did. Vanderhoff has just now sent one of his men with a message. You are to bring ten million dollars to Cartagena or never see your daughter alive again. You are to contact no one and bring your boat and anchor it in the harbor. You will then be contacted." He looked at Sarah and me. "You will be on the boat when the man gets there, but you won't make the trip to Cartagena. The crew will take the boat there, but you won't be aboard. You have better things to do. It seems that you are to lead a US Army commando group into Vanderhoff's camp. You are also to rescue your daughter and her nanny. This has to be done to account for the disappearance of the compound and the entire drug manufacturing facilities there. This has to be done without harming any Brazilian-forced labor workers. The Brazilian government will send in planes to burn and destroy the poppy fields and the army Vanderhoff has gathered, as well as the mansion and other buildings. We don't want some other drug cartel to pick up where Vanderhoff left off."

Sarah jumped in here. "We could have done all that without putting Liz in danger."

Jabril shook his head. "Yes we could, but there were other factors that only Liz could accomplish. You will see some of those in a few minutes. The others you can't see, as Liz has to acquire those from the minds of Vanderhoff and his crew. We have to know the extent of involvement of the dark forces and just how far it has spread. We don't know if just the underground compound of the dark forces and Vanderhoff's camp are our only targets. She had to wait for a visit of your friend with the mind-reading ability to again visit Vanderhoff. From him she will be able to gain everything the dark forces are up to. When the invasion comes, you will have to make your way alone to his residence and face him. You will then see why it is so important that Liz has to be a part of this mission." He didn't explain further. He already knew. For some strange reason, he wanted me to see for myself. I felt that my old friend was hiding many secrets.

Jabril looked at me as a father to a son and simply said, "And when you are ready, you will know them all."

I heard Sarah's gasp. She had read my deep thoughts, but Jabril's answer to those same thoughts caught her by surprise. I sent her as private a thought as I could. *For some reason I think we need to heed the advice of this man.* Jabril didn't appear to have picked up this thought, but I'm sure he did.

As we watched the screen, we saw Liz locked into the cell. As soon as the door closed, she went into action. She looked around the room to see what she had available. The toilet was dirty and had the only water in the cell. The bed had a rotting mattress on a set of springs strung on a metal frame. Liz took out one of the springs and after making several bends inserted it into the rear of the lock on the door. An instant later we heard a click. She opened the door and looked outside. The guard for her cell hadn't been posted yet. She closed the door and relocked it and began her exercises. It seemed like a good thing to do to pass the time.

Jabril moved the scene to the kitchen area. The woman in charge was giving Jenny instructions. Her Spanish was not very good, but Jenny wouldn't let on that she could speak anything else. She was busy scanning the lunch area for the guards that would be stationed outside Liz's cell as well as her own. She implanted the idea for the woman to make her refill all the wine glasses of the men having their dinner. This gave her the opportunity to spike the appropriate drinks with time-release knockout drops. The selected guards would doze off on watch at midnight and wake three hours later. This too had been preplanned. Jenny sent Liz a thought. *Phase three accomplished.*

The screen moved to the middle of the night outside Liz's cell. There were only seconds between the time the guard nodded off to when the cell door opened. By scanning the people in the complex, Liz could avoid any contact as she made her way out of the main floor back entrance. She avoided the sight of the outside guards by staying in the shadows. She was heading across the commons to an area outside the camp. We thought she was trying to escape. We were wrong. She came upon another sleeping guard. This one was on watch outside of a prison complex that housed the local forced labor from the neighboring village. She gently borrowed the guard's keys and entered the complex through the barbed-wire gate. She moved to the roughly made shelters to find workers trying to get some rest. Most were already awake when Liz came through the open door. Not only were men and women here, but also children that were old enough to do manual labor. Most were either sick or suffered from beatings from the guard. Liz had seen them on previous scans, but nothing had prepared her for the real thing.

Those here were at first scared because they didn't know what to expect from the strange girl in their presence. Their fears faded as Liz explained that she was there to help. She spoke perfect Portuguese. She even had the same accent as the workers. She surveyed all the people and scanned their needs. It almost made her sick. An hour had passed, and she knew she only had two left before she would have to be safely locked back in her cell. It couldn't be helped as she left and made her way to the supply buildings where she found an abundance of food and medical supplies. She filled a sack with all she could carry and made her way back to the prison complex. She gave the people food and rubbed salve on the wounds caused by the guards. She knew that the salve wouldn't help, but she needed a reason to use the healing powers she possessed that she had learned from the university and practiced for hours on end before the mission. Her healing touch brought sighs of relief from the pain that the people were suffering. It seemed that the children were treated the worst.

She suddenly realized that time was short, and she promised to come back every night with food and salve. She also told them that shortly help would come and they would suffer no more.

It wasn't long before the angel with the flaming hair was on the lips of every worker.

The scene changed to the next day in the fields. The workers had a new spring in their step and didn't appear to tire from their work and for the first time were singing local songs as they worked. The guards were stunned but didn't care as long as the work got done. They also didn't use their whips as much. It also seemed that the production had increased. This pleased the supervisor of the guards. He commended them on doing such a great job in motivating the prisoners.

Jabril went forward again. "This process was repeated every night.

After you get there, Jenny and Liz can fulfill Liz's promise to those people. This was phase four of Liz's mission there."

Jabril zoomed in on the cell containing Liz once again. As soon as he got there, Liz faced us as if she could see us. She gave a two thumbs-up signal. "That was her signal that she had scanned the human go-between and got the information we needed. It came just in time as Vanderhoff's spies finally tracked down your yacht. This scan was only this morning. A messenger should arrive at your boat in about three hours. You are to meet him. Make him think that you will do anything to get your daughter back. I hope you're half as good an actor as your daughter."

A knock at the door brought a smile from Jabril. He personally went over to the door and opened it. There stood King Dresden and a man we hadn't expected to see. It was Eric. We had not seen him since that first visit to Atlantic Base. He had long since finished his work there and gone to work on the outer rim. We were surprised and pleased to see him. Sarah went over and gave him a big hug, which brought that familiar blush to the man's face. He still looked like a teenager though he was even older than me. We greeted King Dresden, and the two came into Jabril's office.

King Dresden started by saying, "It seems I found this no-good pacing back and forth at the base of the tower here. He says that he is to take you to someplace in China. He said it is strictly a volunteer mission and he wouldn't let anyone else do it. Since he was already stationed in the east, we thought it might be a good idea. After all, it won't be too far from where he should be working."

All this was said with a smile. The king held Eric in high esteem but would never let him know it. I too thought of him as my first and best friend of the Hidden World. He was my first guide. He stood by my side from the time I arrived here to the final battle itself. He still stands right behind me on the golden statue at the entrance of my castle. All the people of this world have declared him a hero. He is much more to Sarah and me.

Eric thought he needed to speak up. "Well, I was back here for my first harvest in ten cycles. Jabril asked if I would like to go. I'm sure that Aaron and Sarah can handle it by themselves, but Jabril thought that we should leave someone on the boat just in case. He said he might need a warrior. He said that except for the royalty, I was the only one he knew."

Jabril had a hard time to keep from laughing. Sarah and I couldn't. We both laughed with glee as we again hugged Eric. He still couldn't see what was so funny. He always did have a dry sense of humor.

We sent a private *Thank you* to Jabril and received a smiling nod in return.

King Dresden looked over at Sarah and me. "I know that Sarah would like to go with you on this mission, but we need her here to watch over all the aspects of the mission. She and Jabril will follow closely what is going on and pass on any changes that need to be made. Jeff has set up a watch post, so we will be watching events in real time. We also think it appropriate that she be the one watching over her daughter. She will start when you two return from China. It will take your boat two weeks to reach the rendezvous in Colombia. By that time, both of you will be on station. The boat is only used to give you time to set up the attack and insure that no harm will come to Liz. Vanderhoff will wait until he sees the money to act. Unfortunately no money will be there for him or anyone else." He paused. He looked over at Jabril before continuing. "Liz has become much more than just a student at the university. She is an inspiration and friend to all of us. The decision for her to go on this mission was not made lightly. There are higher reasons for this than you can at present imagine. Please keep this in mind should you receive any strange requests from her when you see her."

This didn't make sense. I don't think it was supposed to. King Dresden's mind was just as impenetrable as Jabril's. I had seen his ability to foresee the future before. Could this be one of those times?

I looked over at Jabril, who was deep in thought on some subject.

"Jabril, why are we going through such an elaborate ruse? Why don't we just go in without all this about the boat in China?"

Jabril's answer made a great deal of sense. "Up to this point, we didn't know just how many people Vanderhoff had under his control. We used his greed and quest for vengeance. We knew he would pull out all the stops and use every resource he had to locate you. It worked. We now know all of his recruits and all the dark forces involved. Liz and Jenny did their job well. Now it's your turn." I could see the pride in his face for our daughter. I also saw that all the loose ends of our problem with Vanderhoff were neatly tied up. I was impressed with the way it had been carried out so far. I just hoped the final phase, which meant me, would go as nicely.

FINAL PHASE IN BRAZIL

Sarah and I left the university and made our way back up the hill to Zaron. Eric would be going along. He was lagging behind in close conversation with King Dresden. The students around seemed impressed with the royal group as we headed up the hill. As usual, many students had gathered around Zaron to view the fabled sword and greet us on our return. We knew we had to be in Shanghai in only a few hours. We would have to board the boat while it was totally dark there.

Sarah was deep in thought. I could see her concern. "Why do you think they gave Liz such a build up? I know she's exceptional, but is she truly that exceptional?"

I put my arms around Sarah's shoulders. "I think she's exceptional, but I think it's something else. It's like the plateau that we couldn't cross before our journey up the mountain. She has to come face-to-face with something and break through some barrier that is holding her back. I got this much from feelings I got from both Jabril and Dresden. I think we'll have one of the answers Jabril was talking about before this mission is over."

Sarah looked up into my eyes. "I felt it as well. It's also strange that I got the feeling that both of them felt that Liz being on this mission was far more important than the mission itself. How do you explain that?"

I shook my head. "I think that we have a long way to go in more ways than one. Look at how far we've come, and I don't think we've even scratched the surface of the knowledge and awareness that we need."

Sarah put her arm around my waist. "We'll get there together."

It was a simple statement but carried meanings that went far beyond words.

Eric and the king approached as we were talking to the students. Dorin interrupted, "I'm sorry, but you must be going. Time is short." He shook our hands and some unknown thoughts passed between Eric and King Dresden as they shook hands. Eric was somber as he headed up Zaron's ramp. We followed close behind.

Greetings, Masters. It's good to have Master Eric once again on board. This improved Eric's somber attitude and brought a warm *Thank you, Zaron* from all of us.

We left Avalon and headed south to the rift. It wasn't long before we were again in Atlantic Base. There was a flurry of activity as we arrived. We were rushed into Dorin's quarters, where we quickly changed into civilian clothes. We were a real sight as we emerged wearing the latest tropical fashions complete with sunglasses. Sarah looked really good in her tank top and white slacks. We were both wearing white deck shoes. Eric, on the other hand, was wearing a stripped T-shirt with white sailor paints and white shoes. He informed us that he was to be our valet, butler, and all-around handy man. This would give him the excuse to take *The Alien* to the rendezvous in the harbor at Cartahena. He smiled at the thought of Vanderhoff learning the name of Charles and Sarah's boat.

We boarded Zaron and left the base. We had to pause below the surface because a cruise ship was much too close and it was full daylight. We moved underwater until we were beyond visual range and left the ocean at a very rapid pace to the upper levels of the atmosphere. We headed east out over the Atlantic. It wasn't long until night had fallen below. At this altitude, we would look like a meteorite streaking across the sky. We arrived over Shanghai harbor about an hour before dawn. It was cloudy and dark as we went down into the waters not far from our rented boat. We traveled underwater until we were on the ocean side of the vessel. Zaron eased out of the water and hovered over the open bridge as she let down her ramp. I gave her a command to wait on the bottom of the harbor below the vessel. We left the craft and climbed down from the open bridge. Turning around, it was impossible to see Zaron as she eased back into the depths of the harbor.

The hired crew was expecting us, but they didn't know when, and all were asleep. So far, so good. Eric broke open a bottle of drink that had been stored on board previously and poured Sarah and me a glass as we settled in the deck chairs on the stern as we watched the sun come up. The drink looked like red wine but was our favorite drink of Shambala. We gratefully sipped our drinks and waited.

We didn't wait long before the first of the crew awoke and came topside. He quickly returned down below and we heard a scurry of activity. The captain hurried topside still adjusting his cap as he tried to apologize for not being there to greet us as we came aboard. "We didn't hear the shuttle at all. The galley will prepare you a breakfast right away."

I was amused. "Thank you, but we ate hours ago. Our man has taken care of everything." Here I nodded toward Eric, who was standing by with a white napkin over his arm and what appeared to be a wine bottle in his hand. He was standing at attention by our table. I was impressed. I think the captain was more so.

The captain looked confused. "What are your orders, sir?"

"We will wait here for a while. We had planned to go to Tokyo from here, but we haven't made up our minds. Have you plenty of fuel?"

"Yes, sir. We topped off the tanks as soon as we arrived." He looked a little nervous. He was getting paid a lot more than his usual rate, and he didn't want to offend.

171

"Good thinking, George. Just keep up the good work. We'll let you know if our plans change. Until then you can just relax and keep us informed on the weather."

Captain George looked impressed that I knew his name. He saluted us. With a very impressive "Yes, sir," he turned and went below.

Sarah smiled over at me. She was beginning to like this game. She had her feet propped up on one of the deck chairs, sipping her drink like some kind of heiress. She was pretending, but I could still see the worry in her eyes. Liz was still in danger, and as long as that situation lasted, she would not be at ease.

Our contact was late. The inner world had not taken into consideration just how hard it was for a Brazilian with a fake passport to get through the Chinese customs. It was well near noon before we heard the *put-put* of the Chinese sampan pulling alongside. There was only one passenger. An older Chinese fisherman was at the helm. The fisherman cut the engine, and the sampan bumped along side.

The sweating, heavyset man in the stern yelled, "Ahoy, *Alien*."

I got up and went to the side and looked down at the man. "Who hails the *Alien?*"

"My name is not important. I am looking for Dr. Charles Jennings." He took a red handkerchief and wiped his forehead.

"You've found him. What do you want?" I wasn't going to make it easy for him. I didn't much like his looks anyway.

"I have an important message for you." He reached down and picked up a satchel that held a military field phone.

"I'm on vacation, and I'm not taking any messages." The answer made the man a little agitated.

"It's a matter of life and death and very important that you speak to me now." Again he wiped his forehead.

"That's what they all say." The man was now sweating even more.

"It's about your daughter." At these words, he lifted the field phone out of the satchel and held it up toward me.

Sarah joined me at the rail. "What is this about our daughter?"

The man gestured with the phone. "You'll have to hear for yourself."

We let the man come up the rear ladder just far enough to hand me the phone. "Just press the button on the side to speak, and let it up to listen." The instruction was unnecessary, but I fumbled with the phone like I hadn't ever seen one before.

I pressed the button and said, "Hello, who's there?"

I let the button up and heard Vanderhoff on the other end. "Never mind who this is, Dr. Jennings. If you want to keep your daughter alive, you'd better listen."

"If you've hurt my daughter in any way, you'll pay." I didn't have to pretend to be mad.

I heard a chuckle on the other end. "It's you who will have to pay, Dr. Jennings. I'd say about ten million dollars American money, or you get your daughter mailed back to you in little packages."

"How do I know you have her and haven't hurt her?" I tried to sound forceful and angry.

"Listen for yourself."

There was a pause, and I heard Liz on the other end. "Daddy, these men are bad, and they are keeping me locked up in a nasty place." She sounded pitiful. I tried not to laugh in spite of the situation.

Vanderhoff grabbed the phone and laughed. It was a truly repulsive sound. "That's enough. Get me ten million to Cartagena, Colombia, by this weekend or she dies a most horrible death."

"Even if I could get my hands on ten million dollars today, I couldn't travel through normal channels with that much hard cash. It would be impossible." I was stalling while Vanderhoff thought this over.

I could tell Liz had implanted an idea in his head. "Bring your boat to the bay in Cartagena and have the money with you. We'll contact you there." He just found a way to get a yacht along with the money. I wouldn't need it after I was dead. I could even hear the smile over the phone.

"I'll get the money from my company here in Shanghai and sail directly for South America." Our plan was going along fine. "It'll take two weeks at full speed to get there. You just make sure my daughter is okay when I get there."

With a smirk, Vanderhoff came back with, "Just make sure you bring the money."

The line went dead. I threw the phone to the man at the rail. He missed it as it bounced into the harbor. He groaned as he watched it go out of sight. He climbed back on the sampan, and the fisherman started the engines. The little sampan puttered its way back toward the docks.

I knew they would be watching. Sarah looked at me sideways. "What company do you own in Shanghai?"

"When we were back home, half of what I wore came from here. I should have a small interest in several companies here."

"That's not quite the same thing." She smiled at my lame excuse for the lies.

"They will watch what we do, so we need to go ashore. We can extend our wardrobe and pack about three suitcases. They will think that we have the money, and the shopkeepers will be happy."

Sarah smiled. "It's been a long time since I've been shopping. This should be fun."

I went forward and pressed the intercom. "George, this is Dr. Jennings. Could you come topside please?"

Ten seconds later George was saluting me. He stood there until I acknowledged his salute with a nod of the head.

"You don't have to salute me every time you come topside." He looked a little relieved. "Get on the radio and order us a limo and get us a shuttle to run Sarah and me ashore."

"Yes, sir." He saluted again. I smiled as he realized what he had done and disappeared below.

It was less than an hour that a much more modern shuttle came along side. She was powered by mercury outboards and had great lines. It was much better than the sampan that our friend had been able

174

to get. Sarah climbed aboard, and soon we were headed back toward Shanghai.

We arrived at a private dock where several yachts similar to ours were tied up. We expertly pulled up to the dock and stepped up to be greeted by a limo driver complete in proper uniform.

"I'm at your service, sir. Just follow me." He led the way to a limo. It was a BMW and a new one at that. He held the doors, and we got seated.

When he got in, he let down the partition between the front and rear compartments. "What is your desire?" He spoke good English. It wasn't like the cab drivers back home. They could hardly speak English and said, "Where to, bub?"

I think I preferred the Chinese. "Just take us to a good department store where we can shop for some new clothes."

"As you wish. It'll only take a few minutes." He was off. He was an extremely good driver as he dodged at least a hundred smaller two-wheeled vehicles plus numerous people who were on foot. The life of a pedestrian in China must be very short.

We stayed ashore for most of the afternoon before returning to the dock. We started to pay the driver, but he waved it off. "My fee and gratuity have been more than generous already. Thank you, sir." He too saluted and turned and took the three suitcases out of the back of the limo.

One of the crew from the shuttle that had waited all afternoon for us to return gathered them and placed them on board. We followed.

The sun was going down just as we climbed back on board the *Alien*. It seemed that this crew also had been previously paid handsomely. We watched as they sped back to shore.

One of the crew that we hadn't seen before rapidly took our suitcases below to our cabin.

We followed him down the stairs. One of the crew with a chef hat motioned for us to go to the dinning room. A banquet had been prepared and laid out before us. Candles lit the table, and soft music came from overhead. The crew was anxious to please the owner. They had no idea that the boat was leased, and we'd have to repaint the name before it was returned. I smiled over at Sarah, and we both looked over at Eric, who just gave a slight shrug of the shoulders.

We went on about how nice the table was and how good the food looked. We ate slowly and made sounds about how good everything was. Our drinks that Eric supplied helped hide our true feelings. Our food from the Hidden World was again appreciated. We had taken it much too much for granted. I asked the waiter to tell the captain that I would like to see him.

He left and only a few seconds later reappeared with George in tow. George came in and started to salute. "Yes, sir, you requested my presence?"

"Yes, George. I want you to pull anchor tomorrow morning and head for Cartagena, Colombia. Sarah and I have to take an early flight. We will be picked up later. My man, Eric, will accompany you on the trip. We should join you there. Should there be any questions, Eric has my complete authority to make any decisions necessary."

"Yes, sir. Will there be anything else?"

"No, thank you, George. That will be all for now. I'm sorry we didn't get to know all of you better, but you know how business is sometimes." I gave him a reassuring smile and said, "Have a safe journey."

"Thank you, sir." He saluted again, turned, and left. *I guess breaking that saluting habit is a little hard to get over. I don't think Eric will have to cope with that problem. I can't see our captain saluting the butler.*

We were both smiling after our captain. Sarah and I knew we would never see him again, because we would be headed in different directions with different tasks to perform.

We left the table and went topside and on up to the flying bridge. It was dark, and the clouds hid the stars. We sent a mental message to Zaron to scan the area and pick us up.

We heard a thud and looked behind us. Zaron had let down the ramp. *A Chinese police patrol boat will be coming by shortly. Please be welcomed aboard, Masters.* We could sense the urgency in Zaron's warning.

Sarah and I climbed aboard. We were soon off. We didn't get to say goodbye to Eric before we left. He'd understand and hopefully explain our sudden absence from the boat.

We shot up straight through the clouds as we climbed well above normal commercial airliners and turned Zaron due west. At least in this direction it would be dark much longer. We would arrive at Atlantic Base under full sunshine.

After the normal precautions, we entered the underwater hanger and were met by Dorin. Dorin seemed urgent that we get underway. Was it just me, or is it that we always seemed to be late? Everyone always knew just the minute that we were to arrive. There was no time wasted. The usual group was not there. The conference room was empty.

Dorin led us to the table and sat down in front of a lot of papers that he had apparently been going over. They seemed to be some sort of aerial maps. Even from across the table I could tell that they were mostly jungle.

Sarah and I waited as Dorin collected his thoughts. "As you know, we few who have been selected as guardians of the outside world have had our hands full. It must also be added that those same hands are tied when it comes to direct interference except for advancement. Many times in earth's past we would have liked to interfere to prevent mass murder and world wars. In these areas, we have been forbidden. We cannot affect these events in any way. The explanation for this is for you to learn much later. You still have far to travel and more to learn. You and Sarah have had more than your share of responsibilities in events on the outer rim. The reason for this has also been kept from you. You both will know when you are ready. We will know, and so will you when this time comes. Now we have a situation where the dark forces have exceeded this order, as they too have been restricted in the same way. When this happens, they have to pay the consequences. It is up to the guardians of the outer rim to carry out this justice. You have been involved in some of this already. In all of this, we have to refrain from taking human life, no matter how vile it may be. Vanderhoff seems to be a prime example. It was your daughter who first noticed that events happening in the jungles of Brazil did not follow normal human ways. It was then that we found the interloper from your university on the outer rim. He was born in the Hidden World and raised by the dark forces to do their bidding. We had to know more. As you know, our scans are powerful but cannot reach into the minds of those we probe. We needed Liz with her powers to do this for us. We now have to go and confront Vanderhoff directly. We also need to destroy the underground base in the mountains of Brazil from where they are dispensing weapons and technology to Vanderhoff and his army. All this has to be done without the loss of one single human being at our hands."

Dorin stopped and looked over the prints on the table as he let sink in what he had just said. "We are maybe overstepping our position dealing with Vanderhoff. One of our outer guardians is working with the US military. He is the one you will report to on the outside. You are to lead a commando group from the Special Forces into the jungles of Brazil. You will use the group to infiltrate Vanderhoff's camp. You, as leader, will then go directly to Vanderhoff's mansion he has built there and face him yourself. This will be under the guise of rescuing Elizabeth Jennings. This is the daughter of one millionaire that we have become very fond of." Here Dorin grinned at his little joke. It also brought the first smile from Sarah and me.

Dorin continued. "Our man on the outside is Colonel Dick Chambers who is with the Special Forces training facility at Camp LeJeune in Jacksonville, North Carolina. That isn't that far from here. You can travel there from our house at the beach. Jeff has your uniform and makeshift orders with identification in his quarters. He will take you to the beach in less than an hour. Dick will introduce you to your group. We expect some derision as these men expect to work as a group. They don't like newcomers telling them what to do. You may have to prove yourself. Dick can help you with that. It should be interesting."

Dorin again knew something that I didn't. I could tell from the half smile on his face. His mind was a blank wall.

I could tell that Sarah was getting uneasy again. She would be thousands of miles away while two members of her family were in danger of being hurt or worse.

Dorin saw her concern. "Don't worry, Sarah. It's Vanderhoff and his goons that should be worrying."

I appreciated his confidence but didn't see it being all that easy. I got that frown from Sarah again. *Don't go getting yourself killed. I've got too much invested in you to start all over.* The thought was supposed to be a rebuff, but too much love came with it. I reached over and squeezed her hand.

Dorin stood. "It's time both of you were on your way."

We left the conference room to find Jeff waiting. Sarah and I kissed goodbye, and the look in her eyes told me to be careful. Would one day come that we would never have to be parted again?

I watched her walk away and board Zaron before I turned to go with Jeff to change. Jeff placed a hand on my shoulder. He understood better than anyone else about sacrifice. All those at the base did. I wondered if the humans on the outer rim were really worth the trouble that these guardians were going to. It was much later that I would have my doubts erased in a most dramatic fashion, but that is for much later in my journal.

OMEGA FORCE

J eff and I left his quarters and headed toward the smaller craft that stood waiting on its cradle. It was warmed up and ready to go. This would be a very short trip. It was two in the morning on the outside, and no one would be on the beach. No one would see a special service's soldier leaving the ocean without even being wet. The sand and water wouldn't even mar the spit shine someone had put on my boots. My thoughts were of Fort Jackson and what lay ahead. Yes, this should be very interesting. The nametag on my chest just said Jones. Yes, Mr. Jones; this was something new. I also noticed that I only had three ribbons on the opposite chest. One of them was a good conduct metal. Another was for service during the Vietnam War. The last was a unit citation metal for achievement. None of these were going to impress anybody. Yes, I hope our man, Colonel Chambers, also knew what he was doing.

I left the beach house just after dawn. Sitting in the driveway was a beat up dune buggy. I smiled at someone's humorous little turn of affairs. I wasn't the rich dude anymore. I was driving what I could afford. I'm just glad it wasn't raining.

The only one who appreciated my ride was the guard at the gate later that morning. He was more impressed with my vehicle than he was with me. He looked at my identification and then at my dune buggy. "Who are you to report to, sir?"

"I'm to report directly to a Colonel Dick Chambers." I tried to look anxious. It wasn't hard because I was.

"Sir, you will have to get a pass for your vehicle here. You can get those at the personnel office. I will have to get someone to escort you to Colonel Chambers's office as it is in a restricted zone. If you'll just pull to the side and park, someone will be here shortly. Sir, I'm sorry for the inconvenience. Have a good day." With that, he saluted and I drove to the side and waited. It looked like my vehicle could not enter until I had a pass. Maybe the character that got it for me would know to retrieve it. This was the least of my worries, but it passed the time.

Soon, a private in the colonel's jeep arrived and picked me up. With a salute, he got my bag and tossed it into the back. "Sir, the colonel is expecting you. You are to report directly to the training area." With that, we zoomed into the base and went to the far side to a firing range. A group of twelve men were with a colonel. They said nothing as the jeep slid to a halt beside them. The colonel gave the driver a hard look as I got out and took my bag. The soldier saluted and left at a more sedate pace.

He came over, and I saluted. He returned my salute and shook my hand. "Jones, it's good to see you again. Did you have a good trip?" The conversation was for the benefit of the men. He knew where I had come from. His thought was unexpected. *You can tell that these men don't want you here. Just follow my lead. We have to gain their respect, or this will never work.*

He turned to the others. "Jones here will lead the group. You will follow his orders to the letter. He has been sent here especially for this mission." This was no lie, but the men didn't change their minds about me one bit.

The sergeant spoke up. "With all due respect, sir, we were expecting someone with a little more experience."

They didn't want a shave-tailed lieutenant telling them what to do. They had little respect for new officers, right out of West Point.

I was still holding my bag in my left hand. Dick took the bag and placed it on the ground a good ways away from me. *Let's give them a little lesson. Don't do any permanent damage. We need them later.* The thought came with a smirk. Dick was enjoying this. He had wanted a way to clip the egos of this group. They thought they were good. They thought they were too good. They were about to get a lesson they would never forget. He handed me a utility belt with a knife and clips for other weapons. I noticed two forty-five pistols lying on a table by the colonel's side. He looked down at these and smiled. What was he up to?

He called out six names and told them to step forward. They did. "You are the best that the army has to offer in single hand-to-hand combat. At least you think you are. I want all of you to attack this man and kill him. Any man who stays his weapon or is slack in any way will answer to me." They slowly drew their knives and were concerned with what they were supposed to do. Dick could have let them use guns, but that would be showing off too much. "Don't worry about harming him as he's protected. Just make sure your attack is true."

The sergeant spoke up again. "Who goes first, sir?"

Dick smiled. "I don't think I made myself clear. I want all of you to attack him." He looked at the men. "Any time you're ready, sergeant."

They all came at me at once. I have never seen so many knives going in so many directions at the same time. Since all were going for a kill, it was easy to anticipate their movements and even easier to avoid being hurt. I was supposed to dispose of them. I tried not to damage any of their nervous systems beyond immediate repair. To the ones left watching, all was a flurry of movement that culminated with six commandos lying at my feet. I had not even wrinkled my uniform. There was some dust on my boot. I took a handkerchief from my pocket and brushed it off.

I think this impressed the remainder of the group more than the fight, or what they thought was a fight. They would have had a hard time with the ninjas back in Tibet. They were much better trained than these men. I saw why Dick wanted to give them a good lesson. He sent me over a thought. *We had better wake them up before our next little exercise.*

I wondered what he had meant by that. As we both moved among the men, each of us massaged those numbed nerves. It looked as though we were just waking them up. Only someone from the interior could have revived them that fast. Normally they would have been out for hours and woke up with one really bad headache.

As all of them regained the ability to stand, they also tried to remember where they were. As awareness came back, so did the stunned look from the six.

When Dick was sure that they were back to normal, he looked over at me. "Lieutenant Jones, unbutton your blouse."

I did so. Since I wasn't wearing an undershirt my chest was bare.

"Jones isn't wearing any body armor, and I don't see any scratches on him anywhere." He feigned a confused look. "I thought you men were good. It seems that I may have been mistaken."

He called out two more names and two more stepped forward. They hoped they didn't have to fight me like the others. Dick handed each of them one of the two pistols on the table.

"At the end of the range are fifteen targets. I want you two to take out as many as you can in ten seconds." He knew that the targets would be almost out of range of normal accuracy for the military forty-five.

The targets popped up, and they unloaded their weapons toward the targets. One of them got lucky and caught one target in what should have been a kneecap.

Dick shook his head as if he was really disappointed. He took the pistols and reloaded them.

"Jones, you have fifteen enemy targets, and you have to put them down in five seconds. The time starts now."

He tossed both weapons at me. I caught one in the right and one in the left by the butt and flipped off the safety. One second was gone. I had seven rounds in each pistol. I rapidly fired them at the targets, concentrating on the head. Three more seconds were gone. I tossed the pistols to Dick, and with the same motion, I retrieved the knife from my belt and threw it at target number fifteen. Even though the target was more than eighty feet away, second five found the knife protruding into the heart of number fifteen.

All of the men rushed forward to get a close look at the targets. Every one of them had a hole in the middle of their foreheads. That is, except for number fifteen, which now had a knife protruding from the direct center of the heart-shaped target on its chest. The sergeant removed the knife. He slowly walked back to where I was standing.

"Your knife, sir. I hope that you haven't been offended by anything I've said. I sure wouldn't want you anywhere but on my side in a fight."

"I believe that's the whole idea, Sergeant." I smiled at him, and he looked relieved.

The sergeant was impressed, and the rest of the men were too stunned to speak. Dick was pleased.

He raised his voice a little and asked. "Any more problems with your commander?"

No one made a sound. They looked a little more humble than when I first arrived.

I sent a thought to Dick. *Should we have been so rough on them? It seems a little unfair to take such an advantage with their inferior training. I feel a little sorry for them.*

He smiled and sent back, *They needed to be reminded that no matter how good they are, there is always someone who is better. They will never take for granted that they are indestructible ever again. You have done them more good than you can imagine, and they will now follow you anywhere. That's what we were after.*

Dick looked over at the shaken group. "Omega group will be in the briefing room in one hour. Be packed and ready to leave." He looked over at me. "Jones, we need to go over some last-minute changes. Come to my office." He turned back to the group. "Omega group, dismissed."

The group saluted as one and turned and jogged off toward the barracks. We watched them go. Dick sighed. "They're the best we have. It would be a shame for them to know that they are being sent in just for show. They can't possibly realize that you alone could handle the mission much better. You have to let them play their part. The Brazilian government will expect to be impressed with their ability."

"I'll give them as much responsibility as I dare under the circumstances. I wonder what their reaction will be when I tell them I have to penetrate the guarded mansion of Vanderhoff's alone."

Dick looked back at me. "We can't let them see what will take place there."

Dick paused and looked around. When he saw the area was clear, he reached into his pocket and brought out a disrupter. It was one of the new ones and could fit into the palm of your hand. He tossed it to me. "You may have some use for this. Jabril insisted that you take it with you. Don't lose it. On full power, it could destroy a whole city. I'm glad it'll be in your possession and not mine from now on." He tossed the disrupter to me. I placed it in my jacket pocket, trying to come up with what reason there would be for me to use it. Like Dick, I couldn't think of any.

We both headed back to Dick's waiting Jeep. Colonels didn't have to walk, and I appreciated the time it would save in getting us to his office. One hour didn't give us much time to talk.

Dick's breakdown of the mission was short and sweet. He only hit the high points of my responsibility. I would hear the rest in the normal briefing.

Dick became serious. "It's important that you keep to the timetable. At the instant you arrive, Liz and Jenny will have all non-target personnel out of harms way. You will have to return with Liz at your base camp to establish that you have fulfilled your mission. The men are to return without you only minutes before the Brazilian Air Force arrives

185

to demolish the fields and buildings. A second force is to destroy the mansion and living quarters of the army. Jeff is to destroy the underground bunkers of the dark forces at the same time and make sure the Brazilians have done a complete job on Vanderhoff's complex before returning home. You, Liz, and Jenny are to return to Atlantic Base before sunup. I'm not sure how that is to be done. It seems that Jabril and Sarah are taking care of that. Liz and Jenny will know."

Dick looked up at the clock. "I never realized just how much the outside world was ruled by the clock. It's time we were going. It wouldn't be good protocol for the leaders of Omega Force to arrive late."

As we entered the outer office, Dick's secretary handed him a piece of paper. He nodded and thanked her. I scanned her thoughts and saw that she was just a normal army private and not from the inner world.

We left Dick's office and headed across the compound to the briefing room and all came to attention as we entered. "As you were. Have a seat. We don't have a great deal of time. I just now received word that your transport will be taking off sooner than we had expected."

Dick covered almost everything that we had talked about in his office: that this was a stealth mission, no firearms without silencers—and only then if it could not be helped. The main body of the camp should never know that we were there until it was too late. This was a rescue mission. The little girl and the imprisoned workers were to be freed. All household Brazilian workers, no matter which side they were on, would be removed from the compound under darkness before the Brazilian strike force arrived. From landing to execution was to take only three hours.

At this, I heard an intake of air from the group.

Dick picked up on this. "Jones will go in alone and secure the mansion, remove the workers, rescue the girl, release the imprisoned workers, and all while the rest of you keep the perimeter secure. You are not to retreat until you see him arrive. If after exactly three hours he has not arrived, you are to move in and remove any obstacle in order to bring the girl and Jones out, dead or alive."

I sent Dick a thought. *Thanks for the confidence.*

That was for them. We don't want them to think that you're invincible. Who knows, you could be killed. Dick smiled.

The briefing was soon over. The men looked a little uneasy. They found out that our jumping-off point was Guantanamo Bay, Cuba.

It wasn't long before the transport from Fort Jackson was underway. The flight was over before we knew it. We didn't even leave the field when we arrived. An attack helicopter was waiting for us. We moved into it, and it too was soon underway. This time we had an opportunity to get suited up. The chopper was to meet a tanker just off Panama to give us enough fuel to reach Brazil. We skirted through Panama to be able to go across Colombia into the mountains of Brazil. We would cross the boarder just on time. It had been dark now for over an hour. We would reach the base camp location by twenty-two hundred, local time. The chopper went into silent mode a hundred miles out. The landing was smooth and quiet. The chopper cut her engines. The crew was ordered to stay put until we returned. In the event we didn't return by zero one hundred, they were to leave and not look back.

We moved out. Each of us was armed with silenced Berettas, knives, and grenades. The point team had silenced long-range rifles with infra-red sights. The six that were to come with me wore new night-vision goggles. Since anything that would make a noise would result in my death, I would go alone and only carry the combat knife strapped to my leg.

I posted the first six on the outer perimeter to protect our back. The next six were to go with me to the barbed-wire barricade surround-ing the mansion and living quarters of the workers and guards. To the south was the army barracks. There were over a thousand here that Vanderhoff was going to use to take over Brazil. It took us another thirty minutes to reach the fence. It looked like it was electrified. I knew the generators at the mansion were at their limit. Vanderhoff wouldn't trade his air conditioning for an electric fence. I felt nothing emanating from the fence and gained even more respect when I grabbed it with my bare hands and took the cutter and made a hole just big enough for me. I sent the other six in an arc that placed them fifty yards apart to watch my back.

I waited just long enough for the men to get settled and well hidden before I made my move. I slipped through the fence and scanned the area. There were two guards on the grounds on this side of the house. They were walking together. There were six others at different locations around the perimeter closer to the residence.

I knew that Eric and the *Alien* would be coming into the harbor in Cartagena just about now. Vanderhoff would be waiting for a call confirming that. He would not be asleep. He had doubled his guard. He thought he wouldn't be taking any chances with ten million dollars on the line.

I came up behind the first two guards. I put them into a much-needed sleep and drug them into the shrubs surrounding the pool area. The other six guards took more time than I wanted. I had to take them out when they were out of sight of the others. All were taken care of on the outside. The inside would take a little more care. Vanderhoff didn't need to know that I was coming until I was there. To gain access I had to climb to the second floor and enter a window that had been left open. I wondered if Jenny had anything to do with it. I would bet my bottom dollar, if I had any, that she had. I was able to come downstairs unseen by the guard at the entrance. He too found it a good time to take a nap.

All the guards were now taken care of. Vanderhoff was the only one left. I scanned the area and soon found him upstairs. He repelled me even at this distance. I didn't have much time left. I had to face Vanderhoff.

I reached the room. The door was locked. Evidently he liked his privacy. I could hear him on the phone. He seemed very pleased with himself as he hung up the receiver and sat back down in his overstuffed recliner. I could smell the sweet smell of his Cuban cigar as he contemplated his good fortune.

I used a small lock pick to unlock the door. The only sound was a slight click. I hoped that it would go unnoticed by Vanderhoff.

It hadn't. When I flung open the door, Vanderhoff was standing there with a pistol in each hand. A general never goes far without his weapons. Vanderhoff was forever the general. I had pulled my knife as I entered. It was my only weapon.

Vanderhoff laughed at my apparent predicament. "Well, son, just what do you think you're going to do?"

I didn't answer. There was something about the man that I couldn't put my finger on. It was during this pause that a light came on in his brain. "I don't know how you got in here, but you're never going to leave." He let loose with both pistols. All shots were for my body. I knew where he was going to aim, and I simply wasn't there.

He was surprised when the smoke had cleared and I was still standing. He felt smug as he knew he always kept one unfired bullet in the chamber just in case.

"That must be some new type of body armor that I haven't heard of. I'll make good use of it when you're dead."

"Better than you can imagine." I was still trying to figure out this vile man before me. Even his thoughts were too vile to read. I was going to have to take him out despite my warning to the contrary about taking a life.

I started forward when a very familiar voice said, "Wait, Daddy." I had not heard her or even felt her arrive. We would have to talk. I'd like to know how she did that.

Liz stood there with her hands on her hips and a very serious look in her eyes. "Take a close look, Daddy. Isn't there something familiar about this man? Something that reminds you of someone in your past that you despised?"

Now I knew. He reminded me of the dark lord. Now I saw what she had meant. Vanderhoff wasn't human. This is what confused me.

Liz almost snarled as she said, "He's a half-breed. Bred by the dark forces and placed in the outer world."

189

I had taken my eyes off Vanderhoff as I listened to Liz. She was wearing the Sword of Truth across her back, combat style.

Vanderhoff was taking all this in with no understanding at all of what we were talking about. He felt no threat from either of us. He turned his attention to Liz. "So the brat arrives too. That's good. I won't have to go looking for you to put a bullet through your brain."

This only reminded Liz of why she was here. She removed the sword from the sheath with one swift move, and the flame from the blade lit the room.

Vanderhoff's eyes widened. Not from fear but with greed.

"Well, it seems you are very healthy for someone that hasn't eaten for a month. I'll make sure your guards wish that they were never born. Sneaking food to prisoners is punishable by death." He snarled as he looked over his choices. Would he take a little girl with a sword or a man with body armor who carried a knife? He started for the girl.

I started for Vanderhoff when Liz stopped me once more. "No, Dad. I have to do this."

Both Vanderhoff and I stopped for two totally different reasons. I was told to listen to Liz. Could this be why? Vanderhoff was just confused. He didn't know whom to kill first.

Liz faced the man. "This man poisoned my mind and soul before I had learned how to protect myself. His evil has tainted me. I must now destroy this evil and cleanse my soul of his filth." There was fire in her eyes as she turned back toward Vanderhoff.

Vanderhoff didn't like the way this conversation was going, and he didn't like the look of that sword. The kid could get lucky. He raised his gun and fired at Liz. The Sword of Truth flashed in front of Liz, and the bullet hit the blade. It didn't bounce off. It just stopped and fell at Liz's feet.

Vanderhoff was impressed but now wanted the sword even more. Greed was bred into this creature along with his hate and quest for power. It all made perfect sense now.

He slowly circled the room, keeping an eye on both Liz and me as he thought over his next action. He looked me over carefully and noticed I carried no weapon other than the knife still in the scabbard strapped to my calf.

You could see his mind working as he carefully prepared his next step of action. He felt he could take the man but the girl and the sword had him worried. He could not afford to turn his back to either one of us.

His eyes turned to me. "Just how much would it take to buy you off soldier?"

I looked him straight in the eye. "I already have all I need. I'm Charles Jennings and this is my daughter you have taken. I don't think you have enough money to get out of this."

This caught Vanderhoff off stride because he had never seen me before. His arrogance was suddenly replaced with fear. Fear of the unknown and just what we were capable of.

He knew he would have to act fast. He would have to take out the girl. With the sword in his hands he would make short work of this Charles Jennings. A snarl came to his lips and an inhuman growl came from his throat. His true colors were coming to light.

He pulled a knife from behind his back and sprang for Liz. He would teach the brat a lesson she would never forget. He did. Unfortunately, his head reached Liz before the rest of him did.

Liz slid the sword back into the sheath slowly as she looked at the creature at her feet. "I know now how you felt at the final battle. I feel clean once again."

I thought back to that battle. I remember the creature at my feet. I remembered how Eric felt it necessary to cleanse the world by destroying the remains.

I reached inside my jacket and pulled out the disrupter. There was a flash, and then there was no sign of Vanderhoff. I heard Liz sigh as she looked back up to me. Tears now flooded her eyes as she ran and jumped into my arms. "Daddy, I love you so much. We can't let things like that come into our lives ever again."

"I know, Princess." I hugged her back with all the love of a father and kissed her forehead. "We'll make sure the world stays clean of creatures like him for all eternity." It was a promise I was determined to keep.

I looked down in her now bright eyes. "Tell me, young lady, just how did you get your hands on the Sword of Truth?"

"Mom sent it. She thought it might come in handy, and we needed a ride back, so Zaron came all the way from Avalon." She beamed up at me with that winning smile of hers. She was as tall as her mother and just as pretty.

This brought up another question. "Who was doing the flying?"

"No one. She came here all on her own. Mom just gave her the coordinates, and presto, she's here." It seemed simple to her but left more questions about our little friendly UFO. So Zaron didn't need a pilot. It seemed she had a mind of her own. Maybe this was another mystery that I would learn about later.

I stepped back and looked my daughter over. She didn't seem to be any worse for wear. She certainly didn't look like a captive who had been starved for a month. "Where is Jenny? And what about the captives and house workers?"

"I released all the prisoners and Jenny got all the household workers to go along. The head of the house didn't want to go along. The gardeners persuaded her that she had no choice. She had already planned to spend all the money she was supposed to be making on a wild fling in Colombia. She didn't realize that no one ever left the compound, much less got paid a dime for what they were doing. Jenny will be waiting for us with Zaron when we get there."

"Speaking of which, we must get back to my men. If I don't return now, they will be swarming in to get me."

I turned to leave, and Liz jumped on my back and flung her arms around my neck.

"Just what are you doing, young lady?" I turned my head so I could look into her eyes.

"Why, Daddy, you're rescuing me from this horrible place. I haven't had any food for a month, and I'm famished. You wouldn't want a poor, starving child to have to walk, would you?"

Well, in some strange way it made sense. We made our way back to the perimeter fence without encountering anyone. We crawled through the fence and were greeted by the sergeant. He looked over the girl on my back and especially the sword slung to her back. He made no sound as we were still in stealth mode. We gathered the other five inner guards and proceeded back to the outer perimeter. When the team was again assembled, the sergeant took point and the rest of us followed. Jenny was still on my back. She was enjoying this too much. She was also putting on a show. She acted like a poor child who could barely hold her head up. We would have to talk.

When we reached the chopper, I realized that we didn't have too much time before the air strike. "Sergeant, take your men back home. The mission is a complete success. I have called in a special pickup. I have to get the girl out. My ride is waiting just north of here. Tell Colonel Chambers that Vanderhoff is not with us anymore."

The sergeant came to attention. "Will do, sir, and may I add that it has been a pleasure to have worked with you. I just wish I could have been there to see you take out Vanderhoff and his men." I felt Liz give me a punch in the ribs. I tried not to notice.

The sergeant looked at the sword on Liz's back. He couldn't stand it. "Where did you get the sword?"

With Liz listening, I couldn't lie to the sergeant. "The sword belongs in a museum. I couldn't let it be damaged by the bombing. It's a cinch that Vanderhoff didn't have any use for it any longer."

I sent a thought to Liz. *Well, it's the truth. It just isn't the whole truth.*

The sergeant seemed satisfied as he saluted and joined his men.

They rapidly entered the chopper, and the pilot brought the craft up and out of sight. We watched them go.

I turned and looked over my shoulder at Liz. "You can get down now, young lady. You look healthy enough to walk."

She grinned and slid off my back. We headed into the jungle.

193

Jenny was waiting.

We entered Zaron. *Greetings, Masters* was the expected response from Zaron. We took off and zoomed straight up to about ten miles and waited. We had Zaron zoom in on her vision screen that took us visually to treetop level.

We were just in time to see two waves of attack aircraft move in and bomb the complex. In five minutes' time, there were no buildings still intact. We couldn't tell if there were any survivors, but if there were, they would be picked up by a ground force from the Brazilian army at daybreak. The second wave dropped incendiary devices on the poppy fields and sheds. The last of these planes hit what was left of the mansion. The whole area was soon ablaze. There would be nothing left but ashes.

The scene switched to an underground complex of the dark forces. Zaron explained, *We have a projection from our attack force, Masters.*

Jeff was keeping us up to date on what was going on. We watched as deep, penetrating sonic blasts hit the area. The jungle shook for miles around. The dark forces were once again buried within the earth along with their human-like go between.

This mission was over. We waited until Jeff had gone and scanned the area the best we could. The weapons were destroyed beyond recognition. No evidence of alien technology was left.

With a sigh of relief, we started for Atlantic Base once more. Liz popped up. "Daddy, could we go a little faster? I really am hungry."

Jenny and I laughed at our young lady as we indeed sped at high speed to the ocean off the North Carolina coast. We would soon be home.

Zaron came in with another message. *Masters, I have a message from Master Jabril. He would like to inform the young princess that the warehouses of the three drug cartels have mysteriously burned to the ground. Local authorities are investigating the late-night sabotage. It is suspected to be drug related.*

Liz clapped her hands in glee. She looked like a little girl again.

"Well, there are several human lives that won't be ruined. I just wish we were allowed to do more, but Master Jabril said he was pushing it to allow me to do this much. He said it was as much for me as for the outer world that it was allowed. He said I should return with a cleansed soul before I could go any further with my training."

I had to agree with Jabril. Liz had been affected greatly by the monster of Vanderhoff and the unlawful and deadly drug trade. She had come far, but like Jabril, I knew that she still had a great deal of training to go. All those that had ever met Liz wondered just how far this girl could go and Jabril and I both knew this but wanted to make sure we would never change the qualities that made Liz the person she had already become.

We arrived at Atlantic Base with the usual cheers and greeting. It seemed that my family was building up quiet a reputation among the workers here. We had returned here after several missions to be greeted the same way. They had watched a play-by-play at the mansion from Jeff's scanners. They too had been surprised at who Vanderhoff actually was and were very impressed with the way Liz had handled herself. Several of the workers went aboard Zaron to see the sword that Liz had returned to the holder.

We spent the rest of the day going over the implications of our mission, and Liz assured everyone that no technology had left the camp. There was also only one human, such as the go-between, working with the dark forces. Once again the outer rim was safe from the scheming of the dark forces. We wondered how long this would last.

Later, we boarded our friendly craft again to head back to Avalon. Liz was in a better mood since she had been given something to eat and drink. Jenny was relieved that we were both all right. We were both proud of her for the way she handled everything.

It was a happy crew that landed in the garden above the university. It would be good to see Sarah and Jabril again. We felt happy and safe as Liz and I walked down the pathway to the tower hand in hand. We returned the waves of the students that knew both of us.

195

HOME ONCE MORE

When we reached Jabril's office, we found Sarah waiting patiently. She had seen everything, and her nerves were still on edge. She felt much better as Liz ran into her arms. Seeing them together made me realize even more how much like sisters they were, but the special feelings between mother and daughter would never change. That kind of love is eternal, and no words are needed for each to feel it.

Jenny stood behind me, and I could feel her pride in the little princess.

Jabril watched the two with the smile of one who knows. No one who watched the two together would doubt how they felt. As a father and husband, I could not have been more proud of the two people standing before me. I knew that my feeling was not prejudiced, for they were truly special people.

Jabril caught my thoughts and smiled. "It's good to have you back home. You need some time to rest and relax for a while. Harvest in Shambala starts within the next two cycles, and I think you all need to be there."

He turned to Jenny. "That goes for you too, Jenny. A little relaxation wouldn't hurt you either. You've all done an excellent job. Now get out of here, and let me get back to work."

He smiled and was surprised when Liz ran over and gave him a kiss on his cheek and hugged his neck. "Thank you," was all she said. There was much more that went unsaid between the two. I don't know what it was, but I knew it was profound.

We were soon back to our normal activities in Shambala. It seemed like our time there was much too short before our trips back to the university.

We enjoyed the harvest times when they came and equally enjoyed our studies back at the university. Many, many cycles passed without interruption of this process. We were happy and carefree. Liz grew into a mature young woman with great abilities. Her mother astounded even me with the amount of wisdom she had gained. I had gained many, many insights into the history of the world, as well as the universe. I had studied many sciences and worked on technologies that would even astound the people of this world. It would be beyond comprehension on the outer rim. I was just about to get the hang of it all when I got my next call to Jabril's office.

As you know, time means very little to this world. I'm afraid that it meant just as little to me. It wasn't until I was in Jabril's office that I realized that in outside time it had been fifteen years since my last visit. I had been keeping up with much of the news from the outer rim. I saw many instances where they were not allowed to destroy themselves over the past few years. It seemed that fighting and small wars never ended. Sometimes I wondered if our efforts were worth it. It was a cold assessment of the human race, and I regretted the thought immediately. After all, here was Jabril. Not only was he the headmaster but the guardian of the human race on the outer rim. I wondered what was up as I entered his office once again.

Jabril was pleased to see me. He motioned for me to have a seat in front of his desk. He asked about Sarah and Liz just to be polite. He knew perfectly well that they were just great. He finally got to the point of the visit.

"I've been monitoring a young man who has been on a quest now for thirty earth years. He is seeking an angel. One he met on a beach many years ago when he was a boy."

I remembered Gavin. He had thought I was an angel. I smiled as I remembered his face on that September morning. Was that really thirty years ago? That means that in outside time it had to be the year 1994. I had gotten updates on him several times. I had even read some of the articles he had written in various newspapers. He was a student of the unusual and spiritual, and I knew it had to be my fault.

"What is he doing now?" My question was expected.

"He still writes. He moves from place to place and never stays in one place too long. It's because of that touch from God that he received so long ago. He is now forty-one years old but looks more like twenty. This tends to bother some people. It bothers Gavin even more. He doesn't realize that he is more like us than he knows. He doesn't realize just how special he is. He also doesn't know why."

Here Jabril stopped. He was serious as he asked the next question. "Aaron, where is your journal?"

I hadn't thought about the journal for years. "I have it in a safe place back home."

"That's good. I think it's time for Gavin to take your journal and transcribe it into a form that can be published for the world to see."

"Surly we can do that here much better." I was confused.

"Of course we can, but we need for Gavin to do it. He needs to know from where his newfound powers and youthful appearance come. The people of the world may not be ready for us, but Gavin is. We have to make him aware that he is no longer alone. It is important to his future growth." Jabril brought up a scene of a young man sitting in a restaurant writing in a notebook. I recognized the bright eyes I had seen that one morning. "He feels alone and like a freak. He doesn't understand, and it's our fault. I think it's time to make it right."

Jabril stood up. "It seems that Gavin is living in your old hometown. You need to get your journal to him with instructions to convert your handwriting into printed pages suitable for publication. You also need to avoid any old friends that you might run into. It might be a little awkward explaining just why a man of sixty-five looks thirty."

Wow, was I really that old? I used to think that sixty was ancient. Here in this world I'm still just a kid and felt like it. I think that this is why Sarah so many years ago had gotten research started on the outer world to increase awareness and decrease aging. So many were finishing up life when they should just be starting it. Maybe my journal would accelerate that process. But were they ready?

"Not yet." Jabril had been tuned into my thinking. "But Gavin is. Tell him to be patient and wait. We'll find him when the time comes."

It would be good to see the outside again. It would be especially good to see Gavin.

I stood. "I'll get the journal and take Zaron to Atlantic Base. Jeff can get me to the outside."

"Jeff might be too busy. He's head of Atlantic Base now. Dorin is back home catching up on some much-needed work here. You might be surprised who has taken Jeff's place. His name is Eric. It seems that knowing you gives people greater incentives."

I smiled. My old guide is now flight leader at the base. He had always wanted to go into space. He probably has had his share of it. I had heard that they were carrying on some very advanced research that even I was not privileged to know. It seems that my training hasn't advanced to that level as of yet. I wonder if anyone here ever learns too much.

Jabril smiled. "I don't think that you have to worry very much on that point."

Jabril was still grinning about his little joke as he led me to the door.

I took Zaron back to Shambala where I explained to Sarah and Liz about where I was going. Liz seemed excited. "I have been watching

Gavin very closely on our space scanners. He is a very interesting person, and he writes the craziest things. I like him."

I had not known that Liz was so involved with the boy that I met. She had learned about him long ago from stories at the university. She wanted to know what was to become of someone who had been touched by God. She already knew more about him than I did. It seems that many at the university also followed the career of Gavin Graham of Dayton, Ohio. It was time that we again met. Liz wanted to go too, but I persuaded her to stay home. She and Sarah were due back at the university very soon.

MEETING GAVIN GRAHAM AGAIN

It was good to be flying Zaron once more. We took our time going to Atlantic Base. I had my journal still in the old metal briefcase that Peter had gotten for me so long ago. It brought back a lot of old memories of when we first came to this world. Could it really have been over thirty years ago? I looked over the journal. The pages of the ledger had turned yellow over the years, but the writing was still sharp and clear. I hoped that Gavin wouldn't have any trouble reading my writing. Some day he would get my second one. I placed the journal back into the briefcase and gently closed it. Maybe some reader's life would be changed by it as much as my life had changed within it.

Jabril was right. My old friend Eric stood at Zaron's ramp as I came out of the craft. I couldn't miss that smile. We shook hands, and Eric bombarded me with questions about the old crowd from the outer world and what they were doing now. He asked about Sarah and Liz. We could have talked for hours. It took some time before I could ask him about himself. His mission in the east had been accomplished ahead of schedule, and he was posted here as assistant to Jeffery. When Jeff took over as base commander, Eric took his place as flight leader. He was in charge of all comings and goings from the base as well as base security. The new systems could monitor any craft of any kind within five hundred miles from the base. This was used to make sure any sightings of UFOs in the area weren't his. I knew he had extensive time in space, and I never did ask him if he had ever seen any real aliens. I don't think I wanted to know. It was hard enough learning about my new world without learning about any others.

Eric took me to his quarters where I changed into up-to-date business attire. The casual slacks, shirt, and loafers seemed to have replaced the old shirt and tie. I needed to fit in with the public. I was given an ID just in case of emergency. My real outside name and old address was on the driver's license. I checked my birth date. It seems that I was now thirty years younger. That would make me the same age as I was when I entered the Hidden World. My wallet also contained enough currency to take care of any needs that might arise. I was also given a map with directions to Babe's Café in Dayton, Ohio. Apparently this was where Gavin came to eat and write. It was thought that we should meet in public and not go directly to his small apartment. I also learned that I was to drive from the beach house on Emerald Isle all the way to Dayton. I just hoped that I could still handle a car. It wasn't like flying Zaron. With a car you had to do all the work. It was supposed to give me some time to view the changes on the outer rim and also give me some time to adjust. It was going to be quite a change.

Eric had a smaller craft brought to the hanger. He would take me to the beach. Again, like so many years ago, it would be nearly dawn when I arrived.

When we did finally arrive, Eric actually took me to the beach. When I looked shocked, he explained. "Invisibility. The surface is coated with light-bending technology. All light goes around the craft, and no one knows we're here. It won't pass close examination, so you'd better get before someone decides to take an early morning stroll." I left the craft and was surprised to only see a light haze where the craft should be. I couldn't even see Eric leave. I just hoped no one saw a man suddenly step out of thin air. That would have been even more of a shock. I scanned the area, and no one had seen me arrive. I didn't bother to go into the beach house but went straight to the car that was left to me. I was pleased to find a '94 Mercedes in the drive. The keys were supposed to be over the visor. They were.

I was backing out of the drive just as the sun peeked over the ocean. A quick look at the gas gage indicated that I had a full tank. The car drove smoothly and quietly, not like the older cars I had been used to so long ago. I found Interstate 95 and headed north. It was dark when I arrived in Dayton. I had to only stop for fuel twice. I had enjoyed the drive, but I needed a place to stay, so I pulled into a motel just inside the city limits. From the map, it wasn't far from Babe's café.

I picked up several copies of local papers from the booth at the motel's office and spent the night reading all of them slowly. It seemed like times hadn't changed much. They read much the same as papers did thirty years ago. Either times hadn't changed that much or the style of writing hadn't changed at all. I switched on the TV in time to get the local news and weather. Not much had changed there either.

Because my training had been so intense, I had not kept up with outside events as much as I should have. I went back to my papers. I noticed an article picked up by the associated press about UFOs in Michigan. Gavin Graham originally wrote it. It didn't go into much detail, but it looked like a legitimate sighting. By the description, it had to be Eric's bunch or a real alien. It would be interesting to really see someone from another world. We don't really consider ourselves as aliens or even out of this world, but I guess most on the outer rim would. I would have to ask Eric about all this when I returned. He knew what came and went on the outer rim. With today's technology, nothing in our solar system went without notice. Only three years ago the group at Atlantic Base blasted an asteroid on a collusion course with earth. It would have caused major death in the area of central China.

203

Nothing would have been left of the Imperial City or surrounding area. I wonder if Eric was in charge then.

It was sunup. If I were to catch Gavin at Babe's café, I would have to hurry. I grabbed my briefcase and left the motel.

It was a short drive to Babe's. There were only two parking places left. The locals must really like the food here. I entered and looked around the room. No Gavin. I found a seat near the back and waited. The briefcase was close by my side. The waitress looked at me funny when I ordered a milk and salad. I looked back at her and said, "It's my heart," and tapped my chest with my finger. As she walked away, I caught her thought, *Looks perfectly healthy to me.* I just smiled and waited.

I took my time with the food. The waitress also thought it strange that I didn't use any dressing, salt, or pepper. All I got from her was, *Really strange.*

Little did she know.

I waited completely through the breakfast hours, and Gavin didn't show. I could have found him at his apartment, but we had decided that the restaurant would be better for our meeting.

I tipped the waitress more than I should, and she seemed to think that I wasn't so strange after all.

It was a beautiful morning, and I decided to see just how much the city had changed. I drove through the city and the old university where I used to teach and back out to the airfield where I flew from each weekend in the old Cherokee. It brought back many memories, and I could not believe how much things had changed. There were more houses and businesses and many more cars and trucks. The people all seemed to be in a hurry. *I wonder if I used to be like that.* I knew that I had changed as my rate of speed indicated, much to the irritation of those drivers behind me. I got a few hard looks and some words that aren't exactly worth printing. I smiled to myself. They should have more respect for senior citizens.

The rest of the day was uneventful, and the night was the repeat of the one before. Again, the next morning I left for Babe's. Just as I was going in through the door, a man stopped me.

"Charles?" An older gentleman was staring at me in a strange way. "Is that you?"

I recognized the voice, but not the face. He was actually a good friend and fellow professor from the university. It was Ben Thatcher. I tried to cover up. "Yes, I'm Charles, but I don't seem to remember you."

"It can't be you. You haven't changed a bit in over thirty years. Who is your plastic surgeon?"

"You must have known my father. He is retired now and has moved out of the country with Mom. He's doing fine." I hoped he would buy that.

"Boy, you sure do look like your father. I have always wondered what happened to him since he disappeared so many years ago and was never heard of again." He was expecting an explanation.

I leaned over and whispered, "He was doing undercover work for the government and couldn't contact anyone. Don't let anyone know I told you so."

He seemed happy with the conspiracy story of me being an undercover agent. I was really getting into this but suddenly thought I had gone too far already. We shook hands, and I promised to say hello for him when I saw my dad again.

After I sat down and Ben had gone, my little waitress came over with a smile. "You want the same?"

I smiled back. "That would be very nice; thank you." I moved the briefcase under the table out of the way in much the same way I had seen other businessmen do here.

It wasn't more than fifteen minutes later that Gavin came in and took a seat near the window. I saw from his mind that he liked the light from the window to do his reading and writing by.

The same little waitress didn't take any time at all in going over to Gavin's table with a hot cup of coffee. She had her mind on more than food. Gavin had evidently made an impression on her. He was twice her age, but she thought that she might be just a little bit older than him.

Gavin wasn't interested, but politely ordered breakfast. That was something else she liked about him. He was so polite.

I continued to watch. I needed to find out just how much awareness he had gained since that moment he had been touched by a stranger.

He didn't have any close lady friends. He knew he was different but didn't know why. He didn't want to get involved with someone because he knew he didn't age. A wife would grow old, and he would still be the same. He didn't feel blessed by the fact that he didn't age but felt cursed. He was a freak. He was a lonely freak at that. My heart went out to him. He didn't realize that a whole world of freaks just like him existed.

I now saw why Jabril wanted this man to get the journal. He had to realize that he wasn't alone and he had a higher purpose. I could tell that this man was destined for our world, but he couldn't know it now. It would be several more years before the journal could be released to the public, but Gavin needed something to hang on to now before the pure spirit of the man was damaged beyond repair. Jabril knew this as well.

He sensed he was being watched, but he hadn't spotted me yet. His awareness was keen.

I tried an experiment. I sent him a thought. *Gavin?*

He suddenly looked up. He scanned the room and saw my smiling face on the other side of the room.

I picked up my briefcase and went over to his table and calmly sat down. It was like two old friends getting together again. I could see the disbelief in his eyes as well as in his mind. He knew exactly who I was. I looked back over my shoulder to make sure that Ben hadn't returned or anyone else that might be here that knew the old Charles. All was good.

Gavin about choked on his food. I tried to ease the tension. "Good morning, Gavin. I told you we'd meet again."

Gavin's reaction was expected. He was searching for something to

206

say after waiting all these years. The man before him had changed his life. "How did you recognize me after all these years?"

I smiled because the boy I knew was still right before me. "I've been keeping up with you for years. I've enjoyed some of your writing over the past few years, but I don't think you'll win any Pulitzer prizes." I smiled at my joke, but I was here for a purpose, and Gavin sensed it.

"Speaking of writing, I've brought you my journal. It is time it is brought to the public before it becomes too late." I took the metal brief-case off the floor and moved it over to Gavin.

He was even more confused. He still didn't know who I was. His angel had shown up again. I wanted to relieve the tension between us. I put out my hand. "I'm Charles Jennings. Dr. Charles Jennings—just your ordinary history professor." I wasn't ordinary any more, but Gavin would find that out later. He didn't know whether to take my hand or not. The last time he took my hand his world changed. Little did he know that it would be no different this time but for a completely different reason. He shook my hand, and I could tell that he was a little disappointed as nothing happened.

I tried to reassure him. "Oh yes; the last time we shook hands, your nervous system needed a great deal of work. I could see what your body needed, but it wasn't I who healed your body. You will know more after you read my journal. There is something going on that prevents me from disclosing any more at this time. I want you to take this journal and transcribe it as best you can. I, or one of my comrades, will contact you when we want it to be made public."

I sensed an awakened awareness in the man. He would have a future that he had never dreamed of. I passed this on as best I could at this time. "You seem to have become involved in this mystery more than I first realized."

Gavin seemed flustered. "What mystery? Where are you going now? I've got a few thousand more questions."

What could I tell him now? How could I help him understand? What could I tell him that would get him through the many more years of waiting that was to come? Nothing. He would draw upon his inner strength and keep up the faith. I would need to send him something from time to time to keep up his spirits. I decided the journal would have to be enough for now. "Just read the journal, and remember to keep it safe. It's much more valuable than both our lives."

As much as I wanted to, I couldn't get any more involved in Gavin's life. I stood and gave Gavin my hand. It was all I could do now. "Till we meet again, Gavin." He was still numb from our meeting. There was a mixture of awe, fear, and excitement as he looked down at the briefcase. I went out of the restaurant and left Gavin with his thoughts and my journal. I moved my car and watched as Gavin left the restaurant with the briefcase and started back to his apartment. I wanted to be there when he finished to scan his reaction, but thought better of it. I needed to get back to Shambala as I too had work to do. Once again we went our separate ways as I sped down the road to our little beach house on the coast. It would be another long drive, but it would give me time to think about Gavin and how his life would be after this moment. I hoped it was for the good of Gavin. I knew it would be better for mankind in the outer world.

BRIEFING WITH DORIN

B efore I knew it, Eric was picking me up on the beach. I almost didn't find the ship. It was the fine mist that revealed her presence.

Eric was glad to see me again. "We watched your meeting. I want to read that journal myself when it gets printed. Am I in it?"

Eric hadn't changed that much after all these years. "Yep, you're almost on every page. After all, you were thankfully like a shadow on my first trip to the Hidden World. I couldn't have made it without you."

Eric seemed pleased. He would now be known on the outer rim as well. I hadn't realized that before and smiled. It's a good thing that Eric's ego doesn't affect his work.

We slipped beneath the surf and headed out to sea in the direction of the base. Soon Eric took the craft down into one of the larger airlocks. The airlock opened onto a very large hanger that I hadn't seen before, even on my tours with Dorin. Jeff was there to greet us. The others who were used to seeing this craft didn't pay much attention to our arrival, which seemed to please Jeff. He escorted me across the hanger to an assembly area for some of the larger craft that I saw here. He explained as we walked. "We assemble and fly all of our deep-space craft from this part of the facility. Only the most advanced students pull their internship at this location. We have made some great strides in this area thanks to some extraordinary breakthroughs. You may be aware of the old theory that gravity warps space. Maybe I can show you better than I can explain."

We reached the elevator and took it down to the next level. Here were labs that I also had never seen before. We went over to a table where some diagrams had been spread. In front of the table was a view screen.

Jeff indicated the screen as he began to speak. The screen showed a view of our galaxy, but it was from outside the rim. I could tell it was a scan. "You may recognize that this is a real scan of our galaxy from more than fifty thousand light-years away." He looked over at my old friend. "Eric took it on the test flight of our new drive. He rode alone, as there was a possibility he would never return. As you can see, he's back." Jeff smiled, and he brought up a diagram on the screen. "You know about how we project our mass and gravity ahead of us to allow us to fall through space and change directions at fantastic speeds. We have been playing with amplifying this point thousands of times more, generating an area of gravity equivalent to a black hole the size of a grapefruit. Not only are we propelled to this point at fantastic speed, but we also warp or fold space just ahead of the craft. Since we've warped space in front of us, we travel from point A to point B like jumping from the top of one wave to the next without having to go through the valley. The distance we have to travel is now measured in thousands of miles instead of light-years. If we are careful and exactly copy our procedure when we turn around, we travel back to our starting point and arrive safely. We still haven't gotten it completely right. When Eric made his trip, the time he traveled and what time elapsed here was different by over an hour. He actually moved ahead in time one hour. This caused us to be a little concerned. If the trip had taken him back in time on or before he left, we would have had a paradox, which would have wiped out both Eric's. This whole episode made us stop and do more work on time itself. We are only in the conception of this, but we have finished some extremely interesting extrapolations of the space-time bonds."

Someone placed a hand on my shoulder. I turned and was surprised to see Dorin, the old head of the base. I turned to him. "I thought you had gone back to the inside."

"I did take a break for some time but returned to take over special operations because of the new breakthroughs. We needed someone who knew the base and the people and was acquainted with the new space drive. We have a great deal of work to do before we can declare it safe." He smiled over at Eric. "We were lucky to get back our first pilot. He'll go down in history again as the first man from earth to travel outside the galaxy."

Eric just grinned and held his head down. I was beginning to think that this bashful side of Eric was just a front. Only the most exceptional people on the interior are appointed to that post and then only with the unanimous approval of the base commander and the world senate. The senate is made up of the supreme rulers of each of the interior worlds and the master of the university. That post is considered to be that important, and it wasn't his fame that got him there. It had to be pure capability. You have to realize that fame in our world holds very little importance. It only means that more people know your name.

Dorin looked over at me. "The reason Jeff brought you here is because of another concept of the drive that comes into play." He brought out another chart. There were some calculations covering most of it that I could just barely understand. "Since space and time are directly proportional, if we fold space to decrease distance, we also fold time. When Eric came back with an hour discrepancy between his time and our time, we did some further calculations. We found that the black hole projection increased his speed enough to approach light speed. On his return, it should have been two thousand years in the future; but, due to his warp of space, he only gained one hour. We can now even eliminate that. It took a little tuning of our drives and time of their use. Coming and going has to be very precise." He pulled another chart from out of a drawer.

It's the other factor of time that has intrigued us. We think with appropriate controls in a limited area we can actually see back in time much like looking at a star that is two thousand light-years away. We are really looking at the way that star looked two thousand years ago. In other words, we are looking at that star's history. That is over simplifying it, but the principal is the same. With a union of our most sophisticated scanner and a fold of space in a very limited area, we might be able to see what transpired in that scanned area more than a thousand years ago. If it works, it will be like looking across the room. We would like to travel in time also but realize that, even from our calculations, that only someone or anything that is beyond time and space can transcend time." He sighed. "That is only for God and his angels."

He tapped the chart with his finger. "If we could only see the past, we could answer a great deal about the rise of mankind. Our learning would reach a whole new level."

I was curious. "Just how close are you to making a prototype?"

Dorin grinned. "Hard to say. If all goes right we might, we have something after the next intern cycle. That would be about three years, outer world time."

"Why are you showing me all this now?" I didn't see how I came into play.

"Jabril's orders. He said that when you got back to the university your advanced technical training was to begin. You'll be working on this very problem yourself. Jabril is heading up the research personally. For some reason, he insists that this is at a level that is more important than any project that the Hidden World has ever accomplished." He looked me in the eye as he always did when making a point. "I have never known Jabril to be wrong in anything."

I again felt that Dorin was holding back something. That barrier in his thoughts was beyond my ability to penetrate. He, Jabril, and Liz had that in common, and they all were hiding something. It was something very important and something that I should not know. Jabril had promised that someday I would know these hidden secrets. *I wonder why I can't know what they are now. I just guess that I have a great deal more to learn.*

Dorin was watching me closely. I know he saw my thoughts. He only smiled a knowing smile and put the charts away. He placed an arm around my shoulders as we headed out the door. "We all have to be patient," was all he said as we made our way back up to the hanger to again take Zaron back to Shambala.

He paused as if something had suddenly dawned on him. "Aaron, there is only one thing on this planet that comes from beyond time. You need to look closely at the Sword of Truth." He didn't even say goodbye but turned and hurried off as if there was suddenly something very important that he had to do.

I turned and entered Zaron. I touched the sword by the door. I needed to find out all I could about that sword. I felt it was very important suddenly and that my future might very well depend on that knowledge. It also brought a chill that I had not experienced before. When I got back home, I intended to do some research in the sword's history and really go over every detail of the blade and hilt. I knew it was beautiful and powerful. I now felt that it held much, much more. What Dorin said before he rushed off bothered me. Maybe Jabril had some answers.

I settled into the pilot's seat and took a deep breath.

Greetings, Master. My friendly craft broke the spell.

"Hello, Zaron. Let's go home." It was all I needed to say. Zaron took us out into the ocean and south to the rift. The current was stronger on this trip. Normally we would not have attempted it, but Zaron's new drives went through like a knife through warm butter.

Almost in no time we were heading eastward over the crystal sea to the majestic mountains of Shambala and the spires of a castle nestled a mile above the base. It was the place that I now called home.

Zaron settled down in the lower courtyard. I opened the hatch and let down the ramp, or was it Zaron? When we flew together, we were so integrated with each other that it was hard to tell, especially when my mind was occupied. I got out of the seat and turned to leave. The Sword of Truth by the doorway seemed to glow more brightly than usual. I reached up and removed the sword and scabbard from the mount. It brought back memories of the final battle. I turned the scabbard slowly, marveling at the artwork. The scabbard seemed made of some kind of leather, but I knew that this couldn't be true. Worked into this was embroidery of gold braid going down its length. Between the braid runs were intricate representations of birds. Above this, circling the top, was a winged dragon with rubies inset into its eyes. They seemed to burn in the light coming through the door. Just below the dragon were these words in the old language: *Guardian of the Truth.* This must be why the sword was referred to as the Sword of Truth. Which was the guardian? Was it the sword itself or the one who carried it?

I slowly removed the sword from the sheath. The blade seemed to blaze as the light played tricks on the eyes when the central sun's light bounced off at strange angles. The blade seemed warm to the touch. I had noticed this before. It was always a little warmer than the air surrounding it. It was as if it had a life of its own. I had been told that the blade was not of this world. Dorin had hinted at something far more unbelievable.

The hilt of the sword seemed to be made of pure gold and just as intricately carved. Here the main theme was of a fiery phoenix whose wings spread to the sides to form the hand guard. Its feet seemed to hold the blade in place as its neck stretched up to become the grip. It is said that it is the scream of the phoenix that one hears as the blade strikes. I had heard this sound many times. None as loud as the time my own daughter had used it. On the wingtips of the guard were six diamonds or gems very similar. The eyes of the phoenix had green emeralds that sparkled even in the light inside Zaron. That brings us to the main gem inlaid into the chest of the phoenix. It was a smooth crystal about the size of a walnut. It seemed clear, and then it didn't. It wasn't like any gem I had ever seen. If you looked deep inside under the right light, you could see what appeared to be flowing clouds. These clouds swirled and seemed to have a light all their own. Now that I saw it in a new light, it looked very much like a misty veil.

All of this and I still had no answers. No wonder the students at the university wanted to see and touch it. They probably knew more about the sword than its owner. Suddenly I felt ashamed. I had received much from this world and given so little. I had started to take too many things for granted. *Jabril was right. I have much to learn.*

You will never believe just how much, but I will tell you about that when the time comes. I am writing this now to let you know that what I have just put down on paper happened much earlier. I can't disclose how much earlier, as it would distract the impact of future events. My greatest adventure of this world was yet to come. But I don't want to get ahead of myself. Let's just say everything that has happened to me in this hidden world has brought me to the real reason for my being here.

I brought the sword up at this point because it would play a very important point later, and you have to realize my ignorance of its true power as I was admiring its craftsmanship.

BACK AT THE UNIVERSITY

I took the sword of Apollo, or the Sword of Truth, with me as I stepped off Zaron. Liz and Drake swooped down out of the sky to find out what had taken me so long and to learn all there was to know about Gavin.

She took the sword from me and slung it on her back so she could go arm in arm with me into the castle as I told her everything that had happened back in Dayton.

Both Sarah and Liz were preparing to go back to Avalon and the university. What Dorin had said about the sword kept running through my mind. I remembered an old scroll that was supposedly written by the old ones. No one knew the authorship for sure, but it had mentioned the origins of the sword. Since I had not read it before, it took me some time to locate.

After I read it through, I was still confused. It's impossible to translate, but I'll try to hit the most important points. It seemed that the sword was fabricated on another world very far from this one. The people there were very skilled and very advanced. The sword was made as a symbol of peace. The metal was beaten out of a type of iron that was thrown out of a super nova in the far reaches of the galaxy. It had to be heated up to a near nuclear boiling point before it could be formed. It was thrust into solid stone up to the hilt to temper the metal. When it cooled, there was no metal that could stand up to it. The metal was called the Genesis metal. It was formed at the birth of the universe. The old ones took the blade and fashioned a hilt out of gold and jewels. The phoenix symbolized the fact that it had come out of the ashes of the birth of a new star. The jewel in the chest of the phoenix was added by them also and is said to not be of this universe. Its origin is still a mystery, as well as its makeup. There was no mention of how it got here or why it was placed into the sword. I could not get over the feeling that I had each time I looked into its depths. Maybe I could find out more when we got back to the university.

Soon we were ready, and we excitedly boarded Zaron and left our home in Shambala and headed west out over the crystal sea. Sarah and Liz were both getting close to finishing their training at the university. Liz and Sarah both had been selected for internship at Atlantic Base with Jeff. It seemed that my training was not as predictable. I had been studying the scientific discoveries of this world for the past two years, earth time. Now my studies were to go into high gear on new applications of science that staggered the imagination. So we landed in Avalon with different expectations, but each of us was more than ready to go on.

Studying is probably boring to the outsider but was extremely exciting to me. It was in my third year of these studies that I was placed with Jarod and Jocko. They were extremely glad to see me, as we didn't get a chance to visit as much as we would have liked. They had elected to keep their old names from the outside as they had gotten so used to them. Everyone now knew Jarod and Jocko and both loved their work here. They had evolved over the years, and these men, who were already geniuses, were now more than brilliant. They were in a class all by themselves and working as a team seemed only to heighten their achievements.

217

I can't go into all the details of what we worked on, but it kept us very busy. During our breaks, I would try to catch up with Jarod and Jocko by extra study. It was no mean feat. I also took time to read up on the old ones, as what Dorin had said a few years ago had not left my mind. Jabril would explain it much better later, but I got a rough idea by what had been written about them. It seemed that they were here before man. Much that had been handed down about them was mythological. There were stories about their exploits, and there were at least ten different views as to where they were from. Some said they were from heaven, and others said they were from a distant star. The only true fact that I had found was that their decedents were called the sons of light. This must mean that I had been descended from them. This only increased my ambition to learn as much about them as possible. It seemed only one man knew the truth about them. You guessed it. Jabril knew, but he wasn't about to tell me until it was time. That time would only come when I was ready. I had no way of knowing just when that would be.

Sarah had left for Atlantic Base already, and Liz was also due to leave for there soon. We still got together on our breaks for harvest and festival. We relished these times as we forgot about our tasks and studies and just enjoyed being together.

The outside world events had us worried as terrorists attacked the World Trade Center in New York and another war was started in the east. These terrorists killed thousands in the name of God and thought they were in the right. How many times in the past had this happened before? It isn't so hard to understand that God is the God of all men and not just a handful. No peace can be reached when all sides know they are in the right and God stands behind them. What miracle will ever bring them together? We continued to watch and wonder, knowing that we couldn't interfere. It's hard to know that we had the power to end all this bloodshed. It was another to know our place in God's plan.

After Liz left for Atlantic Base to join her mother, I was left to complete my studies. It was almost a year later that Jabril finally sent for me. It seemed that I was to finally graduate from the university. This wasn't a formal ceremony. We just left our studies and went back to our worlds or were assigned to internship at Atlantic Base. Most picked up their lives where they left off back in their home countries. Many of them had already been married and started new families.

It seemed that I had been selected for Atlantic Base, but not before I had a long talk with Jabril. It seemed that my training wasn't over after all. It was just beginning, but not at the university.

Jabril was waiting in his office. He was alone at his desk when the door opened to admit me. He had a somber look, and his thoughts were beyond my ability to see. I had never seen him look so tense. Something must have been up that I hadn't expected.

Jabril finally looked up and smiled. "Aaron, make yourself comfortable." He indicated a chair at the front of his desk. "It's been some time since we've had a chance to talk. You've far exceeded our expectations here at the university. Your awareness is nearly to your full potential. Your studies and training have been the best that our masters here can give. It is time for you to go beyond that. Time is approaching for you to fulfill your true mission here." Jabril saw that this last statement left me with a few thousand questions.

He only smiled. "There will be plenty of time for questions later, but now we have work to do."

He stood up and started pacing. This was always a bad sign. He always did that when he couldn't find words to explain his thoughts. We spoke in English, and I sensed that much of what he had to say would have been easier in the old language. He spoke English only for the purpose of his words being written in this journal. They were not to be for me alone. They were to be put to paper at a later time for release to the outer world when the time was right. History was being written, and when this happens, I get nervous.

He finally stopped and leaned on the front of his desk and looked me in the eye. "We need to start from the first. That is the only way this

219

whole thing will become clear. There is much that I have to keep from you, as future events cannot be influenced in any way. Just suffice it to say that your world is about to change once more."

He had resumed his pacing. He finally sat back down and pulled an old scroll out of his desk. This was one that I had never seen, and I had seen plenty. It was written in the old language and predated anything that I had seen before.

"This was written when the sons of God were first brought to the garden. Here, in this world, lived the righteous descendents of Adam. The sons of God found favor in these people and took wives. Many people think that these sons of God were angels. They were not. They came from a distant world that was much older than earth. The sons and daughters of the union between the daughters of Adam and the sons of God produced children wiser—way beyond those of this world. They would rule the garden for many years. The seed of these people were known throughout the land as the 'sons and daughters of light.'" He looked at me and smiled. "Yes, you are a direct descendent of these people. It is the reason for your powers of awareness and skills. All that has happened in this world has brought you to this point in time. Some think that the thousands of years of progress and evolution of man was just to bring each one to this point in his life. The lives of millions of people who lived in the past and died were for this one purpose. God's purpose is never clear, but it is still God's purpose and not our purpose. It is still clear to me that your path has been planned, and where you go from this point is of vital importance. Even though our lives are not predestined, I believe that certain events in them cannot be avoided."

This was getting deep. Jabril had returned to the scroll and was thinking again. *How much deeper can it get?*

He ignored my thoughts because I know he saw them. "Dorin contacted me years ago about your sword and its significance on what they were working with at Atlantic Base. He too knows the history of the sword better than most. It was a property about the sword that gained his full attention, and he has been working to that end."

220

He knew I was getting more confused. "You already know that the blade was from another world. The sons of God in the beginning brought it here, and it was their children, or whom we now call the old ones, who replaced the hilt on the blade. It was not the blade that gave the sword the power but a crystal placed in the chest of the Phoenix. This crystal did not come from the world of the sons of God. It came from beyond time. It is not known from what source or how the sons of man acquired this crystal, but it is known that they brought it with them. They called it the 'Eye of God.' There are many rumors about its powers. It is said that from it, God sees all. It is said that the eye sees beyond the surface of man and sees his inner soul. Only a being of pure heart can posses the stone. It has traveled the earth, resting in the sword, and has seen many changes during the history of mankind. It has been admired but never possessed by many kings of the outer earth, and its legend grew and spread and influenced many. Its best-known name was 'The All-Seeing Eye'. This name was given to it during the Crusades as Dresden and three others from this world rode with King Richard to free Jerusalem. It was in this journey that the sword gained fame. No one and no object could stand up to the blade as Dresden and the others fought their way into the city. It was Dresden's mission to retrieve the holy relics there as well as the riches and return them to the church in Rome. Dresden and his men were known as the Knights Templar, and their fame spread before them like the wind. Their society grew and became the Free Masons of whom we hear so much about today. The crystal in the sword was never forgotten, even after all this time, and the 'All Seeing Eye' has become a symbol for religious freedom throughout the world."

I was impressed, but Jabril ignored this. "Dresden, on his return to Rome, saw that the church only wanted power and wealth and wasn't concerned about the true significance of what he and the other three had brought to them. They made a visit to the heads of the church and told them the story of the freeing of Jerusalem. They kept the treasures and only gave the church a small token of the relics and gold that they had acquired. The rest of the treasures were distributed to the other knights according to their rank. They became very rich men. Dresden and the other three had no use for the gold, and they did not want the church in Rome to have it to increase their power. The church rebelled much later and tried to kill all the Templar Knights. Most of them were killed, but the four leaders had already returned to this world. They carried with them the relics and most sacred objects of the church in Jerusalem. The most sacred of these being the cup of Christ. This cup became known as the 'Holy Grail', and it was known to be carried by these four knights. When they disappeared, a crypt was placed in their honor, but, of course, no bodies were there. The Grail became another legend, and it now resides in a special place in the Holy City. Only Job knows of its location."

I had been sitting with my mouth open for some time now. None of this had ever appeared in the historical records of this world or any world that I knew of. Dresden had played such an important part in history, yet his name was unknown. This was definitely by plan and not just a coincidence.

Jabril smiled, as he knew I was starting to understand. "It is not by whim that King Dresden gave you the sword. It was no accident that you and Liz were capable of using it. The stone in the hilt would have prevented any other than you two to use it. It is no accident that Dorin saw the implications of the stone and contacted me. It is no accident that you now have in your possession the only thing on this planet that exists that is beyond time itself. It is the *All-Seeing Eye of God.* It is also no accident that you have been chosen once more."

Jabril looked at me with a look that I had never seen before. "Your next journey will be through time itself."

I was still reeling from what I had heard, but Jabril wasn't through. "As you know, being raised on the outer rim in the United States, that the country was started by a unit of the Free Masons. These men sought to establish a new country and a new birth of religious freedom that would extend to all men of all nations. This dream was written into their constitution with enthusiasm. It would be a law of the land and the backbone of a country founded under God. Later, as times changed, amendments to their words were added that changed the meanings of their words. Those that had different ideas and different religious beliefs, or none at all, wanted change to reflect their rights. Soon the Constitution of the United States was no longer what it once was, but men still fought and died in its name. The country also became a place that was no longer held in esteem by other countries throughout the world. This country doesn't need changing. It needs healing. There is no other way for it to survive without a new rebirth of the freedoms the founders strived and fought so hard to establish. These men were not of this world, but their deeds are still talked about to this day. These principals also need to be relearned by all countries. Your journal will not only carry the truth but a spark that will give people new hope. It is not important that they believe your words, but the spark in their minds will make them again think for themselves."

Jabril looked even more serious. "Your journal is not yet finished. It is your final mission that is missing. For that, you will have to go to Atlantic Base. Your wife, daughter, and Dorin wait for you there." Jabril paused and picked up a note with the seal of Avalon at the top. "This is from King Dresden. He wanted to be here to see you off, but other matters kept him from here." He handed me the piece of paper.

On it was written, "Carry the Sword of Truth with pride. It will see you through any obstacles that the world can place in your path. Your friend, Dresden."

I don't know if I will ever live up to the past of my uncle, but I now have a new respect for the sword that hangs by the door of my spacecraft. No longer will I take for granted anything of this world. This world, even after all these years, brings me new surprises.

Jabril saw my thoughts and smiled. He only stood and extended his hand. "Till we meet again, Aaron, son of Drake. May God guide your path and bless your journey."

Again he was holding something back. I could only shake his hand.

223

I felt a sadness there that I couldn't explain, and the warmth of his hand gave me courage. I thought back several years when he said that one day I would know all. I think that all would overwhelm me just now. I could only turn and leave.

I felt unusually sad myself as I climbed the walkway back up to the gardens. I paused as I entered Zaron to again gaze into the crystal in the sword by the door. It had new meaning to me now. I also felt that the stone and I were linked by some magic beyond my comprehension. I would learn later just how strong that link was.

Zaron felt my thoughts. "*Master, it is a pleasure for me to also carry the Sword of Truth. I have been given the ability to understand its nature by Jabril so as to keep it safe.*"

This impressed me. This was a machine that seemed to know more than me. Maybe it did. "Thank you for that, Zaron. I would trust none other with it."

I settled into the pilot's seat and felt the hum of her drives. "Let's go to Atlantic Base, Zaron. It seems that my future awaits."

As you will, Master

We left the inner world once more as we headed straight south to the rift that led to Atlantic Base. *Is it me, or does the sky and Crystal Sea seem bluer? Is the sun brighter, or is it just my imagination?* I suddenly realized it was because it was my world, my home, and my destiny. I knew that this world was destined to not stay hidden much longer.

Zaron seemed to understand also as we plunged into the sea and entered the blackness of the rift. Zaron was careful this time as the current through the rift was strong. She managed without any problem. We moved into the base and into a smaller hanger where Zaron could be moved easily to the elevators, as she wouldn't be flown again for some time.

I felt a little sad for her as I stood up after she had settled onto the waiting cradle. "Zaron, I hate to leave you this time for I don't know how long it'll be before I see you again."

Never fear, Master. Time is measured only by humans. It was a simple statement that took some thought.

224

PROJECTS AT ATLANTIC BASE

I walked down the ramp to a waiting group of people. Eric, with his smiling face, was in the forefront. We shook hands, and I greeted many of my friends there that I recognized. This was to be my new home. Eric led the way to my quarters that I was to share with Sarah while I was here. Here I changed clothes. The gold jumpsuit was no longer appropriate as I was now just a worker like the rest. I was apprehensive and excited about my new assignment. Jabril's lecture could not dampen my spirits once I saw Liz and Sarah just as I left our quarters. Liz came running, just like a little girl, and gave me a big hug. Sarah came at a more sedate pace but gave me the same greeting.

Sarah was all smiles. "Jabril sent word that you were coming. We both had to leave work to greet you. We both have been very busy lately."

Liz was a little more excited. "You'll never believe the breakthroughs we've had. We've received all of the work you, Jocko, and Jarod have done and built equipment beyond our wildest dreams. There is still a great deal of work before it is completed, but our tests have all been very successful. I can't wait for you to see."

It seemed that there would be no pause for me before I jumped into the projects here. Eric led the way back to the elevators and down to the lower level and the labs. There must have been five hundred people working on different pieces of equipment. Some of this I had seen drawings of, and others were new to me. To see the actual equipment sitting there humming with power was stunning. Liz gave me a kiss on the cheek. "Sorry, Dad, I have to get back to the space labs. We're just getting ready with the new drive, and they can't get started till I get back." She darted on down the hall and was soon out of sight.

Sarah gave my arm a gentle squeeze. "Don't worry, Chuck. I won't be leaving you. It seems that we'll be working together for quite some time."

"Maybe shorter than you think if you don't stop calling me Chuck." She knew I hated that tag. I had gotten it back in school, and she never let me forget it. *I think she called me that just to get me to relax a little more. She knows I am nervous about my new assignment.*

She smiled at my thoughts, in much the same way as Jabril had done. "It seems that I am to accompany you to Dorin's office for orientation. I heard you already got a preliminary one from Jabril. Dorin will get into the project we are working on in more detail. I hope you're ready."

"Would it matter if I wasn't?"

"No."

"In that case, lead the way." I followed Sarah to another section of rooms and offices that I had never seen here before. One of these was Dorin's office. There was no indication on the door or anywhere that it was anything other than a plain door. As we entered, it was another matter. The office was huge. There was a small conference table in the center that had recently been used, as there were many charts spread out on its surface. With all the technology here, these two-dimensional charts were still preferred when discussing a problem or planning a certain portion of a project. In more advanced stages, they had to move to

226

three-dimensional projections that brought out any flaws or improvements that might be needed. Some of these were so real that it was almost on the border of being supernatural. The real thing in the final stages didn't vary, even in the smallest detail, from these projections.

Dorin came over and greeted me. I could tell that he was pleased that I had changed before coming down. "Well, it seems that we have another slave to put to work down here." He extended his hand. "It's good to have you aboard, Aaron."

A buzz from an electronic device on the desk caught Dorin's attention. He pressed a button and listened. What he heard, we didn't. He smiled and said into the device, "Well, let Liz do it."

He was still smiling as he sat down and indicated that we do the same. "We needed the sword from the craft. It seems that our technicians who tried to remove it couldn't and got the wrath of one very powerful spacecraft." He chuckled. "They'll think twice before they mess with Zaron again."

He saw my curiosity. "Liz will bring the sword here. It is the keystone of our project, but you will understand more as we get back to the project. For now, let's just say that for this project to work, the All Seeing Eye plays an important role, and I suspect that its bond to you could be just as important. Liz can handle the sword, but the sword sees you as its owner." He saw the many questions that were going through my mind. "I'll explain more about the sword later too."

A knock on the door interrupted Dorin. He pressed a button and in came a smiling Liz with the Sword of Truth. "Daddy, you need to quit leaving things like this laying around. One of the men got a nasty zap from Zaron. I think that it may leave a mark. He'll wear that brand for a long time."

She chuckled at the thought and handed me the sword. "I bet that fellow who got zapped didn't think it was so funny."

This brought an even bigger chuckle. "But everyone watching did."

This even brought a chuckle from Dorin as well. It's nice to see that

227

humor still pervaded the working people here. They enjoyed their work and never let stress and worry enter into their beings.

You would have to know these people to understand. Liz fit right in, and so did Sarah. I just hoped that I could follow their example.

Liz patted me on the head and left. Dorin seemed amused by this little gesture. Sarah only smiled. The tension I had felt was now gone. I smiled too.

Dorin slipped the sword from its scabbard. The blade seemed to light up the room. He held the sword up and turned it slowly, looking at the jewels and workmanship. The light from the blade sent shards of lights around the room as he did so.

He slowly and with reverence slid the sword back into the sheath and looked into the crystal in the chest of the Phoenix.

It was several seconds before he spoke again. "This is the first time I've had a chance to see this marvelous creation up close. It is truly amazing." He looked at me and continued, "You already know about the crystal." He looked back down at it. "You may not be aware that it isn't really a crystal. It isn't really a stone either. It isn't man made. It isn't of this universe. By all rights and reasons, it shouldn't even be here." He gently rubbed a finger over the surface of the eye. "Just to be able to touch it is beyond reason. I know that you feel strange when looking into it. So does everyone else. Each sees something different. Some see water. Some see blood. Some see stars. You see mists, as do I and all other sons and daughters of light. I think that this mist is the closest any one of this world will ever come to seeing beyond what that veil of mist hides."

He became more somber as he placed the sword and scabbard in my hands. "When you hold the sword, it resonates in a frequency that is beyond human hearing or feeling. Only by chance did we pick it up on our scans when you and Liz did battle. This resonance is most profound when you hold it or even when it is your possession. We don't know yet what that means, but we think we can analyze that resonance." He went over to a piece of electronic device and turned on a switch. A low hum filled the room. It was soft and moved up and down in a low octave scale. "That is the sound of the sword, slowed down many times to be able to be heard by the human ear. There is a power behind that stone that is beyond the comprehension of any of us here. I know that Jabril knows its origin and reason, but he is not sharing that knowledge with anyone. I've never known him to be so secretive about anything as long as I've known him. He wouldn't even divulge what he talked to you about. He only said that he explained the origin of the sword to you."

This shed a new light on why I was here. *Jabril said that I was to travel in time but had not shared this fact with Dorin.* This thought I hid from Dorin. I didn't know how much I should tell him at this time. He must have to find that out for himself.

I had forgotten about Sarah sitting so close by. She gave me a strange look. My thoughts cannot be hidden from her or Liz. She took my hand and squeezed it. *This must be really important, Aaron. When Jabril sent me here, he said that I was to be a very important link to the past. He didn't explain. Now I'm scared.* The thought was only to me.

What have I gotten myself into?

Dorin interrupted our exchange of thoughts. "We need to take the sword to the time chamber and check its changes when we power it up."

Dorin quickly followed up, as he knew that I didn't know what he was talking about. "The time chamber is where we have finally built what we think is a way to get in touch with the past. There is a barrier that we can't seem to break through. We have called it the time barrier. We can tell it's there but can't see it or sense anything from it. We think that only something from beyond time itself can see or maybe even travel through this barrier. The stone in the sword is definitely beyond time. We have to see if there is a link between that stone and the past. If there is, it might just be the breakthrough we've been looking for. Jabril concurs, but without comment. Jocko and Jarod seemed excited about the prospect and came here just before you to work with the sword."

Sarah squeezed my hand even harder. My awareness was working

229

overtime as I felt her concern and no thought was even necessary. I knew that the chamber was in my future. I just didn't know how. Sarah felt it too but kept it between the two of us.

Dorin pressed another button on his desk. Only a few seconds later Eric came in. "Eric, just the man I need. You are familiar with the Sword of Truth. We need to take it to the time chamber to run some tests on it."

He saw the concerned look on Eric's face. "Don't worry. We don't intend to harm the sword in any way. It just might be the most precious object on the face of the earth."

He wasn't trying to impress Eric. I saw in his mind that he thought of the sword in that way. It was one object that he was in awe of. I was sure that he and his crew would treat it with the respect that it was due.

When looking back on those days at Atlantic Base, I now realize that it wasn't respect which was given to the sword but reverence. Dorin truly believed that the 'All-Seeing Eye' was a gateway to time itself and it had a divine nature. He also thought that it was some device that could see all things at any time in both the past and the future. He was not the only one with that belief. This belief was common among those that knew the story of the stone. They did not believe that it was an actual gateway to God but that this device was in someway linked to God. He must be in control of the actions of the stone. I needed to add this at this point to give the reader an idea as to the future actions by Dorin and the crew at Atlantic Base. This was also to give you an insight into the power that they held in their hands.

My thoughts at this point in time were only of curiosity. I wanted to see what Dorin was up to. Sarah hadn't given me a hint as to what was going on. She thought I needed to see for myself.

I didn't have to be curious much longer as Dorin stood and placed his hands on his hips. "I'm sorry. I've waited for this moment for the past three years. The lab is ready. I will not miss what they find for the world." He started for the door.

230

Sarah and I rose and followed. I felt the excitement in Sarah as well. She had been involved in this project since she arrived. Other than Dorin, she knew more about what was going on than anyone else here. I also felt that neither one of them knew what to expect, but it had to be powerful.

Dorin left his office with us close behind. We went much further down in the complex to the lowest level. I knew that we had to be on the outer rim of the base also. The chambers here had been cut out of solid bedrock and reinforced with the strongest material the inner world had to offer. They were not taking any chances with this project. It had acquired a priority one in importance. This meant that, should the need arise, all members of the complex would stop what they were doing and respond to any emergency.

We moved into a secure area that had wall-to-wall electronic monitoring devices. A view screen in the center of the room showed a small vault with the Sword of Truth standing within a glass stand. Standing in front of the screen admiring the sword were Jarod and Jocko. Both turned as they heard us enter. The old enthusiasm of the two was still there as they rushed forward to shake my hand and lead me to the screen. "Fantastic, just fantastic! It's finally time. The power is up to maximum. The monitoring devices will follow the resonance to wherever it might take us. We were just waiting for you."

The others in the room had all stopped and were staring directly at Dorin. He nodded once which triggered a sudden flurry of activity. Screens came to life. Monitors started humming with power. A map of the universe became apparent on the wall to my left, and then, as if on cue, all heads turned to the sword.

A glow started from the crystal in the center of the hilt and soon spread throughout the chamber. The light was so brilliant that everyone had to turn away. It was then that the map on the wall suddenly streaked with millions of bright streaks until the whole map was completely covered. Not even one star shone through the mixture of lines on the map. Activity went to another level as everyone in the time chamber

231

was rushing to take readings. The glow was getting more than we could stand.

Dorin made the call. "Shut it down! Shut it down now! We don't want to destroy the sword. We don't know what the stone will do to it. It might be needed."

The light slowly faded, and the hum of the equipment ebbed to silence. There sat the sword and the crystal in the hilt. Nothing had changed. Evidently the light from the crystal did not carry with it the heat that was usually associated with intense light. This in itself was very strange. Normal light of that magnitude would have evaporated the gold in the hilt. Even from this distance I could tell that every detail of the carving of the Phoenix was perfect. Not even a single feather of the wings was damaged. I was impressed even though it wasn't clear what I had just witnessed.

Dorin became active. "Let's get busy. We need to see what we've got. Everyone retrieve your data and meet in the conference room for coordinating our data at the end of this cycle. Now move!"

He did not have to encourage them as everyone was running around like mice, each gathering information from first this device and then another.

Dorin motioned for us to follow. He headed back to his office without speaking a word. Sarah and I followed. Sarah was scared. Even though she saw the same thing in the room as I did, she saw implications that were still beyond me. Dorin saw them too. He too was scared. It was catching. I was scared.

Dorin went into his office and closed the door as we entered. He turned to Sarah. "Did you see the map?" She only nodded. "It filled the whole universe. That's impossible. We were expecting it to only show paths on this planet. If we hadn't shut down the equipment, it would have overpowered our processors trying to plot all of the paths. We only got a small fraction of them."

Sarah spoke up. "I suspect that there were an infinite number of them. George and his crew will probably confirm this in the meeting. The implication is staggering. Do you know what that means?"

Dorin nodded. "The 'All-Seeing Eye' is just that. It sees everything in the universe in every time, both past and future. It can only mean one thing. The stone is truly divine in nature." He was sweating. I had never seen a man so agitated. "What have we done? Are we walking a path that isn't intended for us? Have we gone too far? Where is Jabril when we need him? He said he wouldn't interfere in any way with the project. He knew. He didn't tell us, but he knew. We have to make future decisions on our own. God help us."

It was some time later at the end of the cycle that we all met in the conference room. Everyone had brought something from their areas pertaining to the extraordinary event in the time chamber. There were charts and lists of numbers and pictures and many strained faces around the table. All seemed just as nervous as Dorin. I had spent the interim getting caught up on the project, and I was now aware what the team was up against. I knew that the whole project was in jeopardy, but Sarah and I still kept what we knew quiet.

Jeff had been called in to help Jarod and Jocko. He had been in charge of collating all of the data gathered from the chamber. That was a job in itself. Dorin looked to him for some answers. "Jeff, what have you come up with, and what do we do now?"

Jeff sighed and stood so as to be heard by the entire group. "There's no easy answer to either of those questions. We were looking for time lines, and we sure got them. We got billions of them in fact. They were all generated from the crystal and spread throughout the entire universe. The 'eye' was looking at every instance in time and space. And what is so fantastic is that it was doing this all at the same time. If I didn't know better, I would swear that the crystal really is the eye of God. One thing we do know for sure is that it is generating time lines from a place beyond time to all places in time."

Dorin interrupted. "Are you saying that these time lines come from God?"

233

Jeff looked extremely uncomfortable. "No, I don't think it is for us to know, but for the crystal to generate an infinite number of lines, their starting points have to be from beyond the known universe. The point they are seeing is beyond our technology to follow. To be able to see that point, we would have to have only one time line and an anchor at the point it is seeing. Only then could our equipment have a stable line to follow. Even then, we aren't sure that it could be done. At this point, it is only theory." He paused and sighed. "Then and only then we believe that one could travel that path with the crystal from here to that anchor point in history."

A murmur went around the room. Jeff was walking on delicate ground, and he knew it. He looked up at Dorin and took a deep breath. "Unfortunately, the timelines are an infinite number, and it is a miracle and great planning that we were able to see even this small portion of them at all."

Dorin interrupted. "Then is it possible for us to use our sensory devices to see into the past using those same time lines?"

"No." The answer was definite. "The time lines are all one way. They go out but don't come back, so to speak. Seeing can only be done from the source. Only the eye can see. We can't ride along and see what it sees as of now because we can't isolate one single time line. Even if we could, we would have to have an anchor or object on the other end of the time line to tune in to. You can't go from A to B when you don't know when or where point B is."

"So you're saying that it can't be done, even with the eye?" Dorin was getting disappointed.

"No." Jeff was just as disappointed as Dorin. "We should be able to duplicate the process in, oh, a billion more years or so."

This got a low chuckle around the room. Dorin wasn't amused. He looked over the people in the room with his stern expression. The room became deathly quiet. He looked over at Sarah and me and didn't say a word. He was going over his options. He got up and placed his hand on his chin and rubbed the nonexistent whiskers there. He stopped and placed his hands on his hips like he always did when he made a decision. "We do it again."

This brought another round of whispers from around the room. "This time we don't do it for so long so we have fewer time lines to evaluate. I want to know exactly what we have." He gazed around the room and found everyone hanging on his next words. "We power up just before next break. All who were there will be there again doing the same job. Everyone look for something we missed the first time. There must be a way around waiting a billion years. I don't think I have that much time."

He looked around the room. "Let's get to work." This signaled a mass exodus from the conference room. We left with Dorin.

As we walked back to his office, I was wondering just what he expected to find on the second trial that he didn't find on the first. I was fascinated with the whole concept and very impressed with the crew. I was even more impressed with the crystal in the middle of my sword.

We went over several of the results in Dorin's office. He concurred with the findings of his group. He finally looked up at us. "We need an early break before the test. We can get something upstairs with the off-going crew. A good drink from Shambala and some bread from Agartha will just about fit the bill. What do you say?"

We agreed. We could use a break from the tension that was building. It had been some time since either of us had taken any sustenance. We needed every faculty at our disposal when the new test started. A little drink from Shambala wouldn't hurt. Sarah was already looking forward to the bread and jams from her family's land. After all, you would expect a princess and heir to the throne of Agartha would like the bread and jams from there.

The air in the cafeteria was a little lighter. We sat at a table separate from the others so we could talk. We got strange looks from the off-going crew. They knew that we were involved in some earthshaking project but didn't know exactly what it was, and they were surprised to see us together here.

235

Dorin ignored their stares as he shared his disappointment from the test. All the equipment was perfect. All the theories were checked and double-checked. What we expected, we got—but much more than we wanted, and nothing we could use. In other words, we were back to day one, as the outer world would say. It seemed that a place where the thing called time meant so little was the place that was taking time to a new level. Right now this project was taking much more time than Dorin had expected. He got the feeling that on this project he was slowly running out of options. This was a place where time means very little. When an option failed, this time was wasted. When you run out of options, you run out of time. Maybe Einstein was right. Time is very relevant, especially to the person who is running out of it. Dorin was not the type to give up. I guess we could keep doing it over and over until we got it right.

Sarah jabbed me in the ribs. She seemed to be doing that a lot lately. She didn't think I should be making light of our situation. *Of course, she is right. She always is.*

That brought a smile this time. I only frowned. Her smile became wider.

We finished and headed back down below.

The time chamber was once again closed, and the control room was a bustle of activity. The equipment was warming up, and George and Jeff were making sure every device was up to speed. In less than an hour, they were ready for the second test. Dorin himself was at the controls of the chamber and watching the sword intently. He would try to watch it as long as he could stand it. He knew that something in the light would give him a clue.

He looked back over the room, and everyone was awaiting his signal. He again nodded, and again the crystal started to light up. When Dorin could not stand the light any longer, he called out, "Shut it down!" The light started to fade, and Dorin sighed and shook his head. He hit the button to the door of the chamber and looked up at me. "Get your sword, Aaron. We shouldn't need it again for the next billion years or so." He looked disappointed again. Maybe he had given up.

I felt sorry for him as I went to the chamber and took the sword. I felt a slight tingle as I lifted it from the glass stand. It must be from the static in the chamber.

I went back to the control room and slung the sword onto my back by the strap from the scabbard. I too was disappointed.

Dorin looked over the room and spoke. "Well, we gave it a good university try. That is all we could do. All of you go now and enjoy your break. You deserve it. We'll discuss our options after break and start all over again."

Everyone left except Dorin, Sarah, and me. Well, that wasn't quite true. The one technician that was left first looked confused and then very excited. He stood there going from one foot to another, which reminded me of a six-year-old son of Sarah's old roommate that had to go to the bathroom. She was the one who always called me Chuck.

Dorin noticed Sarah and me looking behind his back. He turned and was surprised to find Riley still there. "Riley, why on earth are you still here."

Riley was very excited. He showed a chart to Dorin. "Just as the equipment was powering down, the time lines were fading. But just before they did, Aaron touched the sword. All the time lines disappeared except one. Only one time line was left. It faded too when Aaron left the chamber." He watched Dorin's face. He became braver with his theory. "I think Aaron is the anchor. With him in the chamber, under low power we may be able to trace that time line."

Dorin was shocked and excited at the same time. He looked over at Riley. "I think you're exactly right, Riley. Great work."

Riley smiled from the praise of Dorin.

Dorin wasn't through. "Riley, get in touch with Jeff and George, and tell them to get everyone back in the conference room now. This is an emergency. We've got to pass this on to them before their break. We can't leave them thinking they've failed. We start new tests after break and lower power, and Aaron will be in the chamber with the sword."

I raised an eyebrow at this but didn't say anything.

I got a thought from Sarah. *This could be the beginning.* I knew what she meant.

We left Dorin's office just behind Riley. Riley was in a run, and Dorin wasn't going much slower as he headed for the conference room. We arrived, and Dorin sat at the head. Sarah and I sat on either side of him. We waited patiently, or at least Sarah and I did. Dorin turned this way and that while watching the door. It was like his seat was very hot.

Sarah gave me a punch in the ribs. *Be a little more understanding, Aaron. Dorin finally sees the light at the end of the tunnel. This could very well be the culmination of his whole life's work. Don't underestimate the importance of what he's discovered.*

Again, Sarah was right. She could see the importance of this. She just didn't know how I felt. *I'm sorry. I was trying to cover up just how scared I am. We both know that something important is coming.*

The first of the crew was coming in the door. Soon many more followed, and all seemed out of breath. Riley must have put the fear of God into them. In almost no time, the room was again full with Jeff, George, Jocko, and Jarod bringing up the rear.

Riley was the only one who hadn't showed up. Dorin caught this little discrepancy and was irritated until Riley came in with copies of what he had found to hand out to the whole crew. Dorin was again impressed.

Excited whispers started almost immediately. They all knew what they were looking at but didn't know why. Jeff jumped in with both feet. "Dorin, this is a single time line, and it is anchored at both ends. How did you get it? We saw nothing like this before we left." He was extremely excited.

"It was by pure accident. It seems that some of the equipment had not powered down, and we got that chart that you're looking at just as

Aaron picked up the sword. He anchored a time line to somewhere. The other billions of timelines disappeared. I think that when we return from break, we need to put Aaron in the chamber with the crystal and bring up the power slowly and analyze that time line with all the equipment we have. We will also have to make sure that Aaron is not harmed. No project is worth a life, and we'll only do this with Aaron's approval."

Here he looked over at me, as did everyone else in the room. I didn't say anything until Sarah pinched me on the arm to bring me back to reality. I was still going over the consequences of my action when I picked up the sword. "I'm here to help. I'll do whatever is necessary no matter what the consequence."

This brought a sigh from Dorin and smiles from the crew.

Dorin stood up and looked at ease for the first time since I got here. "Go home and get some rest. We continue after the break, so be ready for some excitement."

Boy, was that ever an understatement. It did not even come close to what was to come.

THE TIME CHAMBER

Sarah and I spent our break back at our quarters where I got caught up on my journal. We spent many hours seeing what had changed on the base. We visited Liz at the space labs where she showed us the many things that they had been working on. All was impressive, but none even come close to the one we were about to begin at the time chamber.

Sarah and I talked about all the possibilities and consequences of our project. Some were good and some not so good. She was worried about what Jabril had said about traveling in time. He failed to mention whether or not I would come back. You can see why I was so anxious about the project. I liked all of my trips to be two ways. I had come to like my new world. I didn't want to leave it forever, dead or alive. Sarah had the same feeling of doom with the project. She knew that her feelings were seldom wrong, and this worried both of us even more. I looked at the sword that I had brought with me to our quarters. What secrets did it hold for me?

It seemed much too soon that our rest period was over as Sarah and I headed back down toward the project area. The sword slung over my back drew stares. We were surprised to be joined by Liz as she grabbed both our arms and walked along between us.

"Dorin got me transferred to this project. He thinks that I may play an important role in the experiments. He didn't elaborate. I guess I'll find out when we get there." Liz was upbeat about joining the group. Her excitement was just as contagious as ever. It was a comfort having her along.

We arrived at the complex early. Only a few technicians were there. They were getting some of the equipment warmed up. I took the sword off my back and handed it to Liz.

"It seems that this sword has some link to the past where I'm concerned. Today's exercise is to try to determine more about this link. It seems that this time I'm to be in the chamber with the sword when the equipment is powered up." Liz was now looking into the crystal.

"I don't feel good about this, Daddy. What if something goes wrong? I talked with George about it after Dorin contacted me. No living being has ever entered the chamber with power on." There was a worried look on her face. "He said nothing about you going into the chamber." That little detail was bothering my daughter. The reason was obvious. "He didn't want me to worry about it during our rest period. He knows it will be dangerous."

I hoped Liz wasn't trying to cheer me up. I was worried enough for all of us.

It seemed that the room was filling up. Riley was more excited than the others. There was a lot of tension around the room. They felt a breakthrough was in the making. Dorin, Jeff, Jocko, and Jarod came in together. We could tell they had spent hours going over the next steps of the tests. Dorin looked worried. This didn't help my anxiety much. Jarod and Jocko were just the opposite. They were eager to get started. They saw all of our work back at the university coming to fruition. All in the room were eagerly looking forward to the next few hours.

Sarah squeezed my hand as Dorin came over and put his arm around me. "Are you ready, my friend?"

241

"As ready as I probably will ever be." I tried to hide my worry from Dorin, but it didn't work.

"Don't worry so much. We've gone over every possibility to assure your safety. We think that the possibility that you will be killed is very small." He smiled. I didn't see his humor.

"Thanks!" My sarcasm didn't escape him. He only chuckled.

He turned to the others. "All right, people, let's get started." He looked over at George. "Let me know when you're ready for Aaron."

"We're ready when he is," George came back. Jeff nodded his agreement also. Jocko and Jarod gave me a thumbs-up, a signal they had picked up from Liz.

Liz handed me the sword. "Good luck, Daddy."

I took the sword and entered the chamber. The door slowly closed. I felt trapped and very anxious. I didn't want to use the word *scared*.

It seemed like hours before I noticed the crystal beginning to glow. I knew that everyone was watching and the equipment was slowly powering up. Readings would be starting, and the crew would be very busy back in the control room. The room got brighter as the gem in the center of the sword sent forth energy in the form of light. We were right. There was no heat, but the equipment and the chamber seemed to intensify the power coming from the crystal. I felt a warm feeling coming from the hilt in my hand. We were definitely connected. The light was getting strong, and I put my other hand over my eyes to protect them from the blinding light. The glow started to fade and was soon gone altogether, and the door once again opened. I breathed a sigh of relief. I was still alive and realized that the warmth I had felt from the crystal and the sword was very calming. How could I explain that feeling to those watching?

Liz was standing at the door when it fully opened. "Daddy, are you all right?"

I put my arm around her. "I'm just fine. No harm done at all."

We walked back to the control room. Everyone was excited. Jocko and Jarod were going from one station to another. Riley was fit to be

242

tied. Jeff and George were busy trying to determine just what they had. No one was sure, but it was certainly different from the previous tests.

Riley brought over a chart to Dorin. He didn't speak as he handed him the printout. Dorin looked at the chart. "One and only one time line." He looked like the world had lifted off his shoulders. "It's solid. Its starting point is definitely here with the crystal and goes out." He suddenly became agitated. "Who has the plot with the point B data? Just where is this time line going?" He looked around the room.

Jeff came up with another chart. On it was one line that started apparently at Atlantic Base and stretched out over the Atlantic and faded as it moved toward southern Europe or possibly North Africa. "This is the best we can get from our equipment. We know that point B is anchored somewhere on the other side of the Atlantic, but we can't see where. We also can tell from our readings that it is definitely in the past. Here also we are in the dark. We only know that it is more than five hundred earth years in the past."

Dorin was not satisfied. "We were only at ten percent. Could we get more accurate data if we were at full power?"

"We don't know. We are swimming in new waters here. Do you think it wise to go at full power with Aaron in the chamber?"

"You're right. These are new waters. We know that full power didn't harm the sword and partial power didn't harm Aaron, but we don't know for sure if Aaron would survive full power."

He looked over at me. "Only one man can make that decision."

Sarah sent me a thought and Liz picked it up. *You know you have to.*

I looked at Sarah, and Liz looked at us both. She broke the silence that was suddenly in the room. "Before we go to full power, we need to determine if it is just Dad who can anchor the line or someone else who can use the sword. We need to perform this same test with me in the chamber before we risk Daddy's life again." She was worried about me, and I was never more proud of her.

243

Dorin thought for a moment. "It makes sense." He turned to the group. Get ready to repeat the last test."

Liz reached out her hand. I handed her the sword. She took it and smiled. There was still something she was keeping from me. She had not given her real reason for volunteering for this test, but I couldn't see what it was. Sarah saw the same thing. We would just have to trust our daughter.

Liz entered the chamber, and the door was closed.

We watched intently as the power started up. Liz had the sword in her hand and a smile on her face. I got the feeling that she knew what to expect.

The glow from the stone grew as Liz covered her eyes. When the room was again bright, beams of time lines again filled the universe. This was all that Dorin needed to see. "Shut down everything. We have what we need."

I saw his point. It seemed that only I was anchored in time and only one time at that. We needed to investigate the ramifications of both of these tests before we went any further.

Dorin evidently thought the same. "Get your data together. Consultation meeting in the conference room in one cycle."

Many excited people who had to compare notes and work on summations left the control room for the labs. Each department had to present these summations to Jeff, and he had to prepare his report for Dorin all within this cycle. They would be very busy over the next several hours.

Jocko and Jarod were working on something all their own. They too would be making a presentation. Our next meeting could be very interesting.

It was.

When we had all gathered in the conference room, there was even more tension in the air. All got the feeling that something very important was about to happen.

Jeff stood. This brought an eerie silence to the room. "We have come up with some very interesting data. We need to start from the beginning. We now know that only Aaron has an anchor of only one time line to the past. We also know, thanks to Liz, that only Aaron, and he alone, has that time line. The reason for this we can't possibly tell. We don't think that even with full power we would be able to see that point in the past. That point and any point in time both future or past is hidden from man no matter what his technology. To be able to see that point in time, one has to be there personally." Here he stopped and looked at me. I couldn't tell just what he was thinking.

He looked nervous as he continued. "We think," here he paused and looked over at Jarod and Jocko who nodded in his direction, "that we can send Aaron to that unknown place and time using our equipment and, with his strong anchor here to his family, bring him back within twenty-four hours earth time."

This brought an unexpected gasp from Dorin and a round of new whispers around the table. Jarod stood and walked over to Jeff. Jarod looked at me and spoke. "The line is solid up to a point, but someone with the stone and the sword can travel that line, and the final point in time will become solid or real to him when he arrives. We all think that it's worth a shot. We also think that it is necessary. This link is not there by accident. The only way to know its purpose is for Aaron to take that journey. We would only have one chance for him to return, and that would have to be exactly twenty-four hours from his arrival and from the same point. The earth's rotation must be exactly the same as when he arrived. This is important. It must be explained at this point that should Aaron survive the journey, he should not interact or use his powers to scan anyone or influence anyone in any way as the future from that point on would be destroyed or at least changed from what we know it. This is a very tricky endeavor, but we feel it must be accomplished with Aaron's cooperation and approval. We think that on the twenty-fourth hour Aaron should drive the sword into the earth at the point of his arrival. This will give us the point from which to retrieve him. We will be using the earth force itself to locate his time line." He looked over at Jocko. "It should work."

The whispering had stopped along with my heart. Jeff and Jarod slowly sat down. All eyes turned to Dorin. He was already deep in thought.

I looked first at Dorin and then at Sarah and finally at Liz. There was a smile on Liz's face. She knew. For the first time since I arrived here, I knew too. I would travel in time, and I'd be all right. Even with my insight, I could not see my future from this point on. Was it because I would have no future, or was it because I was not meant to see it? I would soon find out.

Dorin seemed to come to some kind of decision. "How soon can we make an attempt?" He had addressed the question to Jeff.

Jeff looked over to Jarod and Jocko, and they nodded.

Jeff said one word that brought chills to everyone in the room: "*Now!*"

Dorin looked at me, and I too nodded. "Back to the time chamber in one earth hour. Aaron is about to leave us."

The room cleared in a hurry. Sarah and Liz came over, as I had not yet stood up. What had I gotten myself into again? They walked with me hand in hand back to the time chamber without a single word. Just being there was enough.

THE ULTIMATE JOURNEY

E ric met us at the door. He gently handed me the Sword of Truth. He smiled. "I always knew you were meant for something great." The words of encouragement were greatly appreciated.

"Thank you, Eric."

I started to place the sword on my back but was stopped by Jarod. "Not so fast, young man. You can't go into the past looking like that." He looked around the room. "Where is that boy?"

As if in answer, Riley burst into the control room carrying what looked like a bunch of cloth. Jarod smiled and took the cloth from him. What looked like just cloth turned out to be a garment made from material that seemed to be Hebrew in origin and a long pouch of the same material that would just fit my sword.

"We think you'll be ending up somewhere near northern Africa or even Egypt. Your dark skin from the central sun and your size would make you stand out. We think these garments worn by the people of northern Africa would give you better cover. The garments are Hebrew, as we know that there was a Jewish settlement there. You would fit the

247

bill for being one of their warriors. Riley will take you somewhere to change. All of your old clothes will have to be left here."

Riley took me, and soon I was clad in the long cloak and hood. Under the cloak, I wore a short, heavy kilt of the same material. Over the brown material of my shirt I had leather armor. Riley explained. "We had it in a museum. Jarod sent for it as soon as he thought that you might be going." He pointed at the sandals behind me. "They came from the same place. We don't think that twenty-four hours of wear will damage them any. Jarod thought your mission was more important."

I was quite a sight as I returned to the control room. Eric had placed the sword into the makeshift cover. The rope handles on the cover fit over my shoulder nicely. Should I need the sword, the top flipped open with just a motion of the hand revealing the hilt, but I already knew that this was a no-no. I could not use the sword other than for travel without changing history.

Liz and Sarah looked more beautiful than I had ever seen them. Was it because I loved them so much, or was it because I might never see them again? They did not want to say goodbye because they did not want to think of it that way. They needed to feel that I would come back.

All conversations had stopped. Only the hum of the equipment insured me that I hadn't gone deaf.

There was nothing left to be said. I went toward the chamber.

I really felt alone as the chamber door closed. Soon the gem started to glow, even through the cover. I knew that the equipment was coming up and this time it would be full power. I covered my eyes as the light became unbearable. Even through my closed eyes and hand covering them, I could still see the light. I felt warm all over, and a tingle went throughout my body. The warmth that I now felt I had felt before, and always it was associated with God himself. It was then I knew that this journey was to be made only with God's blessing.

It was the cool breeze on my face that made me remove my hand. It was a spring breeze that had the scent of flowers.

248

I was in a grove of fruit trees on a small mountain. From the sun I could tell that I was in the outer world, and it was early morning. There was not a cloud in the sky. It was very pleasant here. The trees had just started to bud, so that meant it was early spring.

I walked to a clearing so as to better get my bearings. To the west, I could make out a large city. I was trying to determine just what African city that could be. There were no people in sight. Over to the north, I made out a road. It too was deserted. I thought this strange, as the city that it was leading to was pretty large.

I knew that I couldn't find out anything here, so I would have to go down the mountain. I only had twenty-four hours here. I marked the time by the sun and piled up some rocks at the very point I was standing when I opened my eyes. I was amazed at my movement through time. I had felt no transition at all. I knew that the chamber at Atlantic Base was now empty.

I started down the mountain with my sword gently swung on my back. It was my only way back. It would never leave my possession while I was here, wherever that was.

When I reached the foot of the mountain, I saw the reason for the floral scent in the air. The city had made a garden here, and the early blooms gave the air a very nice aroma.

It was not until I got to the road that I met my first people. There were two small boys that, when they saw me, ran to where I had entered the road. "Ho, warrior! Wait for us!"

The language was Aramaic. It was strange that it was spoken here. I must be in another area of the earth or maybe another time from what we had expected. It could be that the two boys were just as lost as I was.

I couldn't avoid them. I would just have to be careful. I didn't want to make any waves, as time itself was fragile around me.

They slid to a halt in front of me. "Where are you bound for, stranger?"

249

I answered them in their language. "I'm just passing through. Where does this road lead to?"

The older boy spoke up. "You must really be a stranger to this land. That's the road to Jericho."

That placed me in the Middle East somewhere. "What are you two boys doing out here all alone?"

The oldest spoke up again. "We wanted to go into the city, but we can't get in without our parents. Children can't get past the guards without a parent."

That made sense. "Just where are your parents?"

The little one spoke up. "Dad's drunk as usual, and he'll just beat us up again if we wake him up, and Mom's gone into the city to see the priest who is teaching near here."

I felt sorry for the youngsters. They were raggedly dressed but had bright faces and pleasant smiles. "What are you called?"

The oldest spoke up. "My name is Rufus, and my brother is Alexander. We live near here."

If their mother had gone into the city to listen to the priest, she was Hebrew, but their names were of Latin origin. "Your names aren't Jewish."

The older boy frowned. "Our dad used to be a Roman soldier before he got thrown out. He married our mom after he was stationed here years ago."

My heart went out to the boys. "Well, just for today I will be your dad. You can go with me into the city and stay with me until we find your mom."

This seemed to make the boys' day. "What do we call you, stranger? If you're going to be our dad, we need to know your name."

Well that made sense. I thought for a while, and the only common name I could come up with for this area was Simon. "You can call me Simon." We started for the north gate of the city. I had not anticipated a Roman guard. He was older than the normal run of soldiers, and I guess he was on guard here because of it.

He looked me over as we came to the gate and especially took notice of the sword on my back. From my dress, he knew I was some kind of soldier also.

He spoke as we approached. "You are pretty brave, Jew, to be carrying a weapon into a city ruled by Rome. From where do you come?"

"I'm only just passing through. I come down from the country." Both statements were true.

I could tell the guard was thinking about taking my sword, but I was a good head taller than he was and muscular. He assumed that I knew how to use that sword and figured that old age was much preferred over the taking of the weapon.

"Just you mind to keep that sword covered while in the city. Besides, you're late for your Jewish celebration. That was days ago."

He turned his attention to the boys. "Who are these children with you?"

Again I hedged on the truth. "Today they are my sons."

He mistook my meaning. "I know what you mean. They grow up much too fast." He had softened his attitude somewhat. He probably had children of his own.

"You may enter, but keep that sword covered or you'll find yourself in the dungeons."

I thanked the guard, and I entered the outer gate with Rufus and Alexander tagging along. It was when I entered the inner gate and looked to my left that the realization of where I was dawned on me. There stood the Temple of Solomon. I recognized it from renderings of it from several old writings. I was in Jerusalem. The temple still stood. That would put me back nearly fifteen hundred years or more. This was really a treat. I wondered if I'd get a chance to also worship in the temple before I had to leave.

We walked on, and I noticed that the streets were nearly deserted. An old man was sweeping the street, and only a few other stragglers were on the streets. The shops all seemed to be closed. "Where are all the people? A city this size should have many more people."

251

Rufus piped up. "They've all gone to watch the execution."

"What execution?"

"This is the day that some criminals are to be executed. Alexander and I wanted to see it, but we couldn't get in. I don't think mom would have let us come anyway."

I frowned at the boys in a fatherly fashion. "She was right. You're much too young to see men die—no matter how bad they've been."

Rufus just shrugged his shoulders. "Mom will be there. If we're going to find her, we'll have to go too."

Maybe he was right. "Just where is this execution taking place?"

"Oh, they don't kill people in the city. They take them out of the west gate and up the hill."

We headed around the northern part of the city and then south along the wall to get to the west gate of the city. It seemed that we had gotten there before the crowd. Why did executions fascinate people so much? We would wait here and try to find the boys' mother.

The boys were excited despite my earlier words. "They will carry signs in front of the men to tell what they have done. They make them walk all the way up the hill before they execute them."

The boys were right. It wasn't long before the first of the criminals came into view along with a jeering crowd of people. Each of the criminals was flanked on each side by four guards and was strapped to a crossbeam member. Evidently they were to be crucified. One of the guards walked in front with a placard containing his crimes. The first two passed, and I stepped back from the crowd because I couldn't get involved in any way with the proceedings. The third criminal seemed to be lagging behind at some distance. I could not see his face because it was hanging low under the whole cross and not just the crossbeam. A chill went through me. Suddenly I suspected that this was not your everyday execution. My suspicions were confirmed as I saw the placard being carried in front of him. It read, "Behold, Jesus Christ, King of the Jews."

No. It couldn't be. I'd been taken back to view the crucifixion of Jesus

Christ. I stepped back farther from the crowd. The man coming to the gate was beaten beyond recognition. The royal robe across his back was saturated with his blood. Blood ran down his face from a twisted bunch of thorns. That was supposed to be his crown.

The man struggled beneath his burden and fell several times before he was across from me. It was now that I felt his pain. It was beyond comprehension. The crowd was jeering and throwing rotten food and spitting at him. The cross too was soaked with his blood.

I could not help it. My agony was almost beyond what I could endure. I knew it was coming from this man, and I hadn't tried to reach out to him with my awareness. Tears ran down my face as I knew that I couldn't get involved. The man finally fell from complete exhaustion. How could one man live after a beating that I knew he had? There was more blood than I had ever seen.

It was when the guard hit Jesus with the whip to get him back up that I sprang into action. I didn't care what I did to history. I burst through the crowd and headed for the man in the street. Jesus Christ needed my help. I ran to his side and knelt beside him. I started to give him a drink from the flask in my cloak. I was kicked in the ribs by the guard, and I sprawled onto the stones of the street. My head bounced off the stones of the pavement. My face was inches from the man under the cross. I could not stand his agony any longer. I knew that I could wipe out this whole garrison of Romans in a matter of minutes. Suddenly I felt a surprisingly firm grip on my arm. I looked into the eyes of Jesus. I let loose my awareness. The damage had already been done. I looked passed the pain. His mind was much like Jabril's, but no wall was there. At that moment, I knew him and who he was and he knew me. I now knew that what was occurring was meant to be. I also knew that here was power beyond my comprehension. He too could have destroyed the garrison and the whole city to boot as well a host of angels to help. This was not to be. The peace and love that was there was more than anything that I could have imagined, and on top of that was the pain and agony. He could have avoided it but didn't. This was all for the benefit of mankind. It was for the benefit of me.

More tears came to my eyes as I felt his pain and saw the reason for it. I stayed my hand. The sword stayed in place, and the guards still lived.

It was the centurion who rode up that broke the spell of the moment. "What's going on here? You're holding up the procession."

The guard stammered. "This Jew tried to help the priest."

"Well, no wonder. You've beaten him half to death already. We can't have him die on the way." He looked down at me.

"Who are you, Jew?" He was wondering about just how I might be killed too.

A small voice screamed from the crowd. "He's Simon, our father. Don't hurt him." It was Rufus. It was mighty brave of him.

"You're from Cyrene, Simon. I've seen your kind before. What are you doing here?"

I rose on one arm and looked up at him. "I have come in from the country." I didn't need to tell him more.

"I can tell you are a warrior, as none other would have had the courage to do what you did. You are strong. If you want to help this man, you carry the cross!" With this, he turned his horse and left to the head of the procession.

I stood, and the guards backed away as they saw the sword on my back. I helped Jesus to his feet. He stood, but I don't know how. I picked up the cross and shifted the sword as I placed the cross on my back. I started out the gate with Jesus at my side. Without the burden, he would make it to the hill just to be killed. The blood-soaked cross was covering me with blood also. I could feel it dripping into my hair and soaking into my clothing on my back. The people had picked up their jeering, and I was now also a target of their spittle and rotten food.

I was way beyond interfering with history. I didn't care. What else was I to do? The trip up to Golgotha was longer than I had imagined.

When we arrived, the two others were already hanging on their crosses. They were now in pain also.

I reached the top of the hill and threw the cross at the feet of the executioners. They didn't like the gesture but didn't say anything.

They drug Jesus to the cross and began nailing his hands to the upper crossbeams. I felt every blow and moved as far away from there as I could. After they nailed his feet to it also, they dropped the cross into the predug hole and placed stones at its base to hold it upright. The soldiers took his bloodstained cloak and backed away to let him die. It was horrible. Even at this distance, I could still feel his pain. Others moved in to be at his side. I knew that one was his mother. There were also two of his brothers. I did not know which was which, and I couldn't get involved any more.

From where I stood, I could tell he was talking with them. It was only from what I had read that I knew what he said. For the next three hours, I suffered too. I knelt on the outskirts of the crowd and prayed to God to end his suffering. At the end of those three hours, I actually heard a cry that chilled me to the bone. It was "My God, My God, why have you forsaken me?"

He hung his head and whispered, "It is done." I felt these words to the core of my sole. I did not have to hear them.

A guard approached him and plunged a sword deep into his side and blood spewed out onto the mount. As the blood soaked into the earth, I felt it heave. The blood from the Son of God had awakened the earth. It shook with a violence that I had never felt. I alone knew that the earth did not shake just under the city but around the whole world, both inside and out. At the same time, the sky went dark. Winds whipped the area, and the darkness was so dense that even torches could not penetrate it for more than a few inches. God had turned his back on earth.

I walked the best I could to the foot of the cross. I spoke in as loud a voice as I could so all the Romans could hear. "Truly this is the Son of God!" None doubted my words. It was some time before the light of the sun returned. It was now nearly sundown. I had lost sight of Rufus and Alexander. I hope they had found their mother. There was nothing I could do here, and I'd done enough damage for one day. I don't know what affect I had already made on history. I made my way back up the mountain to the olive grove. Now I realized that the stone had sent me to the famous Mount of Olives. It did not help because I could still feel the pain and agony. This was only a small portion of what Jesus felt. As soon as I knelt in the grove and prayed, I became sleepy. I laid down in the grove and slept for the first time in thirty years. The dreams I had were much like those I had in the cave of dreams where I was forced to sleep. It was morning when I awoke. By the height of the sun, I knew I only had a few minutes to place my sword into the earth at the point I had arrived.

I plunged the sword into the earth up to the hilt and knelt and held onto the grip and waited. I waited for the light to come over me. It did not come. Minutes turned into more minutes. More minutes turned into hours. I finally removed the sword from the earth, knowing that I would never return. It was my fault, but I didn't care.

I was covered in blood, but the only wound I had was a slight bruise on my head from the stones of the road when the guard kicked me in the ribs. I turned the sword over and over in my hands. It was then that I noticed the stone. It was streaked in blood. Not on the surface but deep within the crystal. It could never be used again to travel through time. What did it matter now?

I sat on the mountain and pondered what was taking place down below. I also knew what would happen on the third day. I also knew that for events to unfold the way they should, I could never again get involved. This tore at my soul as much as the thought of never seeing Sarah or Liz again did. This was much more than a human should be put through. I was in agony. I knew I had done wrong in the eyes of those back at the base, but I did what I thought was right. That was the only consolation I had.

I moved down to the garden where I stayed that night. I could see the people who had come for the Passover leave the city. None came through the garden. I was alone all that day. I was only left with my prayers. I had never felt so alone in all my life. I knew that sooner or later I would have to leave and take up a life of obscurity, but I refused to leave until after the third day.

That night I suffered. That night I did not sleep. Pain, agony, and loneliness racked my whole being. The only solace I had was in my prayers, asking God to protect my family and help heal my battered soul. I stayed on my knees for almost the whole night in much the same way Jesus had done only a few days before.

It must have been near morning when a voice interrupted my prayers. "Be at peace, Aaron. What you did was meant to be."

Even in the predawn light I knew I was looking into the eyes of Jesus. It was the morning of the third day. He had risen. "Forgive me, Jesus." I knelt at his feet. It was morning of the third day.

"You are forgiven. Go now in peace, and carry the truth to the world." He looked down into my soul, and for the first time since that time on the road, I felt at peace.

I kissed his hand as I looked up into his eyes once again. "I will carry your Word as far as I am capable." He seemed to know what I meant. He knew who I truly was. I was not sure why he singled me out alone here in the garden. There had to be a reason.

Suddenly I noticed a man behind him. I could not recognize him as the light was directly behind him. I bowed my head. I did not deserve his attention.

When I looked back up, he was gone.

The man who was with him came forward. He only said, "Take my hand." Those words were so familiar. I did not hesitate as I reached forth and took the hand. I was suddenly surrounded by light, and I was blinded by it. When the light faded, I saw in front of me the ark of the covenant, and the earth was shaking below my feet. I could only be in one place.

I stepped down from the altar, holding the covenant, and went over to the door, which was now opening. My body was weak, and my knees were giving way. I went out the door and fell into the arms of Job.

He looked shocked to see me. "How bad are you hurt?"

I looked into his eyes. "I'm not hurt at all."

This didn't make sense to Job. "Then where did all this blood come from? If it isn't your blood, then whose is it?"

"It is the blood of Jesus Christ."

COMING HOME

Job looked at me very strangely. I had just come out of the house of God covered in blood. I was thought to be dead and never to be seen again, and now I say that I'm covered in the blood of Jesus Christ. You can imagine why he looked at me that way. He knew I didn't lie.

We had started getting a crowd. There were numerous people who had gathered when they felt the earth tremble. They knew to come to the temple. What they saw was not what they had expected.

Job now realized the implications of just what had come through that door. "You must come with me. Now!" He half led and half carried me to the temple.

We entered and went to the rear and entered a golden door that was only meant for the high priest. Job led me inside and finally down a spiral stairway to a large grotto inside a beautiful limestone cave. I could hear rushing water. Job looked very agitated. "You must remove all your clothes. You have to be cleansed."

Job disappeared as I took off my clothes. He returned with a small golden chest. He opened it and removed a bronze cup and delicately placed it to the side. "Put your clothes in the chest. They must not be touched by anyone here. They are now sacred."

I heard him gasp. "There's a hand print on your arm."

"Yes, Jesus stayed my hand when I stopped to help him. It is his handprint."

Job knelt and prayed to God. His words I could not hear, but the impact on him was evident.

I placed the clothes in the chest, and he gently laid the cup on top and closed it. He also saw the question on my face. "It is the cup of Christ. It was brought here many years ago by Dresden. It was placed in my safekeeping. I was told to keep it safe until I was told where to place it for its final resting place. The blood of Christ should go with it. There is power there that no man should have access to."

He took me to the source of the running water that I had heard. Water was gushing out of the mountain into a large pool. After the water swirled through the pool, it cascaded back down into the earth through a large rift in the mountain. I could not hear the water hit the bottom. The water was crystal clear and warm to the touch. I scooped up a handful and quenched my thirst. I heard Job take in a sharp breath.

"Where does the water come from?" The water had an unusual affect on me.

"It comes from within the earth and is blessed by God. This is the headwater of the river of life." He saw my reaction. "It once ran the length of the land that was here. On the day that Christ died, the winds blew, the sea rose, and this land sank, taking with it the tree of life. Only this island was left. The river was diverted back into the earth, and the temple was built over it. This is the only place that the blood of Christ can be washed from your body. Cleanse your body. I will get you other attire to wear." He left. I slowly waded into the pool. The warm water not only cleaned my body but also invigorated by soul. I took my head under water, and the blood of Jesus flowed out into the bowels of the earth. The earth again shook. I understood the reason.

I stood up straight and closed my eyes. I had been washed in the blood of Jesus, and now I was washed in the river of life. When I opened my eyes, Job was in the water beside me.

He only had one question. "What happened to you?"

I looked him in the eye. "I was saved by Jesus Christ."

He laid a hand on my shoulder. He knew my double meaning. "You, like Christ, must be baptized. It is a symbol of acceptance since that morning when John baptized Christ. Do you take him as your savior?"

"I already have. He forgave me in the garden." The memory of his face will live forever in my mind.

"Then I baptize you in the name of the Father, the Son, and Holy Ghost." With this, he laid me back into the water of life. As I came out of the water once more, I knew that the ultimate mission of my life was over. I now started a new life dedicated to this world and the spread of the truth. I would carry out his wish.

I left the pool, and Job slipped a white robe over my head.

Job picked up the sword that I had put by the pool. He noticed the stain in the eye.

I saw what he was looking at. "The stain is within the eye and not on the surface. It is why I couldn't return on the first day."

The implications of this dawned on Job. He smiled. "The eye was once thought to be a gateway to God. Now it is obvious that the only way to God is through the blood of Jesus Christ."

This was not just a play on words. Job knew this to be fact.

We slowly left the river of life and headed out to the sunshine of the Hidden World once more. It was warm as we headed down to the gardens where we could talk.

Job looked me in the eye. "I sent word to Jabril that you were all right. He seemed to be expecting it for some reason. He said Sarah and Liz would pick you up and take you to Shambala to rest. That will give you enough time for you to tell me all that happened."

The water had given me strength, and I walked with Job and told him the whole story of what transpired in Jerusalem. He was amazed and awed at the same time. He knew what I had suffered, but he also

261

knew that I was blessed. The touch of the Son of God had changed my life once again. Those who only take him on faith are even further blessed for they have not seen what I have seen. Their life will change too.

We talked and walked and stopped and prayed. Job had much to tell to the future students who came to the Holy City. This trip in time was not to be kept secret from them. The Word was to be spread through both worlds. The inner world would spread the truth through the universities in all the lands. The truth would be spread to the outer world through my journal. I needed time to rest and write, and Jabril saw this as he had sent Sarah and Liz to pick me up. I would do my writing at home. Home now had a whole new meaning.

It was a silent pleasure when we finally saw the golden gleam of Zaron streaking toward the Holy City. She silently slid below the trees in the garden and settled to the cobblestone pathway in the middle. Job and I arrived at her side just as the golden ramp came down.

Two very lovely ladies ran into my arms. They flooded me with kisses and questions. There would be plenty of time for both later. I persuaded them to wait as I had much to tell. I now saw that Liz knew where I was going. She didn't know all the details, but she knew I'd be coming back. I could now see through that barrier that for so long had blocked me. She no longer could hide any secrets. She saw this and smiled. There would be no secrets between us from now on.

Zaron took us home. The greeting there was much more than I had expected. I think half the kingdom had shown up. Soon the news would spread of my adventures. Now I needed rest, and Jabril had seen to it that I would get it.

I knew that Liz had to get back to Atlantic Base to finish up her internship so she could leave for the assignment at the University of Southern California. She would keep in touch during the next two harvests. It was at the end of the second one since I got back that I was back to my old self. The work in the fields made me feel much better.

It was then that Jabril again sent for me. The message only said, "It is now time. Come."

Jabril was always dramatic, but I felt there was more in his message than just a simple message to come.

I left Sarah and again went back to Avalon. Zaron landed in her usual place above the university, and I walked down the path to the tower. I got several waves from many students and awed stares from others. It was a pleasure to be back here again. I climbed the stairs to Jabril's office with a light heart.

The door opened, and I entered. Jabril stood there with a smile.

I crossed the room and took his hand. It was then that I realized that I had felt that feeling somewhere before. I looked deep into his mind. I was now past his barrier. I saw who he really was and where I had felt that hand before.

"You're Gabriel, the archangel of God." I was out of breath. "It was you who helped roll away the stone at the tomb. It was you who took my hand and brought me home. You were there!"

"Yes."

TRAINING BY THE ANGEL OF GOD

J
ust when I thought I knew it all, something new like this hit me in the face. Standing before me was the Angel of God. I really did have a lot to learn. It looked like all those secrets that I had wondered about were about to become secrets no more. *He had promised that this day would come. Now it is here.*

He saw my thoughts. "Yes, your day has come." He smiled. "In this land where the day is as long as you like, you'll find you have a very long one ahead of you."

Jabril suggested that I have a seat. I needed to sit down anyway.

He remained standing and again started his very familiar pacing. I now knew why. This was to be in my journal.

"It should be clearer now to you why you were involved in so many missions. Why the earth responded to you while you were on the mountain and at the final battle. Why the earth opened for you after you slew the dark lord. Why the earth only responded to you alone and no other. Why only you and your seed were able to use the Sword of Truth. You also can now see why you were brought to this hidden world. Everything that has happened to you was because you were the one who carried the cross. It was ordained by God that you should do this deed. It is not by accident that you stand before me now. You have been led here to take my place. It is clear why you were destined to write of this world and make it known to the outside world. Every aspect of your life has led to this point in time because my work here is done."

I was silent. I wasn't silent because I had no questions but because I was at a loss for words. I was still overwhelmed by who stood before me. This man was no man at all but an angel of God. He, like God, was eternal. The last two thousand years he had spent in the Hidden World was nothing to him. He was only carrying out his mission. God had left him on earth as guardian of the garden. *How many others here knew his true nature?*

He saw the question in my mind. Now I knew why there was nothing that could be hidden from him. "There are only three who know who I am: King Dresden, Dorin, and your daughter, Liz." He smiled. "After this meeting, all are to know—both inside and out."

This made a great many things from my past much clearer. I saw why my friends and my daughter had to keep the secret from me. They had not known my mission but knew that Gabriel did and that it must be kept secret. They had done their jobs. Dorin suspected that my trip in time might be the mission for which I was intended. Liz knew from Gabriel that I would be all right, but she too did not know where I was to go or why. This was why King Dresden seemed to know what lay in store for me. All seemed very clear to me now as I looked back. It was as if someone had suddenly turned on a light.

Jabril was pleased that my insight had improved. He knew that my awareness was now beyond anyone else of this world—and all because of what I had seen and felt two thousand years ago.

He stopped his pacing and smiled. "It is good that you see. I have been called to come home. I have very little of your time to prepare you." He looked deep within my soul. "We have much to talk about."

He came around the desk and extended his hand. I took it as I stood. A warm feeling spread throughout my body. It was familiar. I had felt it in the House of God. I had felt in on a beach in North Carolina. I had felt it in the garden of Gethsemane two thousand years ago. I knew its source.

"Yes, God has now selected you to take my place. You can be sure that he walks with you now and forever. The blood of Christ has cleansed you, and your sins have been washed away in the river of life. Who else could be the new guardian of this world?"

I stood as I still held the hand of Gabriel. He smiled like the friend I knew him to be. "Come. We must walk in the gardens and talk."

We left the tower and went up the hill to the gardens. I had never seen them look so beautiful. Gabriel agreed. "The beauty that God has given us to see too often goes unnoticed. It is good that you can appreciate his creations. You will appreciate them more and more as time goes by. You have yet to grow to who you will eventually become. It is a process that is not to be rushed but taken in time and cherished. You will see many changes, and like the All-Seeing Eye, you will have to observe and analyze. All your decisions will have to be made with the welfare of mankind as your goal."

I was still silent as I was listening intently to his every word. "The sword you carried will hang in your office for all students who come to you will see. The crystal will remind them of what you have seen and the truth behind it. They will carry this forth. It was this crystal also that connected you to God's kingdom. As you watched what unfolded on the hill before the cross, all the angels of heaven also watched and wept with you. You are not unknown in the kingdom of heaven. Your actions in Jerusalem have affected many. Two small boys for the rest of their lives considered the brave warrior they met on the Jericho road as their father. Later they carried the truth in their own way as they started churches on their own. The people who watched and followed you to the top of the hill had their lives changed as you declared the man on the cross as the Son of God. They would never show disrespect to any man again. They would regret for the rest of their lives the way they had treated Jesus Christ."

These were powerful words, and they meant a great deal to me.

We walked and talked for many hours. Many things were revealed to me that I couldn't put into this journal. There were many things that were to come that I would have to manage. There was even more that I had to learn. There were tasks and restrictions. There were writings and histories that had never been seen. There were people who I had never met that held incredible futures, even though I would not be able to see what those futures were. There were others that I was to encourage and help along because of this. One of which was a man who had written my first journal. Gavin Graham, it seemed, was also chosen for a reason. Even the reason for this was kept from me. After all, I was still a man. Knowing what will come is not for man to know; it is for him to live.

Gabriel and I spent many long hours at the university and on many long walks through the gardens. We spent many hours in the projection room seeing many outer world events as if we were there and Gabriel pointing out many things that I would normally have missed.

My awareness was changing, and with the increased knowledge of the worlds and its peoples, I was becoming wiser.

After one rest period had ended and I had returned to the university, I found Gabriel kneeling before the Sword of Truth. He rose and turned to me. There were tears in the eyes of the Angel of God. "It is time." He put his hand on my shoulders and again looked deep into my soul. "I can give you no more. I now have to leave your world and return to mine. I have grown to love all of your peoples and you most of all. I can truly call you friend."

I too cried as I felt his sorrow. I hugged the man I called friend and the Angel of God that had saved my life and taught me so much. "I can't believe you have to go."

"I have to go to the Holy City. I must be cleansed and prepared before I can return. It will take much time and prayer before it is time.

I will have Job send for you when the time is ready. I would really like for you to be there."

He didn't say any more. He left the tower at the university for the last time. There was a special royal craft from Avalon that was to fly him to the Holy City. I sat down hard in the chair at his desk, knowing full well I didn't deserve to be sitting in it. This was one of the saddest moments of my life. Even the fact that I had learned who he truly was had not changed the way I had thought of the man Jabril or the arch angel Gabriel. He was the one everyone always turned to. Now I knew why.

It was about two days outside time when I got word from Job that all was ready. A sudden chill went through me. It was like hearing about the death of a friend, and I was called to say my goodbye. It was hard to again walk up the path to Zaron, who waited patiently once more for me to arrive. The *Greetings, Master* was as if I had only left her a few minutes before.

"Greetings, my old friend. We have to go say goodbye to an old friend." I sat down in the pilot's seat.

I know, Master. He is the one who created and programmed me. It will be hard to see him go. My spacecraft also knew who Jabril really was. I guess that was to be expected.

SAYING GOODBYE TO AN OLD FRIEND

We landed in the courtyard of the temple. There was only one of the workers in the temple that was there to greet us. All others had gathered in the temple. I was led to the steps where I was given a white robe to put on before entering. I quickly put on the robe and entered through the great doors. All members and students of the Holy City were assembled, and all heads were bowed. At the dais stood Job. Before him knelt Gabriel. To his right were King Dresden and Dorin. To his left knelt Sarah and Liz. A space had been left for me between the two ladies of my life.

I walked slowly forward and knelt with my family. Job said a prayer of cleansing and asked a special blessing on those assembled. He spoke in the ancient language.

At the end of the prayer, all heads were raised. Gabriel rose, and we followed his example. He turned to the assembly. He spoke, and his voice seemed to echo around the temple. "For all who see this day, remember you are the blessed among mankind. Your labors have not gone unnoticed. Carry forth the truth to those who follow that they too should know. I leave you now with God's blessings for all time."

At this, he walked down the isle with me right behind, followed by Sarah, Liz, King Dresden, Dorin, and Job, in that order. We headed toward the house of God.

We waited there in silence as the whole of the city came from the temple and gathered around. Not a single word was spoken by the many thousands that now stood behind us. Job came around in front of us. I had not noticed that he carried the golden chest.

Without a word, he handed me the chest. I knew that there was a reason and stayed silent.

We waited. The earth suddenly started to tremble. All there, including me, knelt because we knew this was the sign that the power of God was in the temple. Only Gabriel remained standing. The doors opened, and the light within outshone the overhead sun. Gabriel turned to me. "Go with me, Aaron. There is something you must do."

I stood and followed Gabriel into the House of God. The door closed behind us, and as my eyes again adjusted, I made out the ark of the covenant before us with the flame of God burning over it. Gabriel turned to me. "I would shake your hand goodbye, but I can't be touched after my cleansing. There is one more task you must perform before I depart this world. The chest containing the garments of Simon and the cup of Christ must be placed in the ark. The old covenant to the Hebrew people and the new covenant to all mankind have to be united. It is for you to do this task as a sign to the people and as a right to take my place."

Gabriel moved to the side, and I stepped upon the dais and placed a hand on the lid. I slowly lifted the lid, and the glory of God shone from the inside. I could see within at the contents. The tablets that Moses brought down from the mountain were in the center. Aaron's staff was to its left, and the urn holding the food from God was on the right. Below the urn I placed the chest. It now acquired the same light. This was a sign that it was there, and God had accepted it. I slowly closed the lid and stepped off the dais.

Gabriel took my place there. He looked sadly down at me and said, "It is time." He spread his hands to the side and smiled. The next words I'll never forget: *Till we meet again, old friend.* The blinding light that I had come to recognize now surrounded him. When the light faded, so did the flame above the ark. Gabriel was gone. The doors of the temple opened, and I went back out. All were still kneeling before the house of God.

I made only one statement. "It is done."

FINAL PREPARATIONS

All who waited again stood up and, without a word, headed back to the temple. There was a short service where we prayed for all who lived in this world and that the outer world would soon follow our lead.

It was only up to a few of us to be guardians of the outer rim, but all here were behind those few. Decisions had to be made. People had to be assigned. Posts had to be filled. Meetings had to be attended. I had never realized just how busy Jabril really was. It was only with my new awareness that I could organize and handle all of this. I found great pleasure in doing so.

I took special time out of my duties to put down in my journal all of these events while they were fresh in my memory. I don't think that those memories will ever fade. I can still see and feel everything that has happened in this world. With my new awareness, I can see that many more important events and missions will take place. Some of these will concern many people who you have met in my journals. Some others you will meet much later, but not from my journals.

Liz has been writing much of what has happened to her in a journal of her own that she keeps updated between classes at the university. I must add here that the university I mention is on the outer rim and not here.

Those who started this journey with me have often visited me. Billy and Cindy still reside just south of the university. Their son, Bill, graduates from the university very soon and has been selected for Atlantic Base. This is a great accomplishment for one of the sons of Adam. Peter keeps in touch with me via our communication equipment. He is back in Washington at a new post. He is an advisor to the president of the United States, and I'm sure he will also be advisor to the next. He passes on secrets that only we know of that keeps the world from destruction. Sarah now takes care of the castle and lands back home. I get to go there also between my other duties. Both Jocko and Jarod are working together at Area 51 again through special appointment from Peter. No one there knows their true age. They think they are almost sixty. They would be surprised to learn the actual age. Gavin still waits for a message from me. Each Christmas I have sent those cards, but personal contact has become impossible as much as I would like to see him. I still feel that somehow he is destined for this world.

We have been monitoring the communications in the outside world and feel the time is approaching that the journal that Gavin holds should be turned loose on the public. One of Jabril's predictions was that I would know when the time was right. I feel that it is close.

Liz has been keeping tabs on Gavin and knows where to find him. I'll discuss Gavin and the journal with Liz during her next break, which should be this Christmas from the university. I wonder if I should send him one last Christmas card. I think the beginning of the year would be about right. The outside year will be 2008. I'll know more by Christmas, and so will Liz. We'll make the decision then. She will have to take this journal also for him to get ready for printing. For this reason, I have to close out my journal. I will not have time to write more before that date.

I hope when you read these words that your life too has been affected for the better just as mine has. I still turn and stare at the sword hanging behind my desk. It contains many secrets. Some of them you already know, and many others are for another time. I can only leave you with these words. May you always walk with God.

CONCLUSION

BY GAVIN GRAHAM

That was the last entry by Dr. Charles Jennings, alias Aaron son of Drake, alias Simon of Cyrene, the man who carried the cross, and so much more. I have come to know that man since I've been here. I have visited him at the university and worked with him in the fields of Shambala. I have read his journals and put them to paper. I have eaten with him and talked with him for hours on end. The journals only hit the high spots of this man's life. There is so much more. I have also gotten a chance to read some of what Liz has written, and it is incredible but not yet finished.

Since my arrival, I have been given the chance to stay in this world. I have accepted to stay, as this is the only place that I have ever felt at home. The people I've met are just like me. I no longer feel like a stranger to anyone. I can say what I feel, and feel what other people say. Liz and I have become great friends and have worked together on some very interesting mysteries that have to be saved for a later time as this

275

journal too has to be sent to the outer rim to be made ready for publication. The outside needs to see these words. This story is so powerful.

Like before, the three people I love best in this world have sent a message to be added. Charles, Sarah, and Liz sent this message to the reader. They said you'd know what they meant.

"Till we meet again."